W9-AUB-804

Shimmer

Also by Sarah Schulman

Fiction
Rat Bohemia (1995)
Empathy (1992)
People in Trouble (1990)
After Delores (1988)
Girls, Visions and Everything (1986)
The Sophie Horowitz Story (1984)

Nonfiction
STAGESTRUCK: Theater, AIDS and Marketing (1998)
My American History: Lesbian and Gay Life During the Reagan/Bush Years (1994)

SHIMMER

Sarah Schulman

BARD

AN
AVON
BOOK

AVON BOOKS, INC.
1350 Avenue of the Americas
New York, New York 10019

Copyright © 1998 by Sarah Schulman Inc.
Interior design by Kellan Peck
Visit our website at **http://www.AvonBooks.com/Bard**
ISBN: 0-380-97646-3

All rights reserved, which includes the right to reproduce this book or portions
thereof in any form whatsoever except as provided by the U.S. Copyright Law.
For information address Avon Books, Inc.

Library of Congress Cataloging in Publication Data:

Schulman, Sarah, 1958–
Shimmer / by Sarah Schulman.
p.   cm.
I. Title.
PS3569.C5393S48   1998   98-23798
813'.54—dc21   CIP

First Bard Printing: September 1998

BARD TRADEMARK REG. U.S. PAT. OFF. AND IN OTHER COUNTRIES, MARCA REGISTRADA,
HECHO EN U.S.A.

Printed in the U.S.A.

QPM   10   9   8   7   6   5   4   3   2   1

Acknowledgments

I am very grateful to those friends and colleagues who offered personal and/or professional kindness, support and insight during the development of this book, especially Carrie Moyer, Maxine Wolfe, Jacqueline Woodson (endlessly generous), Don Shewey, Michael Bronski, Peg Byron, Carl George, Jack Waters, Meg Wolitzer, Alison Gross, Mark Owen, Jennifer Levin, Kathy Danger, Laurie Linton, Julia Scher, Mariana Romo-Carmona, Retha Powers, Urvashi Vaid, Jaime Manrique, Alix Dobkin, Charles Flowers, Ellen Geiger, Leslea Newman, Leslie Gevirtz, Kate Clinton, Beryl Satter, Claudia Rankine, Patrick Merla, Chana Bloch (for the epigraph), Erin Cramer, David Sternbach, Judith Halberstam, Edmund White, Octavia Wiseman, Tony Kushner, Rachel Pollack, Erica Van Horne and my editor, Charlotte Abbott. Historical debt to Mel Watkins, David Halberstam, Neil Gabler, *Jazz: A History of The New York Scene,* Clifford Odets (*homage* to *Deadline At Dawn*) and Cherry Jones, whose performance in *The Heiress* provided the narrative arc.

For material support I am grateful to The MacDowell Colony, The Corporation of Yaddo, The Ludwig Vogelstein Foundation, L.C. Hanson and Ann Stokes.

Special appreciation to William Clark.

For Carrie Moyer

The race is not to the swift

1948

BILLBOARD MAGAZINE'S TOP TEN HITS

1. Buttons and Bows.............................Dinah Shore
2. Manana (Is Soon Enough For Me)......Peggy Lee
3. Twelfth Street Rag........................Pee Wee Hunt
4. Nature Boy...King Cole
5. You Can't Be True, Dear..................Ken Griffin
6. You Call Everybody Darlin'.....................Al Trace
7. Woody Wood-Pecker.............................Kay Kyser
8. A Tree in the Meadow.............Margaret Whiting
9. I'm Looking Over a Four Leaf Clover.Art Mooney
10. Love Somebody...........Doris Day & Buddy Clark

CHAPTER ONE

Sylvia Golubowsky

1

Ordinarily, I have a proclivity for bitterness. But it still hurts me that another dear old friend is dead. They'll have to sweep away twice her weight in leaves to open up that tiny plot. No car doors will slam for this funeral. Her frail mourners are barely strong enough to shift the gears. Their rusty doors fall back into place these days relying on luck and gravity. Small, dismissable old women. Mouths sealed shut. They'll stand, chilled, until it's dangerous. So much threat from so many tiny places. Then they'll fold back into those cars.

The past that I shared with the newly dead proved the falsity of the Christian Ethic. Good does not triumph in the end. Suffering does not make you better. There is no divine reason that justifies pain. I know this because I have lived long enough to watch the biggest shits go on to fame and fortune. I see them on TV winning every award. They never had to account. The honorable? They were not vindicated. They melted without resolution. Now that I'm an old lady I still believe what I knew at twenty-five. Certain personality types slit our own throats because we have to. We can't help it, we're about something larger than ourselves. But don't slit your own throat if you're not expecting blood. There is no cure for honor.

My students never ask me about that time. If they would,

I'd have plenty to say. For example, there is no such thing as the secret to the atom bomb. It takes thousands of volumes of information to make an atom bomb. There's no secret ingredient like "just add water." You can't scribble the formula on a Jell-O package. Julius and Ethel Rosenberg were murdered by the U.S. government in 1953 for a crime that could never have been committed. This is the emblematic fact of my generation. The Rosenbergs were working-class people, and I have always believed that they were patriots. They wanted an America that was fair. Why should the rich have everything? My final point is that there is only one country in the history of the world that has ever used an atom bomb on human beings. That country is the United States of America. Whichever brilliant Soviet scientist it was who actually figured out how to make an atom bomb did the world a big favor. She created a balance of power, and atomic weapons were never used again. Try to imagine a United States let loose on a defenseless world, dropping atomic weapons whenever they choose.

My students never bring this up. They're too young, they don't know it even happened. They've been duped into thinking only about themselves. When has it ever been normal to be so greedy? I feel sorry for these kids. What would I advise? Outlive it. You can't beat history, but if you're young enough, try to wait out the historic moment. Everything does pass, but unfortunately so will you. That's why each of us has to try to hurry along the process of change in any way we can, while not becoming its victim. It's an irony of history, but the people who make change are not the ones who benefit from it. This is a bitter pill to swallow.

In our part of the country there are occasional days that stay light until midnight and grow into full darkness by four. Morning, by contrast, is stark and disappearing. Fruit still doesn't come in fluorescent plastic bins in this town, each apple totally green or totally red. There is a soothing river that runs through the middle of Plainfield, Vermont. A food co-op, a good bookstore, a good restaurant, a hardware store, and four churches. Vermonters have excellent taste. When I was young I thought I'd never leave New York, but there came a day when

I couldn't stand all the familiarity. All those horrible people I'd run into on the street, knowing exactly what they'd done. I wouldn't forgive them and it was their world, so I had to leave. I'm old but I still have a job, and not just for the hell of it. Agnes says to relax.

"Charge your groceries on the MasterCard," she says. "Let them try to collect."

But the money does make a difference, and I like having students. They let you change the world, one person at a time. You can make a big impact by showing somebody one great book. I know that the level of influence is deceptive, it doesn't add up. But, in the immediate, it is something worthwhile to do. Those people I was remembering, the honorable? Each one thought she'd at least have a comeback. But how can a whole nation's bad conscience be avenged? They let you survive only if they need an exception to the rule that proves their power. In other words, if they hated you yesterday but can use you tomorrow, they'll love you. Truth is an entirely different matter. How can authority be obscure and poor? This is the one question my students are always about to ask. I can see it hovering quizzically in their eyes. Thank God they're too well bred.

I must retire. It's obvious. The new fascist, money-grubber administrators of this college are breathing down my neck. They want me out. In the meantime I keep inviting students over to our house, tantalizing them—not with fantasies of sex with old professor G., but to let them feast on my shelves of books. My books. All by me. Japanese editions, Greek editions, book clubs, hardbacks, and the subsequent softs. How could a person have written so many books and still not be able to earn a living? Still be so unknown? My students stare at the golden calf obscuring the desperation and disappointment that sits patiently in the middle of the room. The centerpiece of my life. I don't want to touch them. I just want to show them my books, now that I'm on the verge of extinction if existence depends on recognition by others, which it does.

There is one oily seductive student preoccupying my mind at the moment. Mary Louise Prelinger. The one who manages to name her genitalia at every opportunity. She's twenty and completely lacking in the one thing I find irresistibly attractive—a historical view. I wouldn't kiss her boots if she paid my grocery bills. I know that's what she wants. Crosses her legs in class and waves them in all our faces. Always freshly waxed. The boots. She came to school in hot pants, and sporting a newly minted tattoo. Such beautiful legs and she makes a tattoo. I'm so lucky to have had this job. Thousands of people think this is the line you cross to get to safety. A job. She's too young to be sexy. She doesn't know a thing.

As my dear friend's funeral began this morning, I was guilty, still at work. Today in class we sat in a circle, despite my objections. I like it the old-fashioned way. The Socratic method. I want them to know who is boss. They lean back in plastic chairs and balance notebooks on their laps. They think they're going to learn how to write. They don't know that the purpose of these classes is to employ writers. First we had WPA, then the NEA. Now there's only MFA. Without it, how would writers ever earn a living? I'm offended by the whole process. Real writers don't learn it in school. They pick books haphazardly off the shelves, a cacophony of influences. I try to steer them toward books that will make them suicidal, demand a different life. If they're comfortable, I haven't done my job. Yet, I know that I am a hypocrite. None of this matters because they are already doomed. By history. They too were born at the wrong time. One day each of these kids will pray to be stuck in an office with fluorescent lights. They will word process regardless of what they read. You see, in today's economy, even excellence has no reward.

2

Long ago, before my conclusions were drawn, I had a job as a secretary for the New York *Star,* a mediocre tabloid with large type. There were eighteen desks in our stenographic pool, and, according to the girl on my left, Theresa Calabrase, they were laid out just like the cots in a juvenile reformatory. She should know. I kept my eye on Theresa Calabrase and especially on the rough-hewn, surly young men who waited for her on the sidewalk after work. They were always of the same mold–strong, skinny brutes with ancient faces, the descendants of discus throwers and slaves. That was the only time I'd see Theresa light a cigarette. She'd run off the elevator and burst through the old oak revolving doors, gasping for the first chance all day to do *what she wanted*. Then, suddenly, she'd see the tough guy waiting and stop her pursuit of free will. She was surprised to see him every time. Theresa kept a pack of Old Golds in her purse but never actually smoked unless she had to. Unless some thug from the neighborhood came uptown to tell her a thing or two. It didn't take long on the job for me to realize that each girl in secretarial had her own dreams and her eye on the back of the chair behind the next desk, one step up the ladder. But each one also had a mind of her own. And Theresa wasn't the only girl with a secret, secret life.

Every morning the office crackled with anticipation for the great opportunity we'd all been promised. And so it was with immeasurable enthusiasm that each girl came to her first day on the job in a brand-new homemade skirt, shined old shoes, and soft quiet hair. We'd start at desk Number Eighteen, filled with expectations, and slowly come to the sad truth. After all the promises we were actually and simply condemned to our spot until our betters got married or fired or sick of it all or died a sudden death. This is how I learned about competition, gritting my teeth and waiting for the others to get out of my way. After all those stories about my parents and the Old Country, where you didn't have the right to earn a pair of shoes, surviving hunger just to grow up in the Depression was normal American living. I was lucky to have a job after all. Wasn't I? Lucky?

Of course I brought my lunch from home in a paper bag or tucked demurely into my purse. Wrapped sandwiches and pieces of fruit. The ones who still lived with their mothers may have had a slice of homemade cake, all crumpled up in a napkin. But we independent girls never had a moment for baking and either went longing for something sweet or splurged on a store-bought treat. It was all a way to pass time in the trenches, waiting for a sister to conveniently disappear. Then I'd hurriedly empty my drawers, pack up my hairbrush and diary and thermos of hot coffee, and move on over one step closer to my goal. Dependent on time, we wished for fate. For only fate could save the life of a hard-typing, dictation-taking, shorthand working girl.

The matrons at reform school were a bunch of Irish sadists, Theresa assured us repeatedly at lunch. They'd made her parade naked and searched through her pubic hair for lice. They shined lights on her bed in the middle of the night to make sure she was alone and then warned her to keep both hands above the covers. They counted her rags when she had the bloods and watched her wash them out in a basin filled with ice. They locked her in the outhouse. There were worms in the apples. Wild dogs picked through the garbage-strewn yard. The girls ate soup made from potato skins, and rock-hard moldy bread. The only two details she'd never revealed were what criminal indiscretion sent her there in the first place and who those goombahs were waiting on the sidewalk, every now and then, after work.

The higher we climbed on the stenographic ladder, the more individual each girl became. Being underestimated every single day brought out the distinctions in women in a way that the on-going contest for Miss Subways never could. Theresa's hair had grown progressively blonde, her clothing became store-bought and flash. Her lips, more pouty. A little more red.

"Who was that waiting for you downstairs?" I asked finally over the clacking of typewriters.

"Bruno drives a Ford Coupe. What a junk heap," Theresa answered casually, but never taking her eyes off the keys. I knew something was wrong: a good typist doesn't look at her hands. "His idea of a date is the saloon on the corner."

"Nothing wrong with a neighborhood boy."

"Oh, neighborhood boys are great," she said. "If you want to spend your life in the neighborhood."

That evening he was there again. Thick, snarling lips wrapped around a stubby cigarette. Ridiculous suit out of an old

Jimmy Cagney movie. Not even an authentic bully, but a cheap imitation of an out-dated image that had been fake in the first place. That dark skin, more Negro than Jew those Italians were. His twitching stance, more Bowery Boy than hero. His violence. I couldn't take my eyes off of him and his, black and bottomless, insinuated themselves into the bodies and wallets of every woman who walked by. I would have liked to be that slick. I watched Theresa unsuspectingly step out of the lobby and then, on cue, reach for that cigarette the way that John Wayne always reached for his gun.

"How'd you meet this one?" I asked cautiously the next morning, setting up my carbon paper.

"Used to work with my brothers in the fish market on Fulton Street," Theresa said. "Hosing down tables of fishy leftovers and shoveling barrels of fishy ice."

"Sounds fishy."

"Yeah." She sighed. "I don't think he's the guy for me."

"Why not?"

"Eh, Paisans are a bunch of babies. First he orders four rye and sodas. Then his mother stops by and slips him a dollar. He'll grow up to be a worthless big shot, marry some virgin from the Old Country who'll bring him dinner in a basket at the bar."

It was that word *virgin* that I noticed. That's what Theresa and I had in common. We'd both given it up like it was nothing to boys we didn't love. Me, to a nobody nice guy sleaze, and Theresa to whomever. Despite the hysteria we both knew there was nothing to it. That's why I admired her so. She didn't try to cover things up. She just went on with life.

"What's he do for a living now?"

"A living? He's got lots of visible means of support, and I don't want to be one of them. You know the type, a trouble-maker with no guts. I gotta get out of the neighborhood."

I wanted to believe her swagger. But it never did all come together. That was the thing about Theresa, she wouldn't own up all the way. A two-bit punk from Mulberry Street was one thing, but why did she look so endangered every time he came around? The truth was that Theresa loved the threat. She liked being scared. It hadn't exactly taken a lot of living for me to

9

learn about the big divide, girls who get excited by safety and girls who always go for thin ice. It seemed to be a life sentence. Girls who got bored with nice guys always ended up slapped around or extremely content. There was no in between. They didn't have a choice about desire. They just had to learn how to handle it.

"Why don't you move into my building?" I said, setting up a new piece of paper so that I didn't have to look her directly in the eye. "My next-door neighbor got evicted yesterday, and you know how hard it is to get a place."

"Can't afford it on my own yet," she answered softly. "Hey, isn't your roommate moving out?"

"That's not settled," I snapped. This was getting too personal. Why do people always remember the tiniest things that you say? "Rita's probably going to stay."

Charlie, the floor manager, dropped off a new stack of hand-scrawled notes from upstairs. It was shorthand to be deciphered and copy to be typed.

"Still dating those thugs from Catholic school?" Charlie laughed, putting the bulk of work into Theresa's *in* box.

"Who died and made you Mussolini? Mind your own business."

"Sorry, Theresa," Charlie said meekly, immediately defeated. He folded back into his customary blandness with quiet regret.

"It's okay," she added quickly. He wasn't even a contender for a few vocal jabs. "You know I'm thick as an iron stove, Charlie. Never get the message when the guy is a creep. Maybe the next one I go for will be a nice, hardworking fellow. Quiet and clean-cut, like you."

"That's me, the ninety-pound weakling with a heart of gold. Could you make me sound any more boring?"

"You're a real marine, Charlie. You'd never mooch off a girl. You'd rather go hungry, right?"

"Yeah," Charlie said, disappearing. He must have gone into the bathroom five times a day to wet his comb. But if it wasn't for the perfect way his hair was parted down the side, there'd be nothing else to notice. He was blusteringly disappointed in himself. "Well, I guess I'll go jump into a maple soda someplace."

Then he tried to laugh it off, but we wouldn't give him a break.

"He's kind of cute," Theresa said falsely, diving into her new round of tasks.

"Charlie? He's okay."

"Tired?"

"Yeah." I looked up from my machine for the first time that morning and caught the flashing red of Theresa's nails. Her hair was out of a bottle, but it didn't look that bad. I worried about what happened to girls like that.

"You like my nails?"

"Yeah."

"That's a home manicure," she said. "If we live together I'll show you how to do it. Maybe I should just get on a night train to Hollywood and become a manicurist to the stars. It's that or five screaming kids, for sure."

"No, not you," I jumped in, desperately wanting to stop the whole thing.

"Yeah, it's in the cards all right. A fishhead for a husband and a whole tank full of fishy kids. How much did you say your place was?"

CHAPTER TWO

A u s t i n   V a n   C l e e v e

1

I bought Microsoft in 1985, which is enough to establish my authority. This morning I told my grandson to buy ten thousand shares of Netscape and then hold it, just sit and wait.

Now, I've never personally tried out a computer, but I do read the *Journal* every day, and, more important, I read the Advertising column in the *Times* religiously. Advertising is the primary source of cultural influence in the world today. It predicts all investment patterns. In my era, industry wanted its workers also to be its consumers. It was a relationship of dangerous dependence. Then they found other workers in far-away places. Now, in 1996, we've finally found consumers in those same far-away places. No need for Americans at all. I told my grandson to buy Philip Morris, despite those tobacco restrictions, there's always the Third World. My grandson has already cost me a fortune. I had to pay for his detox, and then I had to pay for his rehab. It's so expensive procreating these days. My grandfather was the railroad baron, my father invested in telegraph wires and newspapers. They believed in Business with actual employees and precise products. I just invested, no human element. But my children and their children just spend. That's why our great families are slipping rapidly, replaced by the new money—those information highway robbers and the

Jews running around Newport. There's no exclusivity. The Blacks are moving into where the Jews used to hide. Rap stars at the Hamptons. I asked my grandson if he wanted to earn a million before his twenty-first birthday. He responded to the word *million* but twitched at the word *earn*. Then I leaned over and whispered in his ear.

"Tattoo removal."

He twitched again.

"It is the growth industry of the future."

It's obvious. Open a chain of laser centers in malls all over the country, and they'll come running. Either that or selling ad space in poems.

The trees fell like falling leaves
Buy Nikes from Michael Jordan

I told him to open a chain of micro-breweries in all the Barnes and Nobles. Apricot-Bubblegum Lager. His face went blank. Like all passive people he can't step back from his own experience and commodify it. He actually thinks it's normal.

Some people don't ever panic, even at the moment of death. I knew this about my third wife, Sarah, the day we met. It was the way she interacted. Her skin was a bubbling brine, and I was using her. Everything she did annoyed me, but I couldn't install my own fax. She was twenty-seven, without health insurance, and I was eighty. Cold-blooded, she died immediately. Now I'm on the dialysis machine with no one to talk to except shimmering folding chairs. Shimmering Coke machine. Exit sign shimmering. Too lost to feel bored until my grandson from my first marriage, Calvin Kinsey Van Cleeve, comes to visit. One look at him and I remember that I am dying and should be upset about it.

I insisted on that name because I wanted him to have an edge. When people recognize your name as one of high lineage and authority forged over time, they tend to give you your due without too much fuss. Things are so competitive now. Due is the greatest gift an ancestor can bestow. Only immigrants don't recognize it. But how many immigrants will have power when

Calvin Kinsey assumes the family portfolio? The Indians will, that's for sure. They're climbing a mile a minute. But they will kowtow to that name because it is so English. Veddy, veddy. And they know about protocol. I just do not believe that Dominicans will be running the world by the year two thousand and ten. They don't even know who the original Calvin was and they probably will never know, not if the Pope's marketing people keep doing such a great job.

Calvin Kinsey asked me, dear Grandpapa Austin, for an apartment in Manhattan. He came all the way to this convalescent home in Newport when he could have called me on the cellular. This apartment costs $595,000 for one bedroom and a half study, one bathroom, pre-war Elv. FSB. EIK ovrlkng grdn. A/C 1,000 SF. It is cheaper to have a mortgage, even though we could have paid cash in full. There are tax deductions. He did not know this! That is when I became seriously concerned. I tried to explain the basics to him as simply as possible. After all, I and our kind worked for more than a century to get these protections in place. It was a harsh battle, but we persisted and we won. Now, even if you pay twice as much in the long run, it is actually cheaper. It's all deductible.

"You get tax deductions, Calvin Kinsey. That means you get your money back."

All my hard work and the fool didn't even know this. I actually felt sad. We've won, and he can't even comprehend the triumph. As far as he's concerned, it's just there.

2

In my era, the cigarette girls came by bus and the musicians took the El train, but it was the *swells* who arrived by cab and car. On those hot September days and nights, returning tanned from summer retreats, we barely had to sweat for ourselves. Someone else was driving, someone else opened the door. Someone else cleaned the vomit and cum off the seats the next morning. And once ushered through the playground gates, there was a Chrysler air-cooling system to keep us on our toes.

It was already one o'clock in the afternoon, but Jim was still standing across the street taking in the whole scene. I watched him surreptitiously from behind the heavy door. After all these years it was still a thrill for the man, still a threat. Week after week he approached that canopied entrance, never quite believing that they would let him through. So far so good, but he would not so much as blink with surprise if someday some Joe insisted that he walk in through the kitchen. In fact, he was waiting for it. I enjoyed that about him. It made it all so easy.

I've always believed in hero-worship as a healthy model for aristocracy. It's so American because it's so psychological. The rich are rich because they're better. A New World substitute for the divine right of kings. Some of us enter in from the top and others claw their way up. These two types of individuals must have a relationship of dominance and submission from the beginning, otherwise the newcomers become too desirous and deluded and it ends badly. I've always enjoyed mentoring the upwardly mobile. They're different and more interesting. They need me to explain how everything works. They value my information, respect it. It's temporarily intimate, and I get to leave my mark behind. My own kind don't need what I've got. It's demoralizing. If you like to be needed, you have to reach across the class divide.

At the same time I must admit the benefit of a life without consequences. I had my income and my stature, as no result of my own efforts. Just as nothing I did could give it to me, nothing I do could ever take it away. It was larger than cause and effect. This realization was very freeing and equally fascinating. I saw the structures of human intercourse, and from that moment of revelation on I did what I did because it interested me. I was entranced with the mechanics of social interaction, how I could manipulate situations and what I could make of them. If the scenario didn't pan out exactly as planned, I could marvel at its surprising twists and then start all over again.

Of course I have always had ethics. I never shun someone without letting them know why. It's uncouth.

After summoning up his courage, Jim would finally straighten his tie and move slowly into the Stork Club thinking himself a unique kind of fraud. I'd often watch as he glided down the short hallway, turned past the long bar, and checked himself out in its mirror. Suit from Roger's Peet. New shoes, not a crease in the leather. But the red hair was a fatal giveaway. Here he was, almost middle-aged, and it still had not started to go gray. It just screamed out *Mick*. James Layton O'Dwyer. He'd always relied on his size to hide his fear and perpetuated the name "Big Jim" as a form of protection. He needed a lot of protection. He couldn't accept feeling comfortable in a place like the Stork, and he couldn't accept not wanting to.

Jim passed the main dining area on his way to the Cub Room and once again no one barred his entry. That VIP alcove was the Kremlin for those with gold watches and checkered integrity. We were as identifiable as the club's trademark on every black ashtray, a monocled, top-hatted bird. He deserved it too, of course, this special treatment. But every moment that it graced him could easily be the last. That is what always happens to a man in power who does not come from money, he gets to play temporarily at someone else's bidding. But luxury is never ever a second skin.

I watched him suck in the activity around the room like artificial respiration. It was wall-to-wall solid citizens. We adamant patricians who would have made the right decisions for America if we hadn't been trounced by the New Deal. Here it was, nineteen forty-eight, and we were still licking our wounds. Waiting. But history does bring surprises, and these extended setbacks had an equalizing effect. It made men like me have to sit down to a linen-covered table with the likes of Jim, and it made me learn to love it. That's democracy.

"Austin, how well you look."

Now the two sides of the American coin could square off over cocktails and a three-course lunch, demurely doing battle with the bloody cravings of Roman gladiators. And it was all because of the late Mr. Roosevelt. It was F.D.R. himself who'd gotten Jim a seat at my table.

17

The meal proceeded according to plan. Gossip and small talk until all the chewing was done.

"Nothing like the women at the Stork," I pointed out, slicing the last bite of prime rib. "They wear short, tight black dresses with very high heels. In winter they wear fox coats."

"Not too much jewelry though."

"No, it would detract from their figures."

The Stork's owner, Sherman Billingsley, was ever present, hovering precariously over the line between gracious host and Panderus. His background, notoriously, was trash. Built his fortune from bootlegging, for which he served only three months on a rum-running charge. Everyone knew he fronted for gangsters of the most odious sort. Of course this made Jim look up to him with admiration. He imagined them to be in a conspiracy of two, both having escaped their circumstances. It's the working man's conceit, that there are just a few of them scattered among the powerful. They don't realize how many others are successfully passing. But what was it about socializing with Murder Incorporated that was so terrific? There was always an annoying romance about those thick-lipped Guineas. Supposedly, they lived life to the fullest.

As the waiter cleared our plates I was busy chattering and simultaneously listening in on everyone else's conversation. Always on the alert for tidbits for my column. My father would have preferred to hand me the Business section instead of Gossip, but I predicted the power of the innuendo and had far more social currency on the social exchange than was ever traded on the Dow. I believe I had a William Powell mustache at the time. It was a badge of pre-war aesthetics and cut quite a dashing figure. It was a sign of nostalgia on its way back to power.

From my point of view, the nation had fallen into the hands of dark and alien forces. Roosevelt had been dead for five years, and still my beloved Republicans were in the minority. I wanted to be their champion, a knight in the shining armor of vested interests in distress. Jim watched my fervor with the same internal conflict he brought to everything. He knew quite well that commitment to something was a real gentleman's most important asset.

"But isn't substance also a factor?"

"What do you mean by that, my boy?"

"You see, Austin, the egg at breakfast this morning tasted good. Warm, quiet, and sweet. But the cup it came in was ostentatious and cost much more than my conscience could allow. The same could be said for this luncheon, and yet I am supposed to throw my napkin on the table and sit back, happily knowing it has been a grand old time."

"Slavery is our only hope." I sighed. Being the authentic aristocrat, I was the one who threw down the napkin, officially drawing the eating portion of our meal to a close. The afternoon couldn't move on without that wave of my hand, like Queen Mary baptizing a battleship.

"Now you are getting too extreme. You must be desperate for a punchline."

"No, I'm serious," I said. "The more divided the Democrats become between northern liberals like yourself and the hardcore Jim Crow southern segregationists, the better chance the Republicans will have of walking back into the White House."

Jim perked up. There was something appealingly clean about the way that I proceeded. He too needed to believe in one idea so fiercely that the road was clear. As clear as that telegram from the State Department that said his son was dead. He felt safer when every turn was an uncontestable fact, too obvious. When there was nothing as obstructive as choice.

"After all," I added. "Now that our Lord Franklin D. is finally entombed, Americans need another God. Why not Profit? It lasts longer than icons."

"Americans are a religious people," he agreed. "But if ever there was a deity communicated via F.D.R.'s booming voice . . ."

"Pumped through that propaganda box in every living room in the country."

"Don't be resentful, Austin. Just because he thought of using the radio before you noticed its existence. There are other modes of communication besides the steam room, old chap. Roosevelt was the most professional populist this country has ever known."

"He did have grassroots in every country club in America."

"Austin!" Jim said, settling back into the velvet booth. "You're just a jealous monarchist. Don't worry, we all know that Roosevelt's blood was just as blue as yours."

I looked over at his big, square head. Close shave to hide that red beard. It worked both ways. He liked to remind himself of my lineage, and I liked tussling with a climber sans pedigree. It made me feel slightly risque whenever I could detect one of his working-class mannerisms or rough-and-ready characteristics. After all, Jim battled his way to the top of his profession. But it was I who brought him into the marvelous petty world of delicacy and detail where power really lives. The world of nuance. I was better than a brother because I offered this man something more potent than love. I offered him information. And a man cannot be anyone in America if he doesn't really know how things work. He has to know what it takes to have influence outside his own rarefied little sphere. Presiding over your own dinner table is a dangerous, false illusion. Dominating your wife and daughter can satisfy some prehistoric instinct, but what connections will they ever have? It takes awareness of the big machine to learn, systematically, all the opportunities to get things done. To get them done exactly your way.

CHAPTER THREE

Sylvia Golubowsky

Many nights Rita and I had crept down streets like this one at the most forbidden hours with a wild control. This was really living, the kind of willful dive into the darkness that Jack London wrote about. We went down to the piers, cool sea shimmer worth a foghorn symphony. Rugged old sailors and tugboat captains slowly faded through barroom doors into private territory. But we didn't care. We owned the evening sky. Secret interiors were not the cravings of young girls. We wanted to be let out of our rooms, not locked in.

Some nights we wandered home from a great adventure, every passerby an incredible mystery. The city herself was a gypsy in black veils dancing the tarantella. Each band of her silver bracelets shined with a million lifetimes of romance. All before us. Sometimes the summer's stifling heat made sleep impossible. Then we'd step into the hazy, honey moment where no rules applied. Walking through parks, past young lovers on benches, woebegones staring at the stars for comfort, idealists under a tree. We turned down black, silent streets looking for little treats. The opiated scent of all-night bakeries, yeast like ghosts gliding over fire escapes. Truckers unloading their wares. Streetwalkers unloading their wares. Both catering to a stubborn, strong-armed masculinity, dewy on the dreamy sidewalks. Quiet souls coming off the night shift. Marauders.

"Dr. Greenberg was right," Rita said again. "I'd never forgive myself."

I'd stopped having that conversation days before. I'm not one of those people who can turn something over in my head forever. At some point the solution becomes obvious. My job now was to take history in hand; there was no more room for discussion. My job was to take all the responsibility for morality and make sure that the deed got done. That was love, after all, as I understood it. Doing the dirty work. As for Rita, in the same way that I had to be clear, she needed to be halfhearted in order to go through with anything. She depended on me for the tough stuff. Kindly old doctors back in Brooklyn could not determine the course of our life.

"Here's MacDougal Street."

Theresa, God love her, was waiting next to the closed-up Café Rienzi wearing a black kerchief that could only be right for church. I imagined her, poor girl, in her secret moments of contrition, kneeling before the ivory Madonna, drawing holy water across her chest. I looked up at the night sky and instead saw Rita's naked body laid out on the cross, pierced with arrows like Saint Sebastian. A martyr. There was no way out of the physical pain. Either road would be excruciating. But pain is worth the cost of a higher purpose. Saint Sebastian would not be what everyone else wanted him to be. Death was a greater destiny.

"Do you have it?" Theresa asked.

"Yes," I said. Rita didn't even part her lips.

We walked on silently, the three of us in the sour night. It was less a shroud than a sea of turned milk. Something earthly gone wrong.

All through Little Italy there was silence. Windows lay wide open as whole families slept out by the fire escapes deep into this Indian summer. A confidence in safety, their privacy. My mind leapt to some other fantasy of jumping in through those windows. Leaping under the sweat-stained sheets of three children in one bed and closing my eyes to all this responsibility. A robber could just as easily enter the same way and slash their little throats without effort. I could jump in and bite them, no, lick them. No, slice their little behinds. No motive necessary, just the open window. It was so quiet, no one would ever know.

There! A sign of life. I was saved from my reverie of destruction by a glowing cigarette trumpeting through the darkness. Someone was on sentry duty after all. Over there, a solitary sound from across the street. This soldier was sucking on a piece of ice. I could hear the slurp from one side of the block and then a long draw from that cigarette on the other.

"This way," Theresa said.

We got to Grand Street, across from Ferrara's pastry shop. It had been in New York City for more than fifty years, according to the proud sign behind the plate glass. That store had been in America longer than most of the people I had ever met. We turned into an old-style tenement over a shuttered wine broker, stopping hesitantly in the hall.

"Let me have it," Theresa said, and, for the first time that night, we both turned to look at Rita. She handed over the napkin-wrapped package, this gesture, the sign of her complicity. Her eyes were wide, pretending this was someone else's conclusion. Everything just happened to Rita. She never made the decision herself.

I looked at her and felt strangely cold. Her hair was ironed and somehow ridiculous. Her face seemed pasty and dry. I was overcome, in fact, by a nauseatingly casual indifference that I had never known before. But was more preoccupied by the question of how in the hell people could be so small as to let convention lead them around by the ears. There was a separation between Rita and me at this point. One that only I perceived. It was that distance that accompanies too much knowledge. Too much evidence that the other person is weak.

At that point it had been two years since I first laid out my books, notebooks, and impersonal clothing and placed them in a cardboard valise, expecting a moment I'd recall forever as I moved out on my own. Only, in that hallway on Grand Street, I could no longer remember a thing about it. Not a single telling detail. My memory was just a list of absences. There had been no Mama and Pop hovering by the door waving their handkerchiefs, wishing me well. Instead they looked on me as a monster, fearing my presence in the world. What damage I would do.

Aside from that fear, there was nothing more evident to me than the blank lack of curiosity that made up my parents' reaction to their only daughter. A deep miscomprehension and a refusal of interest. All the enthusiasm had been my own. Mama and Pop offered their stock disappointed resignation. And that's how Rita acted too, on this dark night. Devastatingly vague.

After leaving my parents behind. I'd felt numb at first, carrying that cheap suitcase to the El station on my way to Rita's house. But, by the time I'd run up the three flights of stairs, my heart was turning over like the motor on an aircraft carrier. Rita, of course, was nowhere near ready.

"Rita," I nagged. "There's a new way to pack, you know. It's called *folding things.*"

"Why don't you just help me with it?" she cajoled coquettishly, like a silent film star who'd never make it in the talkies. That's how Rita's father had raised her, to be silent and beautiful. Everything else seemed dangerous and disorienting. But, suddenly desperate to break free, she'd taken a leap into that anomalous moment called *college* where everyone has a chance to defy their fate. Later, I learned the hard way that most revert back to what their parents had in store. But, if any big changes were going to occur, they had to explode void of consequence. Rita's sudden ability to desire beyond what was on her plate was worth more to me than anything in my lonely world. Someone ready to take a chance on life against all the odds, and ready to take it with me? What else is more Godly than that?

"Why don't you help me," she said. "That's your job."

And it was. Rita was a willing student in all the basics, like how to take care of herself.

"Home for dinner?" she'd asked, insinuatingly, that first week together in our new apartment.

"I'm starved."

"Me too," she said. "There's spaghetti in the cupboard."

I figured out fairly quickly that this girl had never been taught how to cook, to iron, to wash out her nylons and underpants at night. But she did learn. It was a necessity. That's what we'd agreed on from the start. The only way our lives could be better than our mothers' was to learn how to do everything. Especially when it came to earning a living. I just did not want some man telling me what to do.

"Come on then," Theresa said, clutching the money in one hand and the nape of her kerchief in the other, leading us farther into the dark.

We were walking among the kinds of buildings that Mama had come to, fresh off the boat when she lived with Cousin Hershy. The hallways were stained in sweat, you could scrape it off the walls and they would bleed with sorrow. The stairs were made of dried-out tears, stomped underfoot by daily defeat. The acrid memory of long-ago kerosene, cigarettes, and gas lamps still hung over each threshold. The dumbwaiter was filled with garbage, and the hallway toilet peeked out naked from behind a rotting door on a single hinge.

Theresa murmured in Italian to an old woman dressed in black, barely distinguishable from the night. She answered in an even more obscure dialect, one Theresa could comprehend but never speak. Then we stepped into a tight, windowless room. Rita was led away so quickly there was no good-bye. I was annoyed and she was simply gone. No one turned on a light so Theresa and I sunk precariously into the soft sagging sofa and sat silently in the dark. After a while, I could hear Rita whimper through the walls.

"It's a sin," Theresa said, finally breaking the quiet.

It was so strange, but for the first time in my life a Hebrew prayer came to me. This prayer has come back many times since, but I never knew until that moment that I was religious. *Dear God,* I thought. *Aveenu Malkaynu. Please don't hurt us. We are so small.*

"There's nothing worse than having it," is what I said, though, and then felt a profound discomfort. "How much is it going to hurt?"

There was an unwillingly edgy hood of regret coming suffocatingly close. Who knew what the sky was like at that moment? It could already be daybreak and not one of us could tell. Rita's whimpering became more obvious but it was fear, not pain. I

25

knew her that well. It was about being terribly alone and trusting no one. Being at the mercy of history and everyone you've ever met.

My back was to the front door, so when it opened I saw a projection onto Theresa's face of the early strands of daylight from the hallway window, and she was illuminated for the first time that night. I saw that the couch that engulfed her was actually green velvet. I saw the crucifixes on the wall surrounding Theresa's head like a halo of devils. But, most revealing, I saw that familiar expression as she instantly reached for a cigarette.

"Bruno."

The door closed again and his footsteps expertly negotiated the overly furnished cell. He bent his head to the glow of Theresa's match and the shadow of their two smoking profiles filled the room. Rita screamed this time and it was not a scream of terror. It was pure physicality. It was her animal. I dug my fingers into the rancid sofa, grime under my nails like strips of flesh. Rita cried out again.

"Don't worry," Bruno said, blowing out the match. "I'll give her a shot."

CHAPTER FOUR

Austin Van Cleeve

The El Morocco opened only for supper and had a decadently nocturnal sense of elegance. Its owner, John Perona, was an ex–prize fighter. He fell in love with a gorgeous Estonian on his way over from Italy and consequently missed going down on the *Titanic*. Saved from a ghastly death by the love of an icy Balt. As a result there was a devil-may-care feeling to the place as its zebra-striped banquets so succinctly conveyed. While the Stork's clientele saw themselves as the Meritocracy, the El was the feed trough of choice for the lazy and untalented rich. What counted most to these people was what others thought of them. They already had enough money.

I'd selected the El because I had business to attend to and the bizarrities of the place would be more unsettling and therefore more intimidating to the man I most desired to intimidate at that given moment. In this case, the object of my predatory exercise was Jim O'Dwyer, and I needled him all the way through supper. He kept hoping for the knockout punch to get it over with and send him to the showers. But instead I turned out to be a gentleman cockteaser and Jim was the first to reach the boundaries of his stamina.

"Well," O'Dwyer finally blurted out, like a man underwater for far too long. "Governor Dewey is the only Republican the *Star* would ever endorse." Then he raised his eyebrows as if he had just that minute come to this decision and had, just at that moment, let me in on the most spontaneous and intimate detail. As an attempted face-saver for cracking under pressure, it was a dismal failure. But I didn't care. I got my story.

"Waiter!" I called out. "Bring me a telephone."

"I've not made a commitment." O'Dwyer smiled weakly, trying to backtrack and finally pulling out a long cigar as a stall, as if there was any way he could turn this moment to his own advantage. "Although I must admit that Dewey is pretty democratic for a Republican. He spoke out this very year that the Communist Party should not be outlawed. 'Can't shoot an idea with a gun,' he said."

Oh yes, you can.

Within a minute I was barking into the phone.

"Operator, give me Butterfield 8–6468. Jim, your paper's endorsement of Dewey for president will make a wonderful piece for my column, provided that I break it before you do."

"Well, break it then, who cares whether or not it's true." He saw my hesitation. "And don't give me that puppy-dog stare like a man punished his whole life who has never done anything wrong. Austin, this righteous anger looks entirely incongruous on you, since you are always totally and unquestionably guilty."

"Flattery will get you nowhere," I smirked, hand over the mouthpiece. "I tell everything I know as soon as I know it, which is often what makes it happen. But I am not at all a fighter. I am a waiter. I wait until someone else places the rope around your neck and then I wait until someone else kicks out the stool. Hello? Mary? Hold my lead. It's Tom Dewey or . . . ?" I looked over at Jim for final confirmation.

"Cherries Jubilee?"

"You love making things hard for me," I said, quietly replacing the receiver.

He did enjoy my obvious disappointment and it was somewhat disconcerting to have such pleasure so baldly on the surface. I resolved to get my revenge. O'Dwyer was a little boy in grown-up clothes, too large for his tailored suits, no matter how well they fit. Gentlemen of my class may get fat, but they never get brawny.

"I do," he said. "I mean, you just can't be so afraid of President Harry, just because Truman rhymes with union."

I showed Jim that I was really listening to him and considering this stunning bit of news. That is how he reassured himself falsely that he did have power, because someone else with power was listening. That's how I knew how much he needed me, and I forged ahead to the next move.

"You irritate me, O'Dwyer. We Americans came out of the war richer and therefore more conservative. Don't you realize that? The elite still feels the way we did in '46. Wrong war, wrong allies, wrong outcome."

"But, Spain—"

"Forget about Spain. To the average taxpayer World War Two started on December 7, 1941, at Pearl Harbor, no ifs, ands or buts. That's what your grandchildren are going to be taught in history class. They're not going to learn about a gaggle of anarchists blowing each other's brains out. Your grandchildren aren't even going to hear mention of it. Spain? Bullfighting, señoritas, and ham."

O'Dwyer winced and couldn't come back. He just sat quietly, stunned. Then he looked ashamed for being paralyzed so quickly. Not knowing what else to do he stared at his hand.

"What's the matter? Oh, your boy. I'm sorry, Jim, I don't know how I could have been so thoughtless. It hasn't been that long. What a horrible way to lose your boy, so close to the end of the war."

"I'm not the only one," he answered, as if to say "no matter." But he was lost. Bad enough that silence now hung over the table, but Jim felt so awkward he actually looked down and examined the matchbook. He was losing all his grace. That's the one thing being ill-bred can never hide, a lack of natural instinct for recovery. "You're absolutely right. Those poor fools who never came back from Bilbao. In another three months no one will even remember that there was a Spanish civil war."

"*Prematurely anti-fascist.* Isn't that what the State Department called them? So," I continued, now that condolences were out of the way. "Is the New York *Star* endorsing Dewey?"

I'd let him off the hook of exposing his grief. Consequently, he should now give me the scoop for my column as a reward and send me home a happy little prince. Then I'd have another feather in my silk stocking cap and the approval of my editor and father, Austin Sr. Later I realized that it was the thought of my father, at that crucial moment, that led me to misstep and blow my chances, push things too far too fast, I'm afraid.

"I know you, O'Dwyer," I jumped. "You worked your way up from a ghetto full of redheads in some Boston slum. It was those fabulous Irish breakfasts that got you to the top of your profession. Big Jim owes it all to that Ulster Fry, one big sizzling slab of pork wrapped in newsprint. That's how you got black ink in your blood."

"I'm sick of playing class war with you, Austin," he said decisively. "You'll have to find another way to impress your Da. Cherries Jubilee?"

"Very well, mock me all you like, Jimmy O'Dwyer," I said. "But America's first families bring the moral grounding that this nation needs to economically dominate the planet."

"Socialism for the rich," Jim answered, victorious. "Free enterprise for the poor. Communism is everywhere, even in our kindergartens. Anyone who can read the *Times* without moving his lips is under suspicion. Is that what you call Christian values?"

Then he signaled the waiter for a delicious dessert.

CHAPTER FIVE

Sylvia Golubowsky

The abortion had failed.

Oh, Rita was no longer pregnant, but she had lost all of her resolve. Rather than granting her the ticket to a freedom she'd always claimed to long for, the abortion had propelled her into an infantalized state. I watched, horrified, as she spoke to Ted publicly in baby talk and from then on conceded to him at every turn. She actually put the food on his plate.

I knew we weren't little girls playing ring-e-levio in plaid skirts anymore, but since when was Rita too grand to climb the wooden fences around a parking lot in order to visit a Puerto Rican kid with a great collection of carrier pigeons?

"Where were you? At the store?"

"No," she answered with that separating tone of superiority that I hadn't yet learned to identify with conformity. "I went to the city clinic. Just a regular checkup."

It was already the next afternoon before I stopped dead on the cobblestoned corner of Thirty-second and First Avenue to realize that the girl had gone for a blood test to get a marriage license. And, more importantly, that she thought this fact made her better than me, instead of worse. Stunned, I looked around for some respite and stared, longingly, through the thick beveled glass on the front door of the nearest saloon. It was one of those neighborhood haunts I've always loved, where the iron chandelier hung from the tin ceiling, a remnant of the poor man's experience of the days before World War. Where now, in the forties, guys in old hats ate liver and onions at the bar with a glass of beer. But I was already late for work, having opted for a long walk to indulge my sorrows rather than suffer another hot morning on the crowded train.

The continuously surprising September heat hung over the stenographic pool, attentive like inevitable punishment for a crime not yet committed. Languid wooden propellers loped in ambivalent circles. They were inadequate memorabilia from the original Golden Eighties newsroom when ink was rolled by hand. Before photographs. Now the stirred air barely ruffled the carbon paper on the desks of eighteen hardworking girls, each one wondering when their boss would finally invest in electric fans.

This particular afternoon, seven of my colleagues were celebrating by eating out at the Automat since Number Thirteen and Number Nine were both on their last day of work. Two September weddings in the New York City heat to two young men who would really make something of themselves thanks to the GI Bill.

The Automat was as large as the City College cafeteria, but had a completely different atmosphere. Instead of a crowd of know-it-all vets and neophyte hopefuls arguing over books, coffee, cigarettes, and newspapers of every language and stripe, it was mostly working stiffs, career gals, and a lot of drifters. These were lost souls staring blankly between tall tales or lonely old people with nowhere to go. That was New York in those days. Every kind of person could eat together at the Automat, poets and beggars and beggar poets.

All the food was laid out in little individual boxes piled high on top of each other against the wall. Each compartment had a carved copper frame and an old-timey slot where you could put in your nickels. The crumpled, tired cashier was popping out of her uniform, grumpy, dispensing those nickels with rapid-fire panache. Like a croupier on a pirate ship.

For those with cash there was Salisbury steak and fried potatoes, or open-faced hot turkey sandwiches on white bread with gravy and french fries for ninety-five cents. But we girls from the stenographic pool tended more toward a bowl of soup and a roll with butter, saving our change for the rivers of hot coffee gushing out of the big copper tureens like gas at the defense plants. The highlight of every Automat meal was a piece of pie, apple or lemon meringue, sitting temptingly in its own little display case. Each slice waited seductively for the indulgent to pop in their nickels, open the tiny glass door, and watch, pie in hand, as the next piece mysteriously slid into place awaiting the next desirous patron. Or, a glob of chocolate pudding in an elegant dessert glass with a little flower of whipped cream sitting on top. The second you committed to it, the pudding too would be replaced with another one, hand-spooned and awaiting its devourer, its savorer. The whole process reaffirmed in each customer's mind that there is a backstage to every event. That even pie requires an elaborate system behind the scenes.

"Today is Wednesday, and I'm just another single girl," Number Thirteen was cooing over her tapioca pudding, the color of a faded rain slicker.

"And by next week, Hasenpfeffer . . . ?" teased Number Four.

"By next week I'll be *Mrs.* Hasenpfeffer to you."

On the way back to the office I stopped at the corner newsstand, toying with the idea of *Modern Screen* or a *Detective* magazine but, as always, ended up buying the *Times* and reading it at my desk for the last few minutes of lunch. The next morning I would be packing my personal items and moving up from desk Number Ten to Number Nine. A whole year on the job and I'd only just gotten halfway to my goal.

"Hey, Number One. Mr. O'Dwyer wants you in his office."

"They're all on lunch, Charlie," I called back. "Me and Number Sixteen are the only ones here."

"Well, you then. Grab a pad and go."

I folded up my paper and gathered my pencils, composing myself for the long walk to Mr. O'Dwyer's perch. Hewitt, the shop steward, would not have liked to see me working on my lunch hour. But everyone knew you had to be industrious if you wanted to get that break. Anyway, the union was supposed to be there to protect working girls, not stop us in our tracks. I passed all the big wooden desks of copy chiefs, phones ringing off the hook, papers piling up waiting for the typists to come back from lunch. Ticker tape hammered out fast-breaking stories coming in over the teletype, while messengers from the mailroom pushed huge wagons full of packages and papers. Copy boys with ink-stained hands ran up and down the newsroom's long wooden aisles.

O'Dwyer's office was a different reality. A different era. Everything was modern. Real twentieth-century spacious. The desk was sleek, metal with a plastic top. Not old, scruffy wood. He had one of those phones where the person listened and spoke into the same piece. It occurred to me that Rita and I should get our own phone. There was a delicious breeze from the bank of opened windows, so high up over the city that no other building obstructed its view. I could see the entire west side of Manhattan like a feudal lord viewing his feifdom, his crops, his offspring and acreage, his streams.

"Mr. O'Dwyer? I'm Sylvia Golubowsky, Stenographer Number Ten, I mean, Nine."

He waved his hand without looking up. "Yes, yes Miss Ski, have a seat." It was that physicality that men display when they're in control. He was huge, healthy, ruddy, well-fed, well-bred, well-dressed. There were no other chairs, so I just leaned against the window ledge, pen in hand, wanting to be a part of it, part of the making of the news. He had the opportunity for generosity. He was secure. That day, Mr. O'Dwyer was my boss. I was just a faceless girl with a foreign last name. But by that time the next year I would be part of the heartbeat of the New York *Star*. I would be a reporter.

"Is this about the Chambers case, sir?"

He looked up then and saw me. I had distinguished myself enough to justify a movement of his chin.

"The Chambers case? That story won't make it to the typing pool until two o'clock this afternoon."

"I saw it in the *Times*."

"You read the *Times*?" he asked, impressed. "A girl like you?"

"I read it every day."

"Really?" He pushed back his hat. That was a real newspaperman, always wearing his hat at his desk. "And what do you think about the Chambers case, Miss Ski?"

I leaned forward on the windowsill, legs crossed under the weight of the steno pad. It wasn't that often that someone who mattered asked my opinion. And I had plenty of opinions to offer.

"Well, normally the House Committee seems ready to investigate anyone. But, in this instance, they really hesitated. If it wasn't for that junior congressman from California . . ."

"Richard Nixon."

"Right, Richard Nixon. Well, for some reason he was just dead set on it and pushed through the whole thing."

"Let me get this right, Miss Ski. Whittaker Chambers exposes the infiltration of Communists to the highest levels of the State Department, naming one Alger Hiss as the prime example. But you attribute all the brouhaha to the career desires of some lowly political neophyte. Is that what you read in the *New York Times,* or did you hear it from some poet on a barstool at the San Remo?"

"Neither, sir."

"See, I know where you kids hang out."

O'Dwyer turned his attention back to his desk, giving me another moment to soak in the atmosphere of his office. Books, papers, files, and a few photographs. His father, his wife, his boy in uniform.

"Do you know, Miss Ski, what Hiss said on the stand this morning?"

"No, sir."

O'Dwyer looked right at me this time. It was a warning masquerading as a suggestion, passing for caring, as though his helpful, personal piece of advice was not at all the menace that it really was. My first professional threat.

"He said 'I am not now and have never been a member of the Communist Party.' Remember those words, Miss Ski. They might come in handy some day."

"Yes, sir."

"Now, what is your name again?"

"Sylvia Golubowsky."

"Sylvia, I've called you here for an important reason. Today is my wife's birthday. What do you think would be a nice gift?"

"Well, what does she need?"

"A good stiff drink."

"Then buy her a bottle of beer."

"For her birthday?"

"A gift is only meaningful if it's personal, sir. If it is individual. You know, it's the thought that counts."

"Perhaps." He swung his feet up on the desk. "Miss Ski, in my closet is a linen jacket. There is a button in the left-hand pocket. Sew it on for me like a good girl, will you? Showing up with all my buttons will be *very meaningful* to the Mrs. It will be *personal*, Miss Ski, and all of that. Do a good job with the button, and maybe you'll get a promotion. What number are you now?"

"Nine."

"Do a good job and we'll take you up to Eight sooner or later."

It wasn't like I'd never experienced that before. *But,* I thought, stepping out into the hallway with his jacket in my hands, *the world should not be the same as your family.* If your family will not be a refuge from the world, then the world should be a refuge from your family. Otherwise, where was the relief?

The professors at City College had smirked at the sight of us, their first class of girls. We'd had to have five points higher on our high school grades than the boys to even be let in, and then they wouldn't let us study what we pleased. Only Education degrees for the ladies, no Bachelors of Arts. How many of my instructors had tried to push me into teaching or social work?

"Jewish girl? Teaching or social work."

And now the restrictions at City made sure that would be the case. In the meantime those insufferable boys from Mosholu Parkway and East New York knew how to get the most out of their opportunities. Professor Wiley in Economics announced on the first day of class that "We all know women contribute nothing to a classroom situation." It cowed a lot of us into dropping out at the end of our first year. All except for the refugees, looking like Christians lost among the Barbarians instead of German Jews that no one else wanted. Those German girls studied more than any American could ever study. Even the Brooklyn boys set on law school or becoming doctors had too many emotions between them and their books.

The point had always been to overcome these obstacles. Do your best and show your best. Some of the girls resolved to stay and fight it out, but I knew it would defeat me. Better to avoid the whole humiliating process and get to work right away. I'd rather fight my way up with one foot in the door than give City College three more years to destroy my will. And now, I could see that I had been right. O'Dwyer was testing me, but he could tell I had a brain. He had to respect that. Especially being the son of an immigrant himself. That's why he had asked my opinion in the first place. He was keeping his eye out for future reporters with a good nose for news.

"Miss Ski," his voice boomed from behind.

For one terrifying moment I wondered if I was being fired. I stepped back into his office, slightly light-headed, pumps clicking away on that old wooden floor, surprised at how naturally I expected defeat.

"Yes, sir, Mr. O'Dwyer?"

"Tell me something, Miss Ski. Who are you working girls voting for this November?"

"Excuse me?"

"Oh, I know it's private and all of that. But, just for my own personal poll. Well, let me put it this way. Who do *you* think the *Star* should endorse for president, Truman or Dewey?"

"Henry Wallace, of course."

"Henry Wallace?"

"I think he has a great chance."

"Henry Wallace? How old are you?"

"Almost twenty, Mr. O'Dwyer. Everyone I know is voting for him."

"You're going to vote for the Progressive Party in November? Where are you from, Flatbush Avenue?"

37

"Originally from Brownsville, sir. But I live in Manhattan now."

"Henry Wallace will get one million votes in Brooklyn and one million votes in the rest of the country, Miss Ski. I assure you that the New York *Star* will never endorse Henry Wallace."

This time the walk to my desk was on a silver carpet. He had noticed me and he had asked me for my opinion. Maybe it would influence his choice of an endorsement, and that could change the whole election. Henry Wallace in the White House and all because of me. Mr. O'Dwyer knew that there is room for all kinds of ideas, and he wanted excellence above everything. Quality above all.

I'm included, I thought. *I'm included.*

Everything that I needed my whole life was confirmed at that moment. If I worked hard and never let go of my desires. If I produced work of great quality. If I was gifted and developed my gifts. If I could sustain the highest level of merit, well then, I could never lose. And, of course I would do these things because then I would get what I needed. I would be a reporter and get my place in this world.

CHAPTER SIX

Austin Van Cleeve

1

"Every moment is filled with regret and nostalgia for this morning's regret. Speech was given to man to hide his thoughts, don't you agree, Austin? Let's have another whiskey and soda."

Jim was dead drunk, and I was taking notes.

" 'Give a woman a couple of kids and she'll leave you alone,' was my father's advice on my wedding night," O'Dwyer blathered. "Da handed it over like the secret password to the Vatican Archives, wrapped in a twenty-dollar bill. I married a wealthy woman and threw his money out the hotel window. I know I'm not the only bereaved parent racing to the office every morning to bury my head in achievement. The streets are full of them. Some still wear their purple hearts. Silent photographs in uniform, unmentioned on so many desks. But the knowledge of a shared national misery doesn't give me a clue as to what the hell I should do with my wife. There is nothing to keep me and Amy apart anymore. There is no third party."

Never, never tell anyone what you really feel unless they don't speak English or are about to be shot by a firing squad. I have never shared a confidence I didn't later regret. But I do encourage indiscretion in others because it always comes in handy.

Amy never actually blamed him. She told me this, sloshy

one night after four martinis. It was 1968, and we had both enjoyed the pleasure of being major donors to the Nixon campaign. Of course, I had contempt for him too, a grocer's son. But given the times, a puppet was the best we could get. All that log-cabin posturing. The hardhats would have been better off with William Buckley, but they voted their sentiments instead of their pockets.

The election night victory bash had been at the Waldorf, of course. Afterward we took a shaker of gin and rode in a horse-drawn buggy around Central Park, pretending to be J. P. Morgan and Lady Astor. Pretending it was still the Gilded Age.

"The government called, and our son did his duty," she said between olives.

Truthfully, I believed her. It's not so much that she'd always been brutally honest, for efficiency's sake, although that was the case. But rather that her statement seemed so true. America had served her father very well, and Amy knew from the time she was a girl that our system required sacrifice. I'm sure that when her son was born she intended him to be of use to the nation, and now he had been. There was no scandal, no shameful conflict or cover-up. He had died in battle and was therefore a hero.

Perhaps it was the gin or the cool evening air, but that night, taking in her gray hair held back by a Hermes scarf, I thought I saw Lady Liberty. In the darkness of Central Park, backlit by the lonely Dakota on one side and the great hotels along the south, she seemed like some kind of apparition. She was an extreme kind of patriot halfway between the lusty Betsy Ross giving head to Big George and the twatless Priscilla Mullins, America's first conveyor of blue balls. I confess I asked her to marry me, two old codgers in a bouncing buggy.

"Moral men have to face their own weakness," was her answer. And I realized what a ball buster she had always been. Not just a crusher but a granite slam. Still, the tension did dissipate, and we were both exhausted. From then on the conversation was quite frank, as though we were old friends. We had never been friends. We had never been anything except for repositories of information about the other. But simply living that long in the same sphere created an intimacy of sorts. A free-market familiarity. Two victorious Republicans on a very clear night.

"Plagued by too many freckles and overly white skin, Jim had gone out for football, true," she told me. "And he was, by all counts, the huskiest entering student at Boston College. Those other eager young men in the class of 1916 seemed to have family connections. That's why Jim had raised our boy to be physically as well as mentally tough. Tough enough to volunteer for the wildest missions."

"Yes, of course. Driver? Could you swing down Fifth?"

"Everyone wants a son who is a war hero, I suppose," she said, never spilling a drop on her mink. "If he comes home to tell the tales. But you can't be the returning champion if you never get in the ring."

There you have it. She was a killer.

"Did Jim serve in the First World War?" I asked, the night air so refreshing.

"He spent it in the classroom excelling in mental combat. That was why he admired our son so enormously. It was a feeling Jim had never imagined a father could have."

I'd heard evidence of the famous Da from the man himself, but they always seemed like inadvertent slips. When pressed, he'd never go any deeper. The old man was a pioneer in the burgeoning insurance industry, I'd gathered. In other words, he sold policies door to door to young hopefuls from the old country. Then he'd dump it all into high-risk, doomed-to-fail investments. A gambler done in by other people's willingness to gamble.

"His father would have loved your Stork Club lunches," Amy said as we rolled out of the forest and down the solid avenue. The most beautiful street in the world. "Drinking old-fashioneds with doctors who play the market with money raked in from abortions and venereal treatments. Lust and savagery among the wealthy, buy drinks all around. That's why our own boy's foolhardy bravery wasn't Jim's fault alone. It ran in the family."

I tipped the driver, and he took us all the way back to the Waldorf, past Bergdorf's, Bendel's, Tiffany's, Rizzoli's, past Best and Company. We turned left on Fifty-seventh Street and rounded the corner onto Park Avenue, the Pan Am Building looming before us. Nixon was president. We were still pulling the strings. History was changing and all of America knew it. This was the beginning of setting things right. The horse's hooves on Park Avenue. It was a beautiful night.

2

"Two more stingers, please. That'll do for me. What about you, Austin?"

"Make it four."

"The Stork is crowded tonight."

"I don't need a head count, Jim. What have you decided?"

"We're endorsing Truman. You can read about it in the morning edition."

I reached for my drink too quickly. "Girl," I called out, snapping for the wet nurse. Fortunately my needs were met by a young thing in a strapless gown and pushed-up breasts that presented themselves quite nicely over a tray of cigarettes.

"Camel, Chesterfields, or Pall Mall?"

"You look charming strapped in between those two leather suspenders," I whined, reaching for a ten-pack of Chesterfields. There was something vaguely familiar about this one. Rarely did the same girl last more than a month. They usually got beaten up, pregnant, or caught stealing gin in a matter of weeks. Wounded by O'Dwyer and in need of some female medicine, I carefully folded a five-dollar bill and placed it, ever so slowly, between the young girl's ample breasts. I owned her, then, with insinuation as quick and inescapable as a flash flood of oil. "How is your box, my dear? Must be a heavy weight to bear."

"Balanced," the girl said, smiling.

She had to smile, I know. It is the chain of command.

"Oh, my," I murmured to Jim as she went on her way with

a little pat on the fanny. "There is nothing less compatible with female beauty than an accent from Flatbush Avenue."

"I had one of those in my office the other day," he answered, delicately ignoring the previous transaction. "A five-syllable last name and a worldview so far to the left it was off of the playing field. But you know, Austin, that was one of the reasons I decided to go for Truman. A paper like ours has to stay in the middle if we want to attract the widest range of readers. Can't go alienating the working girl or we'll lose all those ads for cheap skin cream and third-rate dress shops."

"I am sad to see that you are finally growing up."

"Your father's paper is going for Dewey, I suppose."

"Of course. While you are taking your tips from Wops and Pollaks and any greenhorn washerwoman fresh off the boat, we're following trends in Washington and on Wall Street. The mood there is clearly for the governor."

The band stepped back onstage in their white dinner jackets and bow ties. They opened their set with "I'm in the Mood for Love."

"I, too, am in the mood for love," I cooed. "And that salty little tramp is going to fit my mood to a T."

"What do you mean?"

"Come on now, Jim, you can't be that naïve. There's a little phone number on that fiver bill, and I'm sure she needs something I can help her with. An audition, an abortion, an introduction, an electric bill. But I'll keep my eyes on the blondes, and you keep yours on Washington." I reached for my second stinger. "Do you disapprove? One so fascinated with the unwashed masses? The rank and vile?"

"Waiter, another round, please."

I had to smile, he was so uncomfortable. A big blubbery teddy bear Boy Scout. Then I got serious.

"Listen to me, Jim. There is a certain Mr. Nixon who is on a personal vendetta against every Harvard graduated liberal in the State Department. He was turned down by an angry mob of Ivy League law firms when he graduated, and he won't let a single one of them ever forget it."

"Blood feud? Like at the picture show. Where is that waiter?"

"Right. But this time it's upper-class Commies and working-class patriots. Right up your alley. Nixon has it in for Hiss, but it's personal. Take it from me, O'Dwyer, I have an impeccable source."

"Who? The cigarette girl?"

"Chambers himself."

This time it was O'Dwyer's turn to grab for a drink. Only it was my drink.

"That's my little cherry, O'Dwyer. But, enjoy it. I'll have the real thing soon enough."

"Chambers!"

"We worked together briefly at *Time* magazine, America's number-one breeding ground for skunks. His father was a fairy, that explains everything. Walked out on the family for another man."

The cocktails finally arrived, but Jim was too shaken to even try to finesse his properly. Just drank it down in one swallow like it was bootleg moonshine.

"Well, that's the first time I ever felt sympathy for Chambers. But why should America have to pay? He and Nixon are two peas in a rotting pod."

"Jim, that's true. But it is a very large pod. Besides, Chambers will take a lie detector test and Hiss will not. You can read about it in *my* column in tomorrow's early edition."

I fluttered, right there before him, like Lily Pons in *The Mikado*. She'd never actually sung *The Mikado,* but it spoke to my sense of myself as a great Diva, whispering behind a fan with Oriental cunning, European elegance, and a lethal little list.

CHAPTER SEVEN

Sylvia Golubowsky

"There's a Nigger in apartment 2D," Mrs. Morgan hissed over my shoulder.

"What?"

I'd been staggering up the stairs with two bags of groceries and already had too much to think about for one day.

"There is a Nigger in apartment 2D," she repeated, wringing her hands and twisting the end of her housedress as she followed me into my apartment and then into my kitchen. Rent meant nothing to Mrs. Morgan. Everything still belonged to her. "And I've got to get him out of there."

"Mrs. Morgan, the word is *Negro*," I said politely despite the sudden exhaustion that her anxiety had provoked. "And what is he doing in apartment 2D? Is it a porter?"

"No," she screamed. "A Nigger just moved in!"

I started unloading the shopping waiting for her to disappear. Bread from Bleecker Street, noodles from Mulberry and vegetables from Second Avenue.

"Please, Mrs. Morgan, I wish you would not use language like that."

This was going to be an incredible feast. I'd stayed up late the night before preparing tomato sauce from scratch according to the Calabrase family recipe. Theresa couldn't believe I'd grown up eating ketchup on spaghetti.

"A white girl comes in here last week to rent the apartment.

45

She tells me she's a teacher, he's got a good job. They put down two months' rent, and I gave her the lease. Sneaking little scrit, she didn't happen to mention that her husband is a Nigger. I bet they're not even married. I can't have people living in sin in my building. It's not Christian."

"I'm sure they're married, Mrs. Morgan."

"How could they be? Isn't it illegal? If it's not it should be. Besides, what white girl would marry a Nigger?"

I finally got her out of there and collapsed under the weight of my facade. I knew it wasn't right to let somebody talk that way. It gave the appearance that her attitude was all right with me. But this was my landlady, not some jerk on the El. I would soon be living alone in that place and have to carry all the rent on my own. I couldn't risk getting on Mrs. Morgan's bad side in case I needed a few days of flexibility with the rent now and then. It was a survival situation. Or so I pretended.

The fellows on the copy floor said the most repulsive things all the time, and I'd had to learn to ignore them. Otherwise I'd spend the whole day at work squirming, and a person can't live like that. Not if I wanted to get ahead on the job. Fighting back too much was just a diversion, I had to be strategic. Better to explain politely to Mrs. Morgan the way I had than to run her out of there vowing revenge. It wouldn't have changed her mind.

Anyway, with Negro soldiers fighting in combat and men like Paul Robeson becoming heroes, new ways were no longer just around the corner. They were happening every week on the streets. Since VE Day there had been more Negroes than ever in the coffee shops and movie theaters. Ex-soldiers with better education and raised expectations. That's why the army was going to be desegregated. That was their reward. Robeson was so handsome with that big booming voice singing "Old Man River." A Negro who was both a football star and a Shakespearean actor? That was unheard of before. People like Mrs. Morgan were on their way out, at least in Greenwich Village. Sure, down in the south segregation was still the rule. You could see it in the newsreels. It seemed impossible to imagine Negroes being treated so barbarically. But in 1948, with Lena Horne a big film star, it jut seemed to be a matter of time.

The truth is that I had never lived next door to a Negro before. I had never lived in the same building with one. Barely in the same neighborhood. The line between East New York and Brownsville was the Canarsie train. One side was Black. My whole childhood I really didn't know that Jews were not a majority. I didn't know that there were many other people who were not Jewish. On Christmas, maybe there would be two families in the whole neighborhood who would have Christmas trees. So, the whole idea of wishing that you had Christmas, a favorite complaint of my fellow students at City, never actually entered my mind. I just felt sorry for the Christians because they had to go to school on Jewish holidays. No, the only differences back then were between Orthodox Jews and nonorthodox Jews. There were Jews who kept kosher and those who did not. So, this was good news, having a Negro next door. It was part of being in the big wide world.

I imagined making friends with him and with his white wife. Maybe someday I would fall in love with a Negro. Have sex with him. Someone I'd meet through my neighbors. I had dated a Negro boy once, a City student named Harry. He was a member of the Frederick Douglass Society and they had their own section in the cafeteria. He had a health deferment and was studying hard to keep his grade point average up. He wanted to become a CPA. I'd kissed him against a wall on a windy night in spring. His lips were warm and inviting and that hair, enticing. It was funny, but there was something so much more interesting to me, well . . . attractive to me about being with a Negro boy. I identified with him. Those white ones were too arrogant, they had no fragility about them. No fear.

I thought we'd see each other again, but Harry never asked. After a few weeks of awkward silences I'd invited him to sit with the gang at lunch, but when he found out that some of the others were members of the Marxist Cultural Society he withdrew.

"My family is counting on me to get my degree," he said later, never looking me in the eye. "I can't take a chance with any foolishness."

47

He married Rachel Levitsky whose father lost his citizenship so she couldn't be political either.

Seven o'clock. I got back to the task of preparing dinner, closely following Theresa's scrawled instructions. *Pasta* she called it, plus a tossed salad and a bottle of Chianti from Theresa's uncle's shop. That would be a good farewell for Rita and Ted.

Actually, I was furious with Rita for leaving, no matter how much obligation I was under to feel otherwise. Devastation has always translated into fury for me. It seems so unnecessary, every single time. We'd been through everything together in that thirty-five-dollar-a-month apartment. It was Rita who'd brought home the Moses Soyer reproduction that hung in our kitchen. It was Rita who'd found the Mexican guitar that stood leaning in the corner. All that was packed up now. The place, empty. She did offer to leave the old hi-fi set that now sat deserted in the vacant living room. It was Rita, after all, who had lugged it home on the subway and started me listening to jazz.

When I was a girl Mama and Pop would walk for miles on Saturday morning to hear different cantors sing at different synagogues. Yosele Rosenblatt, Kussevitsky, all the greats. They'd walk to Stone Avenue or to the shul on Sheffield. That afternoon at the kitchen table they would talk over the performances, comparing this one and that one before opening up the shop. Mama always listened to classical music on the radio. She listened at home while she was ironing or at the store, waiting on customers. But this was background music to my life. I'd never had a music that was my own. Not until the night Rita came home and put that first platter on the turntable.

It is still hard for me to separate the music from Rita herself. Those well-worn sixteens and seventy-eights were the score to our two years together. My first shared life.

Rita's granddad remembered all the hole-in-the-walls around Union Square with small dance orchestras from his triumphant days after the Spanish-American War. Only the concert gardens along the Bowey offered up big cabarets. He told us about the Alhambra with its twenty-six-piece orchestra and the despair of song pluggers who had to buy drinks all around to get their lady's favorites played. One night, in our living room, he'd even had a few shots of schnapps and started talking about his bachelor days frequenting the Haymarket, the most notorious red-light Times Square dance hall of them all.

"It was a department store of forbidden pleasure," he said with his big white handlebar mustache. "The rooms upstairs had wide-open gambling. The management created fictitious clubs that held private parties every night. So, on Monday it would be the Welsh Rabbit Society and on Wednesdays, the Piano Tuners' Benevolent Association."

He splurged to hear the First Naval Battalion Band play on deluxe excursion steamers to Coney Island while most people had to settle for humming a dislocated rhythm on the twenty-five-cent round-trip. But the greatest treat of all, Granddad recalled, was the Rockland Palace, a shabby red brick building on 155th Street and Eighth Avenue. It housed the Manhattan Casino and the syncopated orchestras of Manhattan's first Negro jazz bands.

While her grandfather favored the authentic sounds, Rita's dad was more refined and loved dancing to the white interpreters. By the time her father was a doughboy, white dancing to Negro rhythm was the biggest rage since the turkey trot. Especially Vernon and Irene Castle. Their dancing was a *sensation*, he'd say. Particularly their steps to Irving Berlin's "Alexander's Ragtime Band."

"Daddy," Rita said as I watched her slap her father's knee with an unfathomable familiarity. "That's just because you were in the war."

"Oh no, Sugar," he'd answer, equally shockingly American. "I'm not partial to patriotism. It was the fox-trot they learned from W. C. Handy and passed on to the rest of us that won my heart."

I'd never seen my own grandparents but had categorized them according to family stories about my grandmother's reaction to seeing the *tfilen* on the cat. It had no place in the world of aging flappers. My invisible relatives were assuredly ignorant peasants harvesting potatoes and trying to scrape together a crust of bread. Not razzmatazz jazzers switching from pocket clocks to wristwatches, now that they had so many appointments. Mama and Pop might share a little joke or two in the kitchen, but they would never socialize with my friends, treat them like equals with tall tales of enticingly forbidden deeds.

I stood, devastated and therefore furious over the scattered groceries on my kitchen table. Now Ted was going to medical school on the GI Bill, and when he was through, Rita would go back to college and then have children. It was all planned. If only there was a GI Bill for girls. Just getting through the day was like walking a battlefield. That had been a sore spot between the three of us, Rita deciding to become a mother first. Even though Ted knew nothing about the abortion, the whole reasoning behind it was that Rita wanted to be a doctor too. And, she doubted, as I did, that in this marriage her turn would ever come. I suspected that was why Ted pressured Rita to get married so quickly. He was tired of hearing my complaints.

"But you always wanted to be a doctor," I argued again, unable to contain myself despite a mouthful of farewell macaroni.

"Rita's not disciplined enough to be a doctor," Ted interrupted.

"I'm not," she said. "I mean, I like the idea of it and I've always been interested in science. But I don't have a good memory, and you have to memorize so many things if you want to make it through medical school."

I was stunned. Rita was acting out a theater show. This was nothing like what she'd say in private when Ted wasn't there.

"That's ridiculous," I shot back. "You got an A in chemistry."

"That's because I was helping her," Ted said. "And when I'm enrolled in medical school I won't have the time to do her work too."

I knew enough to shut my mouth from then on. It would be the last time the two of us would eat together under our shared roof. It was the last moment before Rita would belong to him. But the last time when Rita would tell me the truth? That moment was already long past.

CHAPTER EIGHT

Austin Van Cleeve

1

One evening our drinking was aborted by Jim's required attendance at the theater. Something about a fellow called "Roberts." We made plans to reconnoiter after at the Astor Bar and stumbled outside together only to be hit by the horrible stench of Fifty-third Street. O'Dwyer was absolutely morbid, and the city's aroma did not revive any last gasps of enthusiasm.

"I have to be at the theater by seven-thirty, but I'd rather be going for a strawberry frappe at Schraft's with anybody's maiden aunt."

That was O'Dwyer. Out of all sixty million Americans, he was the only one heading for a swank night at the theater with his loving wife and closest friends who would rather lie down in the gutter and puke. He was the only one that night who would have gladly given up the greatest players on the greatest stages in the world for the reprieve of ordering a Reingold Extra Dry from some bleached blonde called "Snooks."

The West Fifties were dank, even in the fall. Would winter never come? The streets were held together by old tenements, radios blaring out from crooked windows. Everyone still listening to Walter Winchell, no matter what. We stumbled along past seedy teenagers growing up to be seedy old men who never leave their doorway, just grow fatter.

"A man in Hell's Kitchen keeps on the same undershirt for sixty-seven years," O'Dwyer blubbered. "Until he's laid out in Redden's Funeral Home in the too small suit he got married in."

"This neighborhood," I proclaimed. "It's a jungle of white flesh, yellowed T-shirts, and stark murmurings of the people who don't know how things work."

"And I'd give anything to escape into the sea of them," he said. "Walk among them forever anonymous. I'm so tired, Austin. I just want to rest." I glanced over, and he was a mess. His tie was undone, his hair a strawberry tangle. "I just want to sit on that stoop and be gossiped at. Disappear under a barrage of gossip and fleshy grandmothers who never forget your birthday. In a neighborhood like this, Austin, a birthday is something special."

"Is it your birthday?"

"No."

We took that turn down Broadway, and the intensity of the lights opened up before us like a punishment. The flash and splash of pinball city. Who needs lightning when you've got endless bolts of electricity crackling silently overhead? Who needs natural disaster?

When we approached the theater I stood back and watched as the poor lambie stepped up for his punishment. There was Amy, lovely of course, but very cold, waiting.

"Darling?"

"Darling, am I late? I'm so sorry."

"You're upset," she said. "So I'm not going to argue with you. Oh, Camilla, look, Jim's here."

"How do you know?" he whimpered in front of everyone. "How do you always know?"

"Say hello to Camilla."

Amy was a small woman but fleshy enough. A real blonde, she had a waterfall of tumbling curls that she kept cut short to retain her authority. Big red lips that required lipstick only as a way to tone them down. And she had a crooked face with a lovely large nose, just the kind you'd want to suck on. Pale blue eyes. Her face was twisted so each expression was open to multiple interpretations. It gave her a great advantage, that face.

"Camilla," Jim said, trying to smile. "How lovely to see you. Darling, am I late?"

"We've covered that territory already, dear," Amy answered calmly, taking her husband by the arm as though it was the scruff of his collar. "Come sit down," she said on the way into the theater. "You'll lose all your troubles when the magic begins."

Floor show over, I was left on the deserted sidewalk and decided to go wait out the interim back in my office. I kept a little hideaway on a side street in the theater district in those days. It was away from all the pressures of my father's authority and gave me some respite from the demands of Society and commerce. Besides, I always enjoyed giving one final polish to the next day's column in peace.

—*What two-fisted starlet's new platinum hairdo won't cover up her Red roots?*

—*What all-American he-man can't find a hole deep enough to bury his racketeer father?*

—*What Tammany pol is handing out IOU's faster than crony appointments?*

Who did win the sixth at Belmont? Frankly, that was more pressing on my mind than the burdens of transmitting the intricacies of other people's lives to the general population. But one glance at the Racing Form and it was clear I'd lost another C-note to the Hebes.

The buzzer rang unexpectedly, seeing as it was after eight in the evening. I just assumed it was the night bell for the funeral home downstairs. Someone coming in for a nice coffin, only ninety dollars if he could spirit it out after three A.M. Dying had turned out to be a gold mine, now that America had assimilated Freud and the subsequent guilt. Mortal ostentation made sense in the new economy. A baby born on the charity ward in 1888 could expect to accrue enough for an extravagant funeral by 1948, even if he'd lost everything in the Crash. Amazing how the truly rich could lose "everything" and still be absolutely loaded. I made a note to invest in death as soon as the opportunity presented itself.

I looked up from my desk, which was pristine, even in the

eery light of the single bulb. There, before me like a gift from the Devil, was that trashy piece of human garbage from the Stork that I'd done a couple of times and then promptly forgotten. Teary-eyed tart, she'd made a fair piece of pork. Only slightly overdone. Now, what did she want? This was going to be a good one.

"Austin."

"My dear, what are you doing here?"

I leaned back into my leather chair and looked her over. Lana Turner sweater but just an average set of tits. Never dress like a movie star if you don't really look like one. And no one does, of course. Not unless they're in the movies.

"I missed you, darling," she leaked.

This was going to be good. This was going to be wonderful.

"Oh, Austin . . ."

Tears, I thought.

"Oh, I just don't know who else to turn to." Whimper. Whimper.

"What's wrong?"

"Those dickheads fired me," she said, sitting down on the desk and pulling out a cigarette.

"Well, what did you do?" I asked, deciding to play along. I could use a blow job after all, so I whipped out my platinum lighter and held it under her chin. "Do you like butter, my little buttercup?"

"I mean the house crew is cool, no one's uncouth."

"Of course not."

"But I ran up a bar bill before they told me it was pay as you go. You know, house rules."

"Imagine that. Expecting you to pay. Oh, those beasts."

She crossed her legs, and I noticed her nylons. Not even silk. Legs, fair to middling with an all-important juicy snatch in between them.

"Gee, here we are both getting blue at this hour of the night," she sighed. "I was just sitting at home worrying and then I thought, what's the point of living in a shell unless you expect to be a chicken some day. Right?"

"Absolutely Nietzschean of you."

"I mean losing my night job, well, I'm kind of desperate. My boyfriend says to go be a taxi dancer after hours. But I can't be a dance-hall girl. I'd be ashamed to go home and look myself in the mirror. I'm sick with worry, Austin, and I'm just plain sick of myself."

"Come here, darling. What did you say your name was?"

"Call me June. It rhymes with moon."

"Of course, and also with dragoon."

She looked up over her cigarette smoke with an MGM pout. "Austin, I didn't know you were a poet."

"Yes," I said, "I spend my days on couplets. Rhyming *Jews* and *booze, sedition* and *nutrition, Mommy* and *Commie.* What is it Daddy can do for you?"

"I gotta get out of my mother's place. I've tried to get a room, but they don't rent to single girls. 'Single girls bring single fellas, or else they're up late washing out their stockings in the sink.' How many times do I have to hear that one? I've got to get another night job."

"Poor sweetums. Let me put my little hand on your lovely thigh and we'll see what we can do."

"Oh, Daddy, tell me a story."

"Love to, Junie. Once upon a time, a long time ago, there was a little girl. The water tasted good so she jumped down the well."

2

I waited at the Astor Bar, satiated and in the mood for a new round of drinks, but poor O'Dwyer had forgotten me completely and tumbled home in a cab. Fortunately, for my entertainment, Amy's friend Camilla had invited her out for a drink with the cast since Camilla's favorite pastime was backing up young theater artists. Amy, envious, had gotten into the habit of greeting her husband's frequent desertions with many a late-night adventure among theater people. And, at this point, a drink with cavalier comediennes was worth more to her than the actual performance.

All of this became apparent to me when I saw the two women come into the Astor and join a table of dressers, choreographers, costumers, and set painters, all half-drunk. I'd been listening in on their joviality already, especially perking up when they'd been joined by some actors, fully drunk. They were gathered at a large table right over my shoulder, and I could see their lips moisten in the mirror over the bar. All were filled with hopes and expectations, mostly false and unreasonable. It was delightful. Faith, the gorgeous design of false faith. The velveteen, casketlike embrace of it.

If poetic justice were to be in order, somehow the state of these children's delusions did resonate with Amy's life up to that point. Her own sentimentality had been fading daily. At first she was terribly disappointed, but by this night it had all seemed soberingly predictable. It was a wonder she had been surprised enough to be so bitterly let down.

Everyone in town knew that O'Dwyer had come into the *Star* as a bright eager reporter and Amy's father had liked him right away. She'd always wanted her own father to notice her, and so she placed herself directly in his line of vision by marrying someone who had already caught his attention. That was what she'd been after. And she'd gotten what she wanted.

Yes, I must come clean. Amy did agree to marry me that night in the buggy in 1968 and our marriage survived three forgettable years. It was a marriage rooted in boredom and a last-ditch attempt to break it before accepting the limits of old age. But, since there was nothing truly romantic between us, we spent thirty-six months reminiscing and then filed for divorce. Ho-hum. I'd never acknowledged my pure voyeurism of twenty years before. If I had she wouldn't have told me so many important details. If she'd known I'd been spying on her younger self, she would have withheld the scoop. Even in marriage one has to be ever so careful. After all, marriage is not forever. Thank God. Only by being strategic was I able to learn about that first night, coming home from her parents' with Jim by her side. Amy had felt like Henry Ford watching the first Model T come off the assembly line. All her hard work and her father actually beamed. He'd asked her opinion on a couple of matters and seemed truly pleased when she'd kissed him good night. That was what she'd desired her whole life to that point, and Jim was the one who had given it to her. Her father's attention.

Yes, yes, Jim was a kind and loyal husband etc., etc., and most importantly an excellent newspaperman. Not cynical. No one ever whispered a suggestion of nepotism when he became editor in chief, for it was Amy who had been elevated by the marriage. Not Jim. He was the best man in the office and so, naturally, rose to the top. But then her old man, Harrison, became ill from the pressure of keeping the paper through the Depression and died too young. The next few years were a blur of tears until one day she was waving farewell to a son she'd never even talked to. Sending him off to another blur. She'd never told him a thing about herself. When the telegram came, she still hadn't done with mourning her father and new, metallic grief settled into her heart. Now, by that night in the Astor Bar, she'd developed a razor-sharp curiosity and a keen desire to participate. Jim, of course, had gone the other route. They were as far apart as husband and wife as she had been as mother and son. And I had a ringside seat.

"The existence of the theater is predicated upon the exploitation of actors," Camilla said as they walked right past me toward the exuberant table. "Praise them, Amy, praise them. Tell them to never go back to Kansas. Tell them there was an agent in the wings and a critic on the floor. Tell them you know of a hot new director and there might be a part opening up soon. Give them something to pretend about while they're slinging hash. Then hope, for their sakes, that they get married off before the scenario turns to taxi dancing. We need them, those bright young girls and boys. We need to suck their blood, or there will be no art, art, art."

Heavy gossiping was already underway when Amy arrived, so she plopped down between a dark-haired playwright and a little assistant seamstress. The girl treated the writer with such familiar disdain that she had to be either a knowing ex-girlfriend or the sister who'd cleared his plate for twenty years. Next to her was a Jewish-looking actor with an acquired name like Tad. The three had started on beer and gin sometime long before intermission.

"I was in Hollywood last February," the playwright knowingly let slip. "And everyone I met was waving around a booklet they had just received from the Motion Picture Alliance for the Preservation of American Ideals. It was called *Screen Guide for Americans.*"

"How poetic." The seamstress smiled sarcastically, yet still sweetly. She was advertising a sweetness available for anyone except the Playwright himself, who got only very pointed but affectionately knowing mistrust. "Was it a list of do's and don'ts?"

The girl couldn't help egging on his performance. How intimate.

"Mostly don'ts."

"This is Amy O'Dwyer, everyone," Camilla interrupted, and I could see their nostrils flaring as they each, in turn, smelled money. They smiled lucratively at her and then, being show people, fell right back into the subject of their own desirousness, which always seemed to supersede reality in a delightful way. A seductively entrancing and enticingly delicious way.

"Drink up," the playwright said, flashing his dashing Errol Flynn grin and then forgot all about it, getting back to his first order of business, which was being the center of attention.

"So, tell us," the girl pushed impatiently. "And we'll see how many names you can drop in the process."

"One," he said pointedly, holding up one finger and aiming it right between her eyes. "One. Don't deify the common man. Two. Don't glorify the collective. Three. Don't smear industrialists. Four. Don't be fooled when the Reds tell you they're against Fascism. Their real enemies are Shakespeare, Chopin, and Edison."

"Like to read in the dark, do they?" quipped the girl.

"But," the playwright snorted, grabbing back the spotlight, "Jack Warner says . . ."

"Of *Warner Brothers,*" she underlined.

"Warner says, *Congress can't last forever.*"

"Well, my brother is a law clerk out there," interjected Tad, aka Saul. "And he heard Robert Taylor testify against the Hollywood Ten last year."

Tad adapted his most American Robert Taylor jaw and that seriously empty, handsomely void blank stare. *"I can name a few who seem to sort of disrupt things once in a while. One chap we have currently, I think, is Mr. Howard DaSilva. He always seems to have something to say at the wrong time. If I had my way, the Party would be outlawed and they would all be sent back to Russia or some other unpleasant place."*

"Well, Sterling Hayden . . ." added Playwright.

"That's Name Drop Number Two," Seamstress noted.

"He named his former mistress, not to mention a whole slew of friends."

Playwright had said the word *mistress* in quite an insinuating manner. I'd been watching very carefully through the bar mirror, and he and Amy had not even exchanged glances. But now I could confirm that he'd been calculating his moves ever since Camilla brought her to the table. Must have been desperate for a producer. Or was he just having trouble paying that night's bar bill?

"Well, the guy who wrote *My Friend Flicka* named one hundred and sixty-one people," the girl piped in.

"Now who's dropping names?"

"Flicka? And my agent Lassie, my manager National Velvet, and my director Rin Tin Tin."

"You can't know the whole story, though," Playwright insisted as though it was his future honor on the auction block. "The guy had to make his mark in snow somehow."

"Good artists don't squeal," the girl said, totally confident this time. All the smirky silliness was gone, it must have been a real belief.

"What proof do you have of that, Comrade?" Tad insisted. "Gale Sondergaard took the Fifth, and all she ever made was *Spiderwoman.*"

Now that the table had turned over to politics, Playwright dropped out of the conversation. All his attention was on Amy.

He must have desperately needed a cigarette. Then she lit one for herself and blew the smoke in his face.

"What does your husband do, Mrs. O'Dwyer?"

"How do you know I have a husband?"

"You're not Irish enough for a name starting O apostrophe."

"I've got the best one!" Tad yelled out, grabbing back center stage. "Ginger Rogers's mother testifying before the House Committee that big, bad Dalton Trumbo made her little girl speak Communist Propaganda in that classic 1943 film *Tender Comrades*."

"Oh my, I've never heard of that one. What was the line?" Camilla asked innocently, only to be answered by a chorus of young show-biz fanatics chanting in unison.

" 'Share and share alike. That's democracy,' " all three tumbling over each other with laughter.

"What do you think of the Hollywood Ten, Mrs. O'Dwyer?" Playwright asked, letting his jaw hang slack, just the way he'd practiced it.

"Well," she answered carefully. "They call them the Unfriendly Ten. But really, do these fellows have any talent? Or are they just unfriendly?"

"Talent hasn't a thing to do with it," the seamstress announced, sticking to her guns.

"What are you trying to say?" Playwright threw down the glove. "All evening you've been hinting at some correlation between talent and testimony. Spit it out, girl. Out with it."

"It just seems," she started, and then paused when everyone fell silent. For, finally, there was something at stake before them that mattered. After all, what was more important to these pups than the question of their own abilities and how ethical factors might keep them from getting ahead?

"It just seems," she said. "That if you are really talented you don't have to turn anybody in. You don't have to stab your relatives and friends in the back. Your talents will bring you to your goal. If your work is good, it will provoke people's feelings, feelings about themselves. And they will love your work and support it. It is only the mediocrities without much to say who have to connive and manipulate, build careers by positioning themselves and acquiring connections. That's the only way for them to get ahead. And since there are so many mediocrities it just seems . . ."

"Yes, dear?" Amy asked, suddenly caring a great deal for this young girl.

"It just seems like dangerous days are ahead."

Then none of them were sure of what to do. So they all looked at each other's reactions before nodding in agreement.

CHAPTER NINE

Sylvia Golubowsky

1

"What happened to your face?"

Theresa turned slowly, her neck creaking like a rusty crane. My friend's beating was poorly concealed behind enough powder for the breakfast rush at a pancake house. But she didn't avert her eyes. Theresa just sat there, daring all comers to confirm her defeat.

"Guess."

"Jesus, Theresa."

"Yeah, where the hell is Jesus Christ? I was looking for him last night, but he must have been dead drunk."

Her father, she said, had slapped her around because she was talking about getting her own place.

"Bruno says the old man acts like a pimp, doesn't want to lose a penny of his cut off my paycheck. I'll fix his wagon. Now I'm out of there for good. That's for sure. Let him sell his old jalopy next time the rent comes due."

"Honey," I said slowly. "You can always stay with me."

It's what she'd wanted, after all. Wasn't it? Those hints at the end of the summer. But lately Bruno had been more in the picture, and any ideas of sharing with me had disappeared from our conversations. We were too different. Something about Theresa always scared me, and she knew it. Her life was too big.

Fathers beating up their own children? It's one thing when you're a bratty kid, but grown-up women subjected to paternal bruising? Thank God Jews don't drink.

"You're a doll," she said, smiling for the mere fact of someone actually saying something nice. "But I'm gonna stay at Bruno's. He's all I got, and when you're old maids like us, Sylvia, you gotta keep your guy's eyes off those college babes in varsity sweaters."

"You think cheerleaders are Bruno's type?"

"Don't you give me grief too. His place is okay. No closets though. You know those buildings were made for people who don't have anything. No lights in the hallways. I guess I'm going to be making *his* coffee from now on. It's that or get shipped off one night in an ambulance to Bellevue. *That one's DOA, Doc. Another Wop for the meat wagon.*"

"You think your father would kill you?"

"You never know." Theresa sighed, turning back to work.

How could this be? I was so confused. What kind of monster would beat his daughter to death? How could Theresa let anybody lay a hand on her? It didn't make any sense.

This was a story I couldn't get out of my mind as I brushed my hair in the mirror of the cigarette machine while waiting for the train. I took a long look at my own face. No one had ever struck it. I liked the way I looked. Kind of sophisticated, actually. One of the faces where the beauty just popped out every now and then. Like someday someone who really loved me would look over across the table and be pleasantly surprised by how pretty I looked. On a whim I dropped fifteen cents into the slot and pulled out a pack. Ordinarily I did not smoke. It wasn't like I had never tried it. I'd puffed away behind the laundry with Pete Milliard and then in the cafeteria with Alan Lightman, Heshy Lefkowitz, and the whole sophisticated City College crowd. Rita smoked sometimes at night, late, lying on the couch with jazz on the hi-fi. And there were times, over a glass of Chianti, that I had smoked a few all the way down to the butt. I just hadn't gotten around to a regular habit yet. I hadn't found my brand.

No sign of the train. The elevated platform was empty, and

the cool rainy night felt good. No one from Manhattan was rushing into the boros at eight o'clock on a Friday night. All the traffic was the other way around. Those observing a religious prescription, of course, were tucked away in their apartments while the rest stayed out gallivanting until late. At rush hour the subway was packed with hardworking Brookynites hurrying home to who knows what. But nobody went into Brooklyn for a late dinner on a Friday night. It just wasn't done.

I lit my Lucky Strike in the wind and looked out over the long wooden platform, the weathered wooden shelter and its old long benches underneath. There was something great about standing on top of the city that way, waiting for the train. My destiny. I knew that when I became a reporter I would be standing alone, waiting in every capital city of Europe. It paid to know how to smoke when you're a woman alone. I'd need to look tough, competent, to give myself something to do to pass the time and keep my nerves under wraps. A cigarette would give me a moment to contemplate, something to observe with.

Hanging on to the leather straps as the train snaked across the bridge, I reached into my purse for some Sen-Sen and fluffed out my hair again, hoping no smoke still lingered. No point in making Pop angry if it could be avoided, though compared to Mr. Calabrase, he was starting to look like an angel. Lost in thought, I almost forgot to change at Alantic Avenue, and then plopped down on the yellow rattan subway seats staring out the window of the green car until the Brownsville stop.

If it wasn't for Lou I wouldn't have gone back nearly half as much. It was Lou's presence that made it my home. He was my one true friend, the only one who could telegraph safety under any circumstance because he was really on my side. I couldn't remember a feeling I'd never shared with him, not a single hopeful desire. He knew all my plans. And it was my job to help him keep dreaming even in a tight spot. With all the guys coming home from the service, a young fellow like my brother couldn't find a job for love or money. So, he was going to Brooklyn College at night and still living at home. The competition with the GI's was something else because they all got preferential treatment. Lou couldn't even drive a cab.

Mama was sitting alone at the kitchen table in a housedress, as tired at the end of the week as she was at the beginning. She sat under the yellow table light fingering old photographs kept quiet in a small cardboard box. The young woman in those photographs was a fashionable Polish girl from a good Jewish family, gone slightly wild. Her hair was in a flapper bob, she had kohl under her eyes like film stars from Warsaw. She stood with her family in their best tailored clothes outside of their home in Rohatan. This evening, though, she was extremely plain. Would I dye my hair when I went gray? She didn't. Maybe I would dye my hair before it went gray and then stop suddenly when it actually did.

"Where are they?" was the question she never asked, looking at the pictures.

Mina's mother had already died of cholera by the time that photo was taken. It was that story, about the first war and how the Kaiser's troops had occupied their house. A soldier put the *tfilin* on the cat. Not again. That's all she ever wanted to tell me, one story about a long-lost mother who figures only as an outraged, helpless observer, a joke in her primitive religiosity. It was a story about history, war and occupation. The Kaiser. Its repetition was a substitute for faded memories and a stand in for deep feelings too long past or painful to express. Not about a family, like *the time we all went fishing and dad taught me how to catch,* or whatever it was Americans with short memories talked about. *Making ice cream and cranking up the Victrola.* The Sunday buggy. To this day when I meet a Jew who's stupid, I'm surprised. With epic bedtime stories about global calamities, how could a child not be conceptual? *Yiddishe kopf* meant you were smart. *Goyishe kopf?* Borderline simpleton. But *Yiddishe punim,* you were a wallflower. *Goyishe punim?* A great beauty. Blonde. My grandfather was so handsome, Pop mentioned a couple of times. Blonde. From the Ukraine.

Next to my mother in the photograph were her brothers, Shmul and Solomon, one had been kidnapped by Russian soldiers and taken to Siberia where he married a goy and was never heard from again. He should have painted his eye and shot off his own foot. Then the Nazis would have gotten him instead. How did they know he was married? Mina couldn't remember. The other one? What happened to him? Her youngest brother was not in the photograph. He'd gone off to Palestine to fight with the partisans.

"I used to carry him to cheder," she said.

Maybe someday she'll see him again. But what would they talk about? Her two sisters Dora and Adela. Adela was the intellectual, she taught herself Hebrew and could pray as well as the men. They sent my mother, the youngest girl, to Vienna to a job washing coins in a bank. No one wanted to take her in. She begged her father Simcha to let her stay, but his refusal was their final farewell and she was sent off to America at age twenty-one entirely against her will. Now these sisters had not been heard from in five years. Everyone expected the worst, but *it* had not been confirmed. When Hitler came to power Mina wrote them letters begging her sisters to get out. But she did not have the money to bring them over. She couldn't save them. She had my mouth to feed. They were so stubborn. They wouldn't leave what they knew. They wouldn't give up their status in the community. They didn't want to come to America and wash other people's clothes.

Of course no one took that into consideration when they sent my mother off to New York against her will. I've grown up around immigrants my whole life. I still feel like one. And I swear they are the people that no one wanted, their own brothers turned against them. No one leaves their family by choice. Life was unfathomable and so they had to go. I've heard a lot of stories in Yiddish around the kitchen table from a lot of desperate newly arrived lost souls, and there wasn't a one who didn't cry their guts out and curse waking up in the morning. Lady Liberty and her golden torch? My mother kissed the New York earth when she got off the boat, but then again she thought that food was free. She didn't find out it cost money until she got hungry.

No, when they kicked her out of her own bed and sent my mother to New York against her will, no one cared about how she felt. Yet now, it was her failing, not earning enough in the store to present her sisters with the decisive tickets. They went to Auschwitz instead of Flatbush. And for five years, any day now they could have rung that front doorbell. Then we'd all eat babka and coffee, and my mother could finally tell them off. Tell them how it tore her heart to be sent away. That her own father wouldn't stand up for her. The Kaiser.

"It's almost nine o'clock."

"I had to work late."

Her mother had died when she was thirteen. When I was thirteen I waited, but the dreaded moment passed. Her sisters cooked her food and put it on her plate. She cooked food for Shimshon. She bathed him and made sure he had the money for books and clothes. This is what a sister is supposed to do. I heard these stories my entire life. She loved her brother all of her days, and then he ran off to Palestine and became a partisan, a higher calling. He fought the British and made the desert bloom. Now, this year there was the founding of the state of Israel, and he had done that. That's why you love your brother, so that he can make a new world.

When she was a girl my mother belonged to a circle of Zionist Socialist youth who wanted a Socialist state in Palestine. They sat drinking glasses of tea arguing about politics and literature, all the most modern ideas. She read *Brothers Karamazov* in Russian and *Brothers Ashkenasy* in Yiddish. They argued in German and Polish.

"Your daughter runs around with all the boys," local wags gossiped to her father.

"Oh no," he laughed. "When my daughter is with the boys everyone can see her. When your daughter is with the boys, no one knows."

She was somebody. She was Simcha Leibling's *tochter*.

So, why wouldn't he stand up for her when they sent her off to America? Now she washed other people's underwear, their blood-stained panties and urine-stained sheets. She ironed them perfectly, wrapped them up in brown paper, and tied it with a string. Is that why she went to Gymnasium and had an education.

I couldn't bear to sit at a table and have my mother serve

me food. It made me sick. I couldn't bear anything about my mother's life. That's why I always came home too late to eat.

2

"Don't work so much," Pop said from behind his copy of the *Forward*. "That's all you ever think about, getting ahead. The most important thing is to find a nice fellow. A family is forever. Sylvia, you're in trouble. You're all backed up. You can't find a boy to marry. You're too busy."

Joe Golubowsky's real name was Yosele. He came over when he was only thirteen. His father had died, his mother remarried a man who made him sleep in the cellar. He came to America alone, and every night of his life was a lonely night. My father cried every night. Now, he doesn't cry, he doesn't think about that time anymore, now that his name is Joe.

I never understood my father. I wanted to, but he didn't make any sense to me. His way of operating never became familiar. He would say things casually, almost haphazardly, but they had no implications for how he would act. He'd say, "I only want the best for you." But, now that I had the best he didn't seem to care or even notice. He'd say things without understanding what they meant. He wanted to be a man who did the right thing, but he didn't want to actually do the right thing. He just wanted it to be that what he happened to be doing would somehow be right.

"Pop," I said, hanging my bag in the closet and sitting across from him at the kitchen table. "I've got a great job now. You should come into the city and see my office. It's a big newsroom, like Brenda Starr. The other day I talked directly to the editor in chief. He asked me who I was supporting for president."

"What you do is more important than who you know," he said. "Some things are more important than money."

There, he did it again. He didn't know what he was saying. He hadn't really listened when I was talking, or else he didn't understand what I had said. But why didn't he? It seemed so clear. I tried to explain more slowly.

"No, Pop. Listen. My boss was really interested in my ideas."

"Don't talk back to your boss."

He thought he was being fatherly. He thought he was giving me advice. But he'd never had a father, so he didn't know what that really entailed. He thought that being a father meant providing a critical insight that would unmask the core, true issue that no one else could see. Your children would then have guidance. They would have information, a perspective, and it would all come from you. The father. To agree with them meant to be behind them. It meant that they did not need you. That they set their own example. What kind of authority was that? It was nothing. Fathers have to lead and set the pace, that was more important than what they said. It was the tone that counted. He was only thirteen when he came to America. He was all alone, no one helped him. No one was in charge. His children did have a father. So it was his responsibility to be in charge, no matter what.

"No, Pop, he asked me."

He asked me. Those words were simple enough. Why couldn't my father understand them?

"I should come see your office? Like I don't have anything better to do with my time. I have to go to work, for your information. And I have to read the paper. I've seen plenty of offices. Plenty. When I got my citizenship I was in plenty of offices. They're all the same. Filled with silly girls behind typewriters who became old maids before they turned around."

"Pop."

I couldn't give up. To do so would be to accept that he would never appreciate me. He would never get pleasure from my accomplishments. I had to keep trying so that some day he could understand and on that day he would be happy. I had to keep trying so that I could make him happy.

He put down his paper and looked at me totally confused.

"Pop, don't you want to know what my work is like? What I do every day? Don't you have anything you want to ask me about, Pop? Ask me a question, will you? Ask me a question."

"Not this again," he said picking up the paper. "I don't have time for shenanigans. My only question is, *where is my tea?*"

"All right, already," Mama said, clearing up the photographs and putting them safely away. "I can't make it boil. Only God can do that. Next time you see him, ask him to hurry up."

I sat at the table and picked up a candied orange peel my mother had placed in a glass bowl. It was filled with longing.

"Pop," I said, desperate. "Can't you put down the paper?"

"Here's your tea," Mama said. "Joe, put down the paper. Sylvia wants to tell you something."

"You," he said, popping out again from over a folded page. "You cause trouble every time you walk in here. Five minutes and you've got your mother talking back to me."

"Sylvia," Mama said. "Tell him you're sorry."

"Pop, I got a promotion to Number Nine. Now I'm over halfway to reporter."

I looked pleadingly at my mother, who chose silence. I knew she had been a great reader. Now she didn't have the time, but back in Europe she'd sit and drink a beer and discuss literature, novels, Ida Kaminska's performance when the Warsaw Yiddishe Arts Theater came through Rohatan. Now she listened to classical music on the radio. She read every newspaper, the Jewish, German, Polish, and Ukrainian, following the fate of Europe. Europe once held the key to the future of the world—Socialism. Now it was all down the drain. My mother was born in 1899. She was a baby of this century. In 1914 she was fourteen. In 1929 she was twenty-nine. In 1933 she was thirty-three. How much tragedy can one life contain? If only Mama would speak up right now. If only she would say something to Pop, something that could save my life. But she couldn't. There was too much at stake.

"Our cow had so much milk, you could wash your hair in it," was what came out of her mouth. "We had a beautiful cherry tree, and I climbed it in my white dress and got covered in the juice. My sister . . ."

My mother saw Haley's Comet in 1910. She was ten. She looked up into the sky where all the peasants were pointing toward a fiery broom. The peasants wailed that it was a sign that a great war was coming. A great calamity.

"I always wanted you to go to college. I know that you'll go back and finish." It was the best that she could do.

"When I make full reporter," I said wearily. "I'll take you all out to dinner. To Ratner's on Second Avenue. All expenses paid."

"When I said good-bye to my father," Mama said, "he took me around with kisses."

"Money and connections mean nothing when you don't have a family." Pop looked at me.

"I have a family."

"But we won't live forever," he said.

"I have Lou," I said. "He'll live longer than me."

We sat in silence. I looked at the light green saucer, the cup, scanning the events of my life, searching for one that would attract his attention. One that would make my father ask me a question.

"You know what? A colored man moved in next door."

I regretted it the moment I said it. I should have known better. What I really wanted was to tell my mother and father how alone I felt. How worried I was now that Rita was gone. Who would ever care that way about me again? Who would ever bring home a special record just for me and sit with me all night playing it over and over? Then my parents could listen and sit, taking it all as seriously as it really was. They would be on my side. They could let me cry and rock and assure me that everything was going to work out fine. Mama was sure that Rita and I would be friends for life. But how could I ever say what I really felt if I couldn't even talk about my job?"

"Oh my God, a colored?" Mama said pouring Pop's tea into a glass with a tiny spoon and a lump of sugar for his mouth. I took mine in the pale green cup. "It is shameful the way those people have been treated."

"I tell you not to live there," Pop said, still reading. "No girl who lives in a place like that is ever going to marry a nice boy. You got colored people in the building now? What boy is going to marry you? A colored boy?"

"Why do you tell him these things?" Mama snapped. "You know it makes him upset."

"You come over here," he said. "And in one minute everyone is upset."

My father put down the newspaper and smoothed it out with a big flat hand. He smoothed it over and over like he couldn't control himself, like it was my life he was flattening out under the force of his palm.

"I make the rules in this house," he said. "Your mother doesn't make the rules. I make the rules. You don't make the rules. I make the rules. Your brother—"

Just then the key turned in the lock.

"Your brother . . . your brother is home. Now everything is going to be all right."

Then we all turned at once to face the opening door, like three weary shipwrecked travelers finally finding their place in the sun.

3

After I cleaned up the kitchen and Lou finished his tea, we kissed Mama good night and retreated behind the closed door of his bedroom. There, we smoked my package of Luckies while sitting against the open window ledge on the fire escape and blew smoke rings out over Brownsville.

"I brought over some more records I thought you would like," I said, carefully taking the disks out of my bag.

The first one I handed him had a photo on the cover of a Black man with a goatee beard, dark glasses, bizarre clothing, and a beret hat.

"This is after he left the Eckstien band during the war. Look, Lou, Charlie Parker is playing alto."

"Dizzy Gillespie." He read the name off the record cover. Then he climbed back into the bedroom and put it on the phonograph.

"It's called 'Groovin' High.' You'll love it."

We sat and smoked as the record played. I looked around Lou's room. He was a man now but he still had Joe Dimaggio on the wall. Dimaggio was old too. New players were coming up. What were their names? The familiar sounds of Dizzy's horn reminded me of Rita and how empty our apartment would be when I returned late that night. I could always tell Rita about these visits with Pop. About how much I craved some sign of interest from him, some sign that he liked me at all.

"That was great," Lou said, lighting another cigarette. "That was really Dizzy."

"That was the Diz, man," I joked around until we both started laughing, posing like hepcats with their cigarettes. My greatest wish was that Lou would get what this music meant to me. That he would learn how to think for himself. That way I wouldn't be so alone. I saw him eating up Pop's praise, but I wanted him to know that there were other ways into the world. Ways you couldn't explain. "I'd like to hang out in a jazz bar someday," I told him. "You know, a place to really belong. Be a regular. I'd come in the door after work and everyone would know me. The bartender would have my drink waiting on the bar. Spend the night making snappy comebacks."

"That doesn't sound like you, Syl."

"Yes it is," I said almost defensively. "It is a part of me that hasn't come out yet. You know that Ira Gershwin song. 'If there's a party I want to be the host of it. If there's a haunted house I want to be the ghost of it.' "

"It's a hard life being a musician, isn't it?"

"Suppose so. But all kinds of lives seem hard. That one's a bit more glamorous, I guess. I see them getting off of buses sometimes at the Midtown Terminal after playing in Topeka. Then they head over to Times Square for a late-night plate of chow mein. You should see it."

"You talk like a novel."

"I'm gonna write a lot of novels, Lou. Maybe you can too. We'll write them together. We can write a novel called *Jazz*. It would be romantic. Rita always said that Dizzy is a glamour

boy. That he is the ultimate romantic. Can you hear it? She says
that the battle of bebop is bigger than the battle for the Pacific."

"But how do they make a living?"

"I guess when you love your art, you don't put money first.
It's like loving people, right? I know it takes a lot of bebop to
put the bread crumbs on the table. But some things are more
important than money."

"I don't know," Lou said. "Musicians just seem to be asking
for trouble. The water's full of sharks. Why should some people
just do whatever they feel like and expect to earn a living too?"

"But that's what we should all be able to do. Why resent the
few who can pull it off instead of giving them the credit?"

"Because you can end up in the gutter," he said matter-of-
factly. "That's why it's best to play it safe."

He was just filled with the jitters and who could blame him,
but that was the fear that makes you throw your dreams away.

"Here, baby brother, listen to this album and maybe you'll
change your mind. Dizzy again, but this time with Milt Jackson.
It's called *Anthropology*."

"Who are they studying?"

"Us, Lou."

"Why?"

"Because we're the ones who need to be translated and
interpreted."

"Into what language?"

"Into bebop, Lou-Lop."

While we listened I looked at Lou really closely. He was
staring out at the city, and I could see him loving the music.
He would get into it and it could save his spirit, the way it
saved mine.

"Pop gives me a real heartache sometimes," I said.

"What do you mean?"

"He's always putting me down. He doesn't understand how
hard I'm working and that I'm on my way up."

"That's a shame," Lou said. "Don't let it get to you."

We sat for a while, listening to the music.

"Hey, Syl?"

"Yeah?"

"How did you get that job at the *Star?*"

"Ladies' Classifieds."

"You didn't know anybody there or anything like that?"

"No. Who do we know? Mr. Levy the butcher? That's not a great job lead unless you want to deliver kosher chopped meat."

Lou looked crestfallen, really glum, staring at his own ciga-rette. I've thought about this moment many times over the years, and I have to admit to a private unacknowledged pleasure watching his sadness like that. I wanted him to be vulnerable so that I could help him, so that we could imagine our own way together far from the path of parental approval tightening around my neck.

"So," I said. "Maybe you could put a good word in for me with Pop."

Lou lit another cigarette with the first one still burning.

"Sure, Syl," he said. "I'll talk to him the next chance I get."

There was a cinematic moment then, a blood pact was made. And I leaned back, exhausted, having finally gotten my way.

"Listen to this one," I said, excitedly picking up again on the next cut. "It's called 'Night in Tunisia.'"

CHAPTER TEN

Austin Van Cleeve

There was a wide range of options by the taxi stand. Sky-View, Yellow Cab, or Checker. The driver had just come over from the north of Ireland and wouldn't shut up about it. A partisan of the six counties, same old waxing nostalgic about her rolling green hills. I've never fallen for that one. If the Old Country was so balmy, why in the hell did they have to come over here? I knew the truth the old geezer would rather die than admit. He'd left behind a bunch of hardworking drearies scraping by to throw a cabbage on the table. Damp nights, long days, outdoor toilets, and smoking roll-ups by the fire as your greatest pleasure. No sentimental drivel for me, thank you. They never tell the truth, rather complain about missing out on being a sheep-fucker. As far as I have always been concerned, there is no better place than the comfy backseat of a cab while some poor nonentity takes me where I want to go.

Sick of chatting with yet another drunken Democrat, I sank into the leather and stared out the window as the city unfolded. It was the annual panic that sets in once autumn gets fully underway. All those crazy citizens and fresh-faced immigrants scurrying around making news for me to cover. My power lay in the choice of which acts to amplify and which to obscure. It was the power of selection. There was a slight drizzle that afternoon, and the streets looked cold and cobbled. I was off to lunch on veal cordon bleu, while this fellow was headed for a gravy supper, rotting at the edges like slats of wood in an old brewery truck.

Suddenly I was filled with anxiety and apprehension about getting together with O'Dwyer. Why did we have these meetings? The original premise had been dropped long ago. Now it was something we each looked forward to hungrily, like vampires spotting the proper nape. The threat of what I could do to Jim O'Dwyer had lately begun to feel immense. I know myself, and when that instinct sets in nothing can stop it. I'm the kind of kitty cat that can devour on a second's notice. A real mouser. A killer. I could, on a whim, just by making a phone call, trading gossip, or casually mentioning something to the wrong person, cut anyone dead. A monstrous wall had come crashing down on many a path, and the delivery slip was often signed *Austin Van Cleeve*. That was why I had to be with him. Watch him every minute. I couldn't live without him. He had to stay real so that I wouldn't go in for the kill.

"Austin!"

"O'Dwyer! Why so late, did you take the bus?"

"I know," he said, laughing it off. "I'm a natural-born suspect for public transport simply because I'm not the conventional type."

"Then why are you so predictable?"

"Actually," he said, losing his ability to joust, "I took a cab."

"Waiter," I called out, completely thrown by how dull he was. "Two martinis, please. Straight up with onions. Call them Gibsons if you like. Although you cannot find a Gibson Girl under seventy at this stage of the game. Just make sure the onions are fresher than the girls. And, waiter, even though this . . . er . . . *gentleman* to my right shops at Macy's, he is not applying for a waiting position. He is lunching with me."

"How are you, Austin?"

"Splendid, splendid. Spent the morning chatting with a friend at the Criminal Court. He was not pleased with the *Star*'s editorial on the Chambers case."

"That's fine," he said, restraightening his tie. "The newspaper business is not about pleasing people. Speaking of, how is that girl you've been dating?"

"Dating? Oh my, what a euphemism. Screwing is more accurate. Oh, she's real tasty, Jim. A juicer. Came over the other night with platinum pubic hair. 'How did you get that?' I asked, delighted. Well, I thought she'd sat in a tub of Clorox or something."

Jim never knew how to respond to this side of me. He wanted to go along with it, but frankly, he didn't really care. He liked hearing things about the business, getting tidbits about other people. How else would he know where he stood? This sex stuff, well . . . he was not a man of pleasure. He probably closed his eyes and thought of Susan Hayward.

"So, did she?"

"No," I answered blithely. "Norman did it."

"Her pimp?"

"My goodness, no. She's somewhere between an amateur and a volunteer. No, it was Norman's House of Blondes. Apparently, at night, after closing, all the tarts from the four boros stand in line to dye their pubes. He calls it 'doing the cuffs and collars.' Ah, here are our drinks. Waiter, I'll have the vichyssoise and veal cordon bleu. Jim?"

"Whatever."

"He wants the veal," I assured the waiter. "He just can't commit."

The "21" Club was filled with the usual power brokers jockeying for tables, wanting to be seen breaking each other's balls.

"There's Lillian Hellman," I sneered. "She must be here campaigning for Henry Wallace. Trying to recruit the bartender to the Progressive Party."

"So what did *you* think of my editorial?"

I took a sip, speared my onion, popped it in my mouth, and sucked.

"You don't get it at all," I finally hissed.

"What do you mean?" Jim snapped, hurt and therefore finally coming to life. "Whittaker Chambers appeared before the House Committee as an admitted ex-Communist. He named Hiss, the personification of Roosevelt's New Deal, as a fellow Red. Chambers claims Hiss gave him secret papers that no one has ever seen, which he says he hid in a pumpkin. It's ludicrous."

"I invite you to lower your standards for credibility," I said. "The Committee smashing Hiss works to Truman's advantage, you fool. Not against it. You endorsed Truman, therefore you should endorse the Committee."

"Why?" Jim asked, looking sincerely confused. "Hiss and Truman both represent Roosevelt's legacy."

"That was before," I said slowly, wanting him to get it. "But the war is over forever now. Let me explain to you, Mr. Editor in Chief, what is really going on. Hiss's wing of the State Department just happened to have been presided over by Henry Wallace when he was in F.D.R.'s cabinet. Now Wallace has defected from the Democrats and is running on a third party, threatening to split Truman's votes against the Republican, Dewey. The more Wallace is implicated as a Commie, the happier Truman will be. That's how politics works, Jim. Haven't you even figured out the basics?"

"Well, I don't work that way."

"Get it through your thick Mick skull right now," I said. "No one cares about Communists. They just use it. They use it for professional advancement."

"What is that supposed to mean?"

I finished off my drink. "The Red scare is one big employment agency. It's opened up more jobs than WPA. These guys don't have political convictions. I do have them, so I know the difference."

"And the Communist threat?"

"A convenience of history. It's an aberration that lets little mediocrities climb to great heights. All they have to do is stab another little mediocrity in the back and they can have it all."

"Austin," he said quietly. "You have such a strange expression on your face that it took me a while to realize what it was. You're actually telling the truth."

"Well, memorize the way it looks, I said. "In case you ever come across it again."

"So, how does all this insanity end?"

"It never ends." I laughed in spite of myself. "Little Johnny was always jealous of little Bobby because Bobby had blond hair and got all the girls. Now big man John can squeal on Bob about nothing and watch his car get repossessed while John now gets the girls. That kind of thing never ends."

"Oh God, Austin, I hate martinis. I hate these effete high-society drinks with pickled vegetables on toothpicks."

"Feeling down, Jimmy?" I smiled victoriously. "Don't fret, my boy, just because your life is taking place in a sewer. Learn to love it. Look, here's the address were my tartette works at night. If you get depressed, go out for a walk. There might be another little piece of gash waiting there for you. Be a rat, Jim. It's fun."

1949

BILLBOARD MAGAZINE'S TOP TEN HITS

1. Riders In The Sky (A Cowboy Legend)................
....Vaughn Monroe
....Frankie Laine
2. That Lucky Old Sun.....................Evelyn Knight
3. A Little Bird Told Me....................Russ Morgan
4. Cruising Down The River.................Blue Barron
5. Cruising Down The River..................Frankie Laine
6. Mule Train....................................Perry Como
7. Some Enchanted Evening...................Vic Damone
8. You're Breaking My Heart.................Russ Morgan
9. Forever And Ever..............................
10. Slipping Around...
....................Margaret Whiting & Jimmy Wakely

CHAPTER ELEVEN

Sylvia Golubowsky

1

Everyone struggled to slog home through the January snow.
There must have been ten inches of dry, white dust keeping us
in our place. Swollen, tired feet at the end of a working day.
Every time it snowed the papers recalled the blizzard of '88,
reassuring readers that it could always be worse. But the extra
burden was palpable on the subways. People stepped into the
cars with an extra show of fatigue, an extra sigh.

For me, the snow was a second layer of privacy. I was alone
too much anyway at home in the evenings and over long, long
weekends. Was anything as sorrowful as a Sunday night? But
the snow kept me from the relief of watching how other people
live their lives. Buried in my winter coat, I had nothing to take
in but the constantly strange goings-on at the office.

Truman had been reelected by a dramatic last-minute
squeaker, and yet nothing had changed. In fact, the tension
around the office seemed to have gotten worse as Inauguration
Day approached and passed. Three more girls got married, two
were fired, and two quit. Now I was Number One, the top of
the stenographic ladder. I was only one step away from my
goal of being a reporter, which hopefully would be accomplished
before we got too much further into 1949. Being Number One
had its own responsibilities. I had to work a lot more closely

with Mr. O'Dwyer, which required a better, newer, and more fashionable wardrobe without any more pay. By taking his dictation on a regular basis, I did learn a lot about what went into running a paper like the *Star* and what kinds of dangers lurked behind the production of every page.

Of course, world events were unfolding with great implications and thrilling consequences. Just as Dean Acheson was sworn in to be Truman's Secretary of State, Chiang Kai-shek finally had to leave for Formosa. Washington feared Mao Tse-tung, the new Communist chief who replaced him. I had been studying the map of China, following Mao's triumphs and Chiang's retreats. I'd even gone to the library on my lunch hour and some Saturday afternoons to get a better understanding of that country's history. Not everything, I'd learned, was to be found in the pages of the *New York Times*. China was not a modern state, that was for sure. And I suspected that the Communists would have a great deal of trouble governing it. But their tasks were so large that I doubted they'd even have the time, much less the money, for the world domination everyone else seemed to be predicting. And in my heart I wished them the best in learning how to feed their people.

It was Mr. O'Dwyer, however, who worried me more than China. There were rumors around the office that he was thinking about instituting a loyalty oath. Everyone would have to sign a piece of paper swearing allegiance. Hewitt, the shop steward, was vehemently opposed. Just the other day he had come around with a letter asking people in Stenography and Copy to sign on, declaring that we did not want loyalty oaths in the office. So, the choice was clear. But, I was in a quandary about signing something else, like this petition, on the principle of not wanting to sign anything in the first place. On one hand, if people really were loyal there should be no problem signing an oath. But, if someone had their doubts, did that mean they shouldn't be able to have a job? Besides, no one could agree with everything the government decided. Was that unloyal?

I felt loyalty to myself, that's why I was putting in so many hours. And I still felt loyalty to Rita, even though it clearly was not reciprocated. She never had time for more than a phone call when she was desperately in need. My calls always seemed to be interrupting. And I was loyal to Lou, of course. But did I have to feel that way about Truman too? There was something wrong with the whole business. I just wished it would all come out in the open already so that everybody at work could discuss it upfront and understand all the factors. O'Dwyer could make his case, and then Hewitt could make his. Hewitt said he'd rather strike than sign, but Theresa Calabrase said that scabs would be lining up around the block in an hour, so striking equaled quitting, and she needed her job. Charlie claimed that the oath would only be for full-timers, so the rest of us should go to five-sixths time as a way of getting around it. But Hewitt said it was a matter of principle.

The previous Sunday I'd taken Lou to one of those anti-Communist films. *The Red Menace.* You could tell who the Commie was because they're usually pudgy in films of that sort. Something like Whittaker Chambers or Sydney Greenstreet. They're usually fey and wear white gloves, indoors, in the middle of the afternoon. When the Commie smokes a cigarette he sends smoke out slowly through his nose and he's always got some accented blonde assistant or a dark girlfriend with big features and her bare shoulder showing. Maybe Hewitt was a Communist himself. But, so what? Unions were a working person's right. Everyone knew that. And if what a Communist does is be a shop steward, then hooray for him. The whole thing seemed ridiculous when the people of China didn't have enough to eat.

I trudged to my apartment building, snow piled high on the scrawny branches that lined icy streets, those weedy city trees that Midwesterners like Rita's mother complain about. Cars were snowed in and would be for days. So, I was surprised to see that, despite the snow, someone was moving an upright piano into the apartment next door to mine. The workers were freezing, hoisting it up through the window. I stood still, staring, knee-high in the snow. Lifting a piano through an apartment window took determination enough, but what kind of person could convince others to do it in a blizzard? I looked all the way up, watching the silent, solid object suspended by thick

ropes against a sky filled with endless flakes, hanging, humor-
ously, ominously, against the old brick. That was a picture I
would save for my novel. It was something out of Gogol, a piano
suspended in snow. I wrote it down in my brown notebook
before even taking off my boots.

The notebook was almost full now, soon it would be time
for volume two. I put on some water for a spaghetti dinner and
played Dizzy Gillespie's "*Good Dues Blues.*" There was a pianist
on that record who had real confidence in his music, even
though the rest of it seemed disorganized. This particular troupe
had played at Carnegie Hall and then toured Europe. I followed
all the jazz stars' reviews but had never gone to see any of my
favorites playing live since Rita moved out. It seemed crazy,
with all the clubs and bars within walking distance of my apartment. After all, that's why Rita and I moved to the Village in
the first place.

There was some kind of unarticulated fear that had been
keeping me from really living. There was a sadness, a desire
lately creeping up my throat. A kind of mourning. Maybe everything was coming to a head now that the reporting job was
finally within reach and I had no one to share my anticipation.
No one by my side for the wait. I was almost twenty-one years
old. Maybe Theresa Calabrase would go out with me to some of
the clubs. Lou would, that's for sure. I only had to ask. He'd
love it. It was my job to set him straight about adventure and
discovery, about making your own life. Thank God he would
never be alone. That was one thing I could guarantee.

Some nights he'd stay over at my place when it was too late
to get the Brooklyn train. It gave him a chance to be a little
less under Pop's thumb. I liked walking in seeing him stretched
out on the couch and then take him for walks around the Village, talking over every little thing. But I also liked coming home
to no one at all. I resolved to find someone to go out with me
to hear that new singer, Carmen McRae at Trude Heller's night-
spot on Sixth Avenue. Maybe I'd just go alone. Bring my
notebook.

2

Supper didn't last long enough. I stared at my empty plate. Empty. It took another hour to realize that the faint sound of a radio emanating from the hallway was actually the notes of a live piano. Someone who really knew how to play jazz. Then I thought that it must be the Negro man who lived next door. He must be a jazz musician trying out his new piano.

Now, I have always been a person who embraces hope with the same insane emotion that I bring to the recognition of defeat. All or nothing. All of nothing. What could be more wonderful than to live next door to a musician? And, suddenly, all the fantasies flooded through again. I wanted dynamic evenings filled with friends who lived life all the way. Folks who weren't afraid. Like me, they'd be refugees from uncomprehending backgrounds. I often pictured Lou and me in living rooms filled with friends who'd really understand, each one writing or painting or young dancers from the New Dance Group. Now there would be musicians too, carrying in their instruments after a full night on the town.

Most people wait to find out about ideas by reading them in books. They sit wherever they live and wait for the ideas to appear on the shelves of the nearest shop. But now, I would be part of the people who invented the ideas in the first place. I'd know about them as they were being born. By the time they came out in a book it would be old hat to me. I'd be gearing up for the next big idea and then go home and write it down.

It was the man next door who held the key to all this pleasure. I'd only seen him once or twice at odd hours. He'd nodded his greeting, but then the communication deteriorated into a passive coexistence. I guessed he couldn't be the one to say hello. It might be misinterpreted. And I, as a single white woman, certainly could not be overly friendly. I didn't want to start trouble. But now I knew who he was, that he was a jazz musician. This was surely an omen. I stepped out into the dimly lit hallway and then stood with my ear to the door of apartment 2D.

I could hear the music so clearly. I felt like Mama standing at the back of the synagogue on Rosh Hashanah, listening to the cantor sing. That was the thing about live music. You couldn't own it. You could never have it again. You could not take it home or collect it or show it to someone else. It was temporal.

When I did finally knock, everything stopped. Then, after a moment of silent decision I heard footsteps coming toward me. I realized that I was about to be face-to-face with my Negro neighbor for the first time. And so I was very surprised when a small white woman opened the door.

"Yes?"

"Hello. I'm your neighbor, Sylvia."

"Oh."

That woman's face was blank. She made no move to offer welcome or interest. Not that she was overtly hostile. But she was careful.

"I heard your music."

"I hope it's no bother," the woman answered plainly, despite a strong southern drawl. Her pleasant blandness seemed potentially menacing. "You see, I'm a music teacher, and I need to play regular. Perhaps if you let me know what time you usually go to sleep."

"No, no, I love it," I blurted out. "I'm a jazz fan."

"Oh, in that case," she smiled, opening wide the door. "Come on in. Why didn't you say so in the first place?"

It wasn't long before I was drinking my third beer and yacking like I hadn't had a friend in a year instead of just a few months.

"So," I summed up, "that's what happened. She moved out and got married and hasn't had time for me since."

We'd been sitting for hours in Caroline's apartment on her overstuffed chairs, surrounded by stacks of books, piles of papers, sheet music, and records, records, records. An overflowing desk. There was no housekeeping going on here. It was an apartment occupied by artists. Not just some place to come home to after you've given everything away on the job.

"Poor baby," Caroline said.

"And the thing that makes me so mad is that she must miss me just as much, for God's sake. But she keeps away and pretends it never happened. Like I'm supposed to get over it and forget. But how can you forget being so close to someone for the first time?"

"You can't," Caroline said. She was a small-boned woman with a flat, almost Slavic face. But that was impossible, since she came from Flat Rock, North Carolina. Her hair hung loosely at her shoulders, stringy and out of control.

"I put it up for gigging," she said piling it up on top of her head. "See, I look like a debutante."

She called North Carolina a "Fascist state." She said that Negroes were treated horrible at every turn by her daddy as well as everyone else white. She said that her family was happy to disown her when she'd married a Negro, and that people said nasty things out of the blue to her on the street every single day of her life when her husband was by her side. Alone, though, she offended no one. She wore a soft pair of slacks, gathered high about her waist with a Mexican belt. She was a strange, unknown combination of sloppy and stylish. Happy and terribly sad. She had her own style. She had her own way of feeling things.

"I recall the first beloved friend like that I ever had," Caroline said. "You never forget the first one. Nanette Pomeroy, back home. Her people ran the Pine Grove Café. It was in a pine grove. You know the kind of place." She looked me over. "Well, maybe you don't know the kind of place. Even been out of New York?"

"The Catskills?"

"In other words . . . ?"

"No."

"Well, baby, I hope you get to go. There is a big bad world out there, and it is a fascinating, hard, cruel place. It's filled with beauty and different from anything you can see out the window of the IRT. The land is ecstatic; the people are horrifying. That's America. I hope you get a glimpse while you're still young. Then, come home. Because, when you're special, America can suck your bones."

"Do you think I'm special?"

I still shudder when I think of that moment. I can't help myself, it was the freedom of being noticed for the first time.

"There is nothing," she said, "for a girl like you or me that has more to offer than New York." Then she laughed. "Still, you gotta see what you don't have. Taste that pie. Climb that tree. Ever climbed a tree? Then, when you jump down, you know you did it. You get that special feeling."

"What is it?"

"I can't tell you that, baby. You got to find out for yourself."

"Well," I said. "At least you can tell me some more about the Pine Grove Café."

Caroline smiled at that one. I was to learn that she could be a dangerous smiler. Those lips were just a disguise for her teeth. From the first I could see that she had a strange smile. Must have been her mother's. It was very pleasing and impersonal. It put all the focus back on you.

"The most popular drink was Black Velvet and Ginger. There was a sign on the door that said 'Worms.' If, on a winter morning there'd be a sheet of ice on the lake, you could see a beaver skidding toward the shore. Then, all that evening people would be sitting at the bar discussing that beaver and what it was he was after. *Was it the birch trees?*"

"What else would they say?"

"Oh, sometimes some old codger would tell you *that bear attacked my shed six times 'til I had to junk the thing. I'm gonna send him over to your place, Del. Lay some bacon down around your porch and pour some old maple syrup on your barn.* That would be a big joke. And the fellows would repeat it a couple of times. Then, they'd try it out again the next year when the same thing happened in the same way."

Caroline got up to pour more beer for the both of us out of the quart bottle. She went to change the record on the hi-fi.

"What's this one?" I asked, picking up on a brand-new sound.

"War's over, baby. You don't have to listen to bebop anymore."

"Huh?"

"I mean, Dizzy is the king, but there are new sounds happening in this window of possibility that will probably be called 'post-war' when the next one starts. Sounds like *cool.*"

"How do you know?"

"Playing out. I just think musicians are getting tired of pandering to audiences. You know, they're artists. They're getting more moody and contemplative. Hear that? It's a young trumpet player from Charlie Parker's Quintet named Miles Davis. Studied at Juilliard, that's a new breed. Herbie Fields recorded him at the Savoy. The solos are uneven, but he knows his music. He and Gil Evans have been arranging for trumpet, trombone, french horn, tuba, alto, baritone piano, bass, and drums. I saw them at the Roost in September."

"Is it great there? I've always wanted to go."

I tried to remember where I had been in September. Moping on the couch about Rita going away. But now I realized I could have been living. I could have heard Gil Evans at the Roost.

"I'll take you, honey. Nothing to be afraid of. You're young and in New York. You've got to go everywhere."

"You'll take me?"

"Yes, of course. Ninety cents at the door to sit in the bleacher. But, if you want a drink, it's a buck fifty for a table on a weeknight. They opened for Basie. I had a friend, Bill Barber, playing tuba. He wasn't invited back and took off for France. But, if you ask me, their music was exciting. It was experimental and intellectual, not just pure sex anymore but questions of existence, and it was thrilling. Here's their latest on Capitol. This is called *Boplicity.*"

I fell into a dream more tangible than heaven. This music was so much larger than myself, it freed me from my own stupidity. My own ugliness. I could put music like this on the phonograph and no one could take it away. It was more powerful than any of my dreams because no one could stop it. When I put the needle on the record, I knew exactly what would happen. I knew it was guaranteed to come true.

"It's the bee's knees," Caroline said.

"Do you know these guys?" I asked. "Do you hang with them

and play out with them? Sit around talking music, trying out things?"

For the first time that night I saw something strange in Caroline's face. Something very angry and very controlled.

"I play where I can," she said. "I play around."

"And what about Nanette Pomeroy?" I said, quickly trying to draw her back to some happiness.

"A beautiful girl," Caroline said, lighting a cigarette. "She's got four screamers now and Jesus Christ in her heart. But those quiet country nights deep in the pine grove she was a lovely, lovely girl."

CHAPTER TWELVE

N. Tammi Byfield

1

My mother's given name was Patricia and she changed it to Nzinga. She named me Nubia, and I changed it to Tammi, after the great Tammi Terrell. She wasn't offended. My mother says the point is to honor the heroines who really touch our hearts, on-stage and off. I'm naming my future child after Cassandra Wilson. I just hope no one goes and names their daughter Salt.

We're so much alike, my mother and me. We don't owe anything to the middle class. They're so fucked up. Sending their kids to Jack and Jill, driving those town cars, those Mercedes, those full-length fur coats. We're Jamaican, ancestrally, that means work hard, get ahead. We're not looking for get-rich-quick fix. There's nothing we have to prove.

My mother had a great job with the Dinkins administration. He put a lot of Black women into the city government, and when he lost the election a lot of Black women were out of jobs. And not just in City Hall. Still, actually, it's worked out for her. She got together a consulting practice in Fort Greene helping Afro-centric businesses. You know, exports dealing with those governments. My mother lived in Guinea for three years before I was born and most of her boyfriends have been African or at least Afro-centric. Not American-identified. Until Steve. I don't like him. He's too straight. Real estate broker. Thinks *we're* wild. I do like Fort Greene, though. Even the cop on the beat stops by when you have a barbecue. And I like being in school, after working for Barnes and Nobles this summer. No co-workers, no busybodies to suss out, embrace, and then exclude. I was walking on the Columbia campus last Wednesday and two security guards stopped me because I matched a description. Something about a wallet. This is in my Armani raincoat. I don't think so.

"Do not tell me this," I said to them. The guy from Bed-Stuy was ready to let me go, but the other brother put up his hand to protest my release. Before he even opened his mouth I could tell he was from the islands. I know my own people. We do our jobs too well. That's a West Indian, he follows all the rules, even if they're wrong. Thanks to his strict upbringing I had to go to the chairman of my program. You see, I refused to show my ID. That's the way my mother raised me. The chairman was embarrassed but also uninterested. You have to suss them out, these white people. Once again, I'm lost among them. Once again, the only one in my program. You have to shake them out if you want to find a friend. The guard was cute, but I'm not going to have lunch with him. That is out of the question.

I almost made it through my freshman year at Princeton. It wasn't the fact that I had to eat lunch alone every single time that got me out of there, it was when I got approached by the CIA. I was in Political Science and mentioned to my professor that I still had family in Jamaica. The next thing I knew, the CIA was taking me out to eat and asking if I wanted to be prime minister. That's how they do it. They make all the decisions. I dropped out the next day, switched majors to Literature, and transferred to Columbia. This way I can at least see some Black people on the way to the train. And here I am. My grandfather would be proud. I wish there were three other brown people in the program. Less than that and the look-alikes spend all their time getting us mixed up. At least when you're the only one they remember your name. Right? My mother lived in Guinea, she was practically a Panther. She had that bad look. Big afro, black leather jacket. I'm a race woman, like my mother. She's never fallen in love with a white man, I doubt I could. What do they know? My brother Jamal is an aerospace engineer for the Department of Defense. Where did we go wrong?

My mother and I discuss this over and over. She's very thin. She works out in a gym. It's all about presentability.

"Look like a queen," she says. "It can't hurt."

Me? I'm a big girl, but I can carry it. I have too much to do to go to a gym. That's for the desperate. I don't care for those flashy West African prints my mother imports. It's kind of a joke. That and the fashion plates from the Nation of Islam. Purple silk djellabas with silver trim and veil? I don't think so. I get my glasses at LA Eyeworks. Designer frames make a difference. I like to look good. It's worth it to me. But I like to look good as myself, I don't have to have an expensive body. The clothes will do. My mother's never hidden a thing from me. She always tells me the truth. She knows how I feel about her clothes, but not that Steve is boring.

In the same day I talk to people in so many different ways. I can say "In the case of Caryl Phillips, despite the brilliance of his complex interplay of race, gender, and sexuality, we still find the telltale signs of the emblematic Black writer being excluded from the mainstream recognition awarded inferior whites. Certainly, the fact that Phillips's masterpiece, *Crossing the River,* is the only piece of literature focused on slavery to tell the story of a *white* man making the crossing, should attract white readers who have historically been unwilling to identify with a protagonist who is not a replica of themselves. However, there seems to be little interest on the part of white readers in Phillips's work precisely because they are threatened by the value of his artistic and intellectual achievement. They are threatened by a Black man writing about them, and respond with dismissal and oversight. At the same time, his exploration of the homoerotics of slavery does interject another discomforting and challenging element. The book serves as a prime example of the successful fictionalization of complex historical and personal themes while at the same time revealing what the oppressed know about the inner workings of the dominant mind."

That's a quote from my sophomore paper.

I can say, "I don't like no rappers. Latifah look good, but her mouth is too big. Don't talk to me about Prince. The DL is I love the Bar-kays. They crazy, all right?"

That's a quote from my lunch with the security guard.

The evening after our date, I was so divided in two that I actually thought about going to the gym. I lost it. I cried on the subway home and then I remembered that I am beautiful the way I am. The process was painful, but it elevated me. Then, at dinner, I didn't go so crazy at how dull Steve is. I felt sorry for him because he will never have a great idea. I felt Christian toward him. Generous to Steve and to myself.

So, I needed another credit to make up for what I dropped at Princeton, so I took a class on the history of the literature of New York City. My mother had always had boxes of notebooks and letters and an unpublished memoir by my grandfather who was a writer, so I suggested this to my professor. Guess what he wanted me to write about? The Harlem Renaissance. Ho-hum. They love that story. Those poor great writers. Poor Wallace Thurman, poor Countee Cullen, poor Claude McKay, poor Zora, poor Langston, poor Jean Toomer, who was a good-looking man but too light-skinned. Do you know why we all feel so sorry for them? Because when those white patrons pulled out their dough, that was the end of the Renaissance. And so, we're supposed to learn a lesson. But what is that lesson again? We're supposed to learn that

1) Black art can't exist without white patronage (the official white lesson).

2) But white patronage is bad because it goes away (the official Black lesson).

Therefore? Therefore, what? Therefore *make it on our own,* which is why my mother collects Black artists only. The problem I have with those two official ways of thinking is that these poor victim Harlem Renaissancers are the only Black writers anyone in this country can seem to remember. I mean, who were the writers from the forties? Besides Ralph Ellison? No one knows their names. They only know Langston. So it seems to me that instead of going on and on about how the Renaissancers were dissed, we should be going on and on about how they're the only ones anybody's heard of. Therefore, my conclusion is that you have to get the white man's money or else he's not going to remember you. He'll never notice what you did unless he paid for it. Conclusion. End of story.

So, my philosophy is that Black people should get our own money. But, if we can't always have our first choice, then second best is to go spend theirs. That's what I'm doing at Columbia, spending their money. Not like at Howard where you have to pay to be Black. No, they're paying the bills with the money we made for them in the first place and believe me, it makes them notice.

2

"Your grandfather was a small thin man with a quick gait," my mother said, handing me his photograph and four huge boxes of stuff. He had thick horn-rimmed glasses. I got that from him, good taste in glasses. In every picture from that time he had an ironic squint and saddle shoes, and his face is always younger than his years. Oh, it showed plenty of worry all right. But few wrinkles.

It was on a winter's night in 1949 that this part of his story begins. In his unpublished memoir, this scene is on page three hundred and seventy-nine. But the manuscript has two thousand pages. Moments were very important to my grandfather. They were filled with layers and layers of meaning. It's like he knew too much about his own condition. In a way, he had too much to say. He wanted someone to know all the details. I guess that means me.

Anyway, that night snow was killing business and the employees were staring out at an empty club. No customers. No hamburgers. So, Barney Josephson let them all go home and closed up the kitchen before it was even eleven o'clock.

"You want to hang out?" Joe Mackie asked, slipping on his black overcoat.

"No thanks," my grandfather answered, pulling galoshes over his beloved saddle shoes.

"You are fastidious."

"You never know who you might meet," Cal said. That's my grandfather. Calvin Byfield.

"Okay, Casanova," Joe winked. "See you tomorrow."

But he wasn't off to meet a girl. Cal just liked to look good.

He wandered around for a while that night, enjoying the snow. He'd lived in New York City almost all his life and still couldn't grasp it. Couldn't get on top of it. Nobody could. Nobody ever knew exactly what was going on. It was a humbly invigorating feeling that gave him a bold taste for adventure. I mean, why not? Why not just check in with whatever it was that came onto your path? Otherwise, might as well live somewhere simpler and know what's going to happen to you every single day.

He stopped at the Waldorf Cafeteria on Eighth Street. It was either a coffee with the longshoremen starting fights, or hanging out with the dopers at Nedicks. He was there to jot down overheard street dialogue, which he did all the time. The guy was always writing. He carried a tiny notebook in his pocket and scribbled snippets, images, whole scenes. He spent the everyday writing a play, no matter what else was going on. My grandfather sat in Waldorf's window like a cadaver under the sickly yellow-green light that gave the place its nickname, *The Waxworks.*

Cal ended up, after a while of wandering, at the San Remo on the corner of MacDougal and Bleecker. There was no one else in the place except that old drunk Maxwell Bodenheim trying to sell his poems to nonexistent customers in exchange for the cheapest drinks.

"How's Ruth?" Cal asked politely, taking off those glasses, snow dripping on the black and white tiles under the pressed tin ceiling. The Remo had big wooden booths that you could drink yourself to death in and even huger urinals to accommodate all that beer.

Bodenheim was world famous once. I found a book of his in my grandfather's stuff. You'd never know it by Cal's description of the snot that hung from the man's nose like a stalactite. His poems had been published by someone named Harriet Monroe in *Poetry* magazine, and he was celebrated in the great halls of literature from Chicago to both coasts. Then, instead of reveling in his glory, he drank himself into idiocy. Stupid white man. Any Negro in his place would have been hauled off to jail long before. That was one word I'd had to get used to going through my grandfather's stuff. *Negro.* It was very important to him.

"Ruth is great," Bodenheim said hopefully. "Working at Brentano's."

According to local Village lore, he'd met Ruth Frankel one night in front of the Waxworks. They'd walked around for hours holding hands and got married three weeks later. She'd burned down her parents house back in Michigan and had no other place to go. They moved from flophouse to slop house, in and out of slummy crowded rooms on Bleecker Street.

I went for a walk around Bleecker Street one afternoon just so I could see all the spots my grandfather was talking about. The Waldorf Cafeteria was an apartment building. Nedicks was a chain bookstore. The streets were filled with white people. B and T and A. Bridge and Tunnel and Airport. There were more Eurotrash than folks from New Jersey, and they were all paying ridiculous prices for bland things. I did stop into an ancient Chesshouse that looked like it was the last old thing on MacDougal Street. They had those pressed tin ceilings that Cal kept harping on. Then I found it had just opened and was designed to look retro. There were a couple of old alcoholics who might have been bohemians around his time, but I didn't bother asking if anyone remembered the good-looking skinny Black guy, a writer, with spiffy shoes and thick glasses, who hung out there around 1949. There must have been so many.

"Can I interest you in a poem?" Bodenheim begged. "Twenty-five cents for one. Fifty cents with an autograph."

Bodenheim had created his own Wasteland and T.S. Eliot did not have a thing to worry about. The slob was a walking whirl of dirty clothes, rags, dust, cigarette butts, onions, scuffed shoes, and unseemly socks that no one would ever want to inspect too closely.

"One glass of beer but you can spare me the poem," Cal said. "And don't interrupt once my company comes in."

"Ah, it's a beautiful world," Bodenheim said as the bartender poured the beer.

"Really? I don't think so."

"Why is that my friend?" Bodenheim greedily sipped the head from the side of his glass.

"Because," Cal said slowly. "That quarter I just spent on your beer goes into the hands of Joe Santini, a nice Italian guy who owns this place. The bushel of sweet red apples I bought yesterday paid for an Irishman's daughter's trousseau. My new hat sent a Jew's son to college. But the only Negro-owned businesses in this city are barbershops, and I'm getting balder every day. Or, you can put your money into churches. But that dime on the collection plate never seems to reappear on the street. It goes for elocution lessons for the minister's daughter. The only way I can spend my money to help my own people is to travel up to the corner of 135th and Lenox to buy a boiler with mustard from Pig Foot Mary. There's nothing to invest in that lasts longer than an afternoon snack, Mr. Bodenheim. Does that answer your question?"

"That's a pretty good speech," the poet slobbered.

"Thank you." That's my grandfather. He was so polite he even said *thank you* to a drunk. "It's the opening monologue of my new play, *The Road Beyond the Meadow*."

"Lukewarm."

"The beer or my title?"

"Both. Too sappy. Sounds like a fucking musical. How about *Hercules' Revenge*?"

"Sounds like a lecture at the Art Students League. What am I doing arguing with a drunk?"

"Well," Bodenheim conceded, "you have a good point there. But who in the hell is going to put on this play?"

"Who in the hell indeed."

"I give up," Bodenheim said. "Who?"

"Miss Anne, Mister Charlie. Master Buckra Ofay Faginy-fagade."

"Oh, a whole family of 'em. That's nice. One more beer?"

"Alright. Joe, just pour it."

The bartender was Joe Santini, the one whose name ended up staying in my grandfather's play.

"Look friend," Bodenheim said now that the drink was secured. "It needs some action. It's called a *play* for a reason. Can't just be *talk, talk, talk*. I've got it. At some point Hercules and the old drunk at the bar should get up and do a little jig. Bring in Cab Calloway, and you'll be the darkie Fred Astaire."

"And you'll be the corpse of Ginger Rogers," Cal looked up as the front door swung open and half a snow drift came flying into the bar. "Caroline, thank God you're here."

3

When I came to this chapter in the story of my grandfather's life, I was shocked. A white woman? My grandfather was married to a white woman? How was this possible?

I remember my grandmother very well from when I was a girl and she was as Black as Wallace Thurman's berry, thank you. She was from a very distinguished family. The Woodson family. *Ebony* did a story on her family reunion. Her great-great uncle was the architect for Madam C.J. Walker's mansion on the Hudson. She was not white.

Then I did have a moment of doubt. I have always been darker than my mother. And I have heard from other people who were darker than their folks that their mothers kept them out of the sun and whatnot. Kept their arms covered so they would stay as light as possible. But that is not my case. My mother loves Blackness. She was the one who pointed out how one of the reasons everyone thinks Angela Davis is so beautiful is partially because she's so light. I saw Angela on the Arsenio Hall Show wearing leather pants and dreds, and she looked very, very good for fifty.

"How are you, Angela?" Arsenio asked.

"Fine, fine. I'm still a Communist."

This made Arsenio really nervous. You see there is a reason that revolutionaries do not go on television, and that is because they might say something provocative. You could just see him thinking, *oh shit.*

"What does that mean to you, Angela? I mean, that's kind of a scary word, *Communist.*" And he got all faggotty, pulled his hands to his chest and raised his feet like a mouse had scampered into the TV studio.

"Well, I think that education should be free and students should be paid to go to school," she said, with that soothing deep, gravelly, melodic voice that makes her so convincing. It's not just her light skin. The audience in the TV studio burst into applause. I always suspected a little rivalry on my mother's part. It probably goes back to the wanna-be Panther thing, because in a number of my mother's photographs from high school she has a big natural. It's a lot like Angela's.

But she is light. Kathleen Cleaver was also light-skinned. My mother has made this point several times. My father's dead now. No guns, heart disease in California. But for the first time in my life I wondered if my mother might not have purportedly picked out the Blackest man she could find as a rebellion against her own secret white blood. She was lighter than my grand-mother too, now that I really thought about it. Oh my goodness. Could my mother be half-white?

That would make me the Tragic Mulatto Tammi Terrell.

Herself.

CHAPTER THIRTEEN

Sylvia Golubowsky

Caroline brought me into the San Remo that night. I'd been there as a tourist before, but never with a purpose. Now I was one of those people my old self had watched with envy, desperate to become.

She was deeply in love with him, of that I was sure. We'd spent the evening talking about many things, but I had not seen her girlish side until she threw her snowy arms around him and kissed his brown lips. In front of everyone. I'd never witnessed two different colors kiss in the open like that. My singular embrace with Harry had been in the dead of night behind a wall where no one could see and presumably hurt us. I wondered if the fact of her arrogance was in her mind every time they touched or only every other time. She had a casual grace about such a forbidden thing, seeming to love her defiance as much as she loved her husband. At lease these were my thoughts on that first night.

"Cal." She was red from the cold. "This is Sylvia, our next-door neighbor."

"Pleased to meet you, Sylvia," he said, shaking my hand. But I was taken aback because I'd expected a deep and manly authoritative voice like Paul Robeson, and instead got someone very well bred but kind of squeaky.

"Sylvia loves music," Caroline said, pulling off her layers of snowy sweaters. "She was born in Brownsville, is currently head stenographer at the New York *Star*, and plans on becoming a reporter soon, followed closely by a career switch to great novelist of Brooklyn. Did I get it right?"

When I nodded she turned her body to face me and became a bridge between myself and that Negro man, equalizing us for the first time.

"And this is my husband, Cal. Born in Jamaica, raised in Harlem, USA. Graduate of Columbia University, the great American playwright is currently appearing as head fry cook in the extended run of the fabulous hit *Burger Flipping,* playing nightly behind the scenes at Café Society."

"Well," Cal laughed kindly. "What more is there to say?"

"Let's have a drink." She was already in charge.

"Espresso," Cal said. "I want to work when we get home."

"I'll have . . . a Chianti," I said hoping I'd ordered the right thing.

"Sounds good. Joey? One espresso, two Chianti, please. How was work, Sugar?"

"Cut short, but it gave me time to think over my new play."

"Are you an actor?" I asked.

"I am a playwright, remember?"

"Yes, I'm sorry," I stammered. Poor me, I was so pathetic. "But where do you do your plays?"

"Ah, the question of the century. Yes, it is a puzzle stumping the best and the brightest of Greenwich Village. Where does the Negro do his play in 1949?"

"Well, I didn't mean to say the wrong thing. Surely there are places."

Another couple walked into the Remo. Cal watched me expect Caroline to save the moment, and when she didn't I floundered helplessly. You see, I had never had this kind of conversation before. I couldn't keep from watching myself doing it. Because my own prejudices were repellent to me, I'd never imagined not knowing how to engage a Negro man on his own terms. But there were so many different concepts at stake that I had not considered, and the logic of the situation was not obvious. All the discomfort was rooted in an absurdity, but simply thinking so didn't make it go away.

And of course Cal could read my so apparent thoughts.

"We perform everywhere," he said. "Open decks of slave ships, for example."

I was mortified while Caroline still showed nothing. She didn't even notice anymore.

"Were your grandparents slaves?" I asked, carefully doing my math. I had no idea as to where I was going.

"No, no," he said. "West Indians. Landowning Presbyterians whose eleven children could all read. Could your grandparents read?"

"No."

"Claude McKay grew up down the road. I don't suppose you know who that is."

"No. Were they conservatives then, being landlords?"

" 'How can a Negro be conservative? What has he got to conserve?' Do you know who said that? Marcus Garvey. Do you know who that was?"

"Musician?"

"That's it," Cal said, relaxing as if I had given the right answer. Getting me off the hook. "Garvey was cold strollin' on that trumpet. You win, Sylvia. Let me buy you another Chianti."

It was as though he could see right through me. He could see how shy I was, how afraid of saying the wrong thing, how desperately I needed the two of them, and how much I wanted to be in their world. Their whirl. Now, with everything I've learned since, I can interpret that exchange so differently. My singular special moment was something he'd seen on white faces hundreds of times. And he'd determined by trial and error that diffusion was the best response. We'd work it out. Later. Maybe. Due to his graciousness, of course. But for me it was all entirely focused on the monogrammed ironed handkerchief peeking out of the breast pocket of his suit jacket. A fry cook.

"Oh, let's have a good time," Cal decided. "After all, I'm not the only person in this town with a dream. And dreamers can always identify each other, even across the color bar. In 1949 little Jewish girl typists from Brooklyn grow up to be great American novelists at about the same rate that Negro kitchen help get their plays produced on Broadway."

I had no idea how generous he was being. I did not know the price he was paying. I did not know that this was a rarefied moment of historical hope, an expectation that brought out the very best and then left them stranded.

"It's calm here tonight," Caroline said, looking out the window at the snow. "It is a beautiful night."

"Babies are being conceived tonight," Cal said. "Masterpieces are being created, and new friendships are being made."

"Here's to new friends," Caroline said, raising her glass.

"Here's to new friends on snowy nights in Greenwich Village," I said, drunk with my own authenticity. "With great dreams and even greater futures."

"Hallelujah," Cal said. And then we all drank up.

CHAPTER FOURTEEN

Austin Van Cleeve

1

"It's that Hewitt again," Jim repeated on the way to our increasingly regular pre-theatrical cocktail. "You know I've been dutifully covering the trials of those Communist leaders, when the informer—"

"Which one this time?"

"Charles Nicodemus. But they're all the same disturbed individuals who never fit in, with deep guilt over their Communist pasts."

"O'Dwyer, are you being analyzed? You sound like a walking couch."

"Do you think I'm insane?"

It wasn't a flippant question. He really wanted to know. So, I looked at him, getting bloated from too much drinking, victim of his Irish physiognomy. Pasty skin from living on cigars and bicarbonate of soda. Certainly he was increasingly high-strung, but not yet mad.

"No, not yet," I said. "But don't identify so closely with ex-Communist informers. It's not good for the self-image."

"They're just so grating, Austin. The way they pretend to be patriots while really being stool pigeons. I thought honor was the American way. These betrayals leave a greasy slime over every word of testimony."

"You'll be seeing a lot more of that sort of thing," I warned him. "I suggest you find a place of acceptance for it now."

For some reason we walked right past the bar, even in the rain, and kept on down the avenue. I don't know if he was avoiding taking that next drink or if he needed the cool air to stay awake. Or perhaps he was sensible enough to worry about eavesdroppers at every turn. But not sensible enough to worry about me.

Somehow we ended up walking into that cavernous town square called Penn Station, and I gasped for air, suddenly so overcome by its beauty. All around me the detritus of human frailty. Each item was filled with meaning. The wall of sober wooden phone booths, how many tears had been shed behind those doors? A beckoning parcel depot. Private gatherings of hats and overcoats stamping out cigarettes. A colored porter with shined black shoes led white guests to the Hotel Statler across the street. Assuredly his brother was the porter at the Hotel Ashley, wall phone in every room. And it all started to spin around me. The details. Barbershop. Immunize against diphtheria. *She's kind of shifty.* Ace Dairy, special on cottage cheese. *Our milkman lives on Staten Island.* The clatter of glass bottles in his carrying case. Rooms to let. Beds twenty cents. Free reading rooms. Lodging. Showers. *The Bennet girls of Brooklyn.* Rupert Brewery. Gracie Mansion. Tugboat on the river. *On your way, Sonny.* Over the teletype. If the door gets stuck it's bad luck. *Kettle on the stove.*

"So, when Nicodemus was cross-examined at Foley Square yesterday, he conceded that he had been expelled from the Party because of his attitude toward Negro workers."

"What?" I felt very free, almost ecstatic. The greatest feelings in life are always so fleeting. The city was a beauty. Its people unified in a perfect nonrhythm. Something Stravinsky would have emulated.

"It's Hewitt, Hewitt," he said stubbornly. That's what he was so upset about. "Hewitt is probably under direct orders from Stalin."

"Have you talked with the man?" I asked automatically, not letting this banal discussion impede my sensation of feeling special. There was nothing I loved more than to be at the center of all this feeling. All this consequence. I forgot my real age, my real place. I was the inventor of an arbitrary future. I was awake.

"Hewitt!" he shrieked, drawing the attention of some bum walking around all night and sick of his own thoughts. "I run an impartial, slightly liberal, objective New York City newspaper. Not the *Daily Worker* and not the NAACP. Either Hewitt works for me, or he works for them."

"I'm sure you know what's best," I whispered softly, coming back to my senses.

"This is a lousy business," Jim said. "I should have been a priest like my mother wanted."

There we were at the theater, greeted by Amy's stone face. I looked on her with marvel and envy. I understood so much more about her than her poor dilapidated husband ever would. Clearly Amy Harrison O'Dwyer thought that she should be running the *Star*. She had an organizational mind. But instead of a mate to share the daily intrigues of the human machine that makes a newspaper work, she had a man on her hands who was depressed, drank too much, and kept her waiting again for him to show up three minutes before curtain. He was so sadly predictable stepping out of his cab, lost, angry, and late.

2

I returned after the curtain came down for our equally habitual post-theatrical drink. But O'Dwyer's nerves had gotten the best of him, and I stood across the street watching how Amy would handle her post-encore solitude. Rather than sulking, she also found the rainy night to be a delight. Her flesh luxuriated in it. She was only forty-six after all, nowhere near ready for the nursing home or any level of complacency. So, once the crowd had thinned and left her standing under the marquee, she started walking. We were both such romantics.

In those days tawdry old Broadway booths sold fruit drinks

for five cents each and live turtles for fifty. That was the great divide, of course, the Broadway area. New Yorkers of every stripe passed each other in the night and took a good look in the process. She could turn left at the corner and head toward the Automat where the masses got a hot meal for half a buck. Or, she could take a right and land in the Hunt Room of the Astor Hotel where orchids sold for six to eighteen dollars. Forty-second Street was the most depraved of the district, littered with male and female prostitutes and hustles of such advanced complexity their precisions are beyond the average American's imagination. Poor couples who could afford nothing more than the street display strolled past Hubert's Museum with the world's finest flea circus among other monstrosities and exotica. Across the street, *Kiss the Blood off My Hands* was playing at the Loew's Criterion movie theater. Any fool could tell from the title alone that it was destined to be a forgotten flop. The big neon Bond's sign endlessly flashed its promise of two trouser suits.

Amy was about to enter the Astor and I wondered who she was intending to meet. Then she stopped suddenly, actually blushing and turned abruptly in the other direction. I imagined the detailed picture of what she was seeking. The throbbing genitalia in her mind was suddenly so graphic that she quickly changed her path and headed up Broadway, fully intending to grab a cab to the dangers of her own apartment and poor, deranged husband. But, when she passed by the Automat, she spotted the object of her fantasy, that young playwright she'd met through Camilla, along with his dresser friend and a Negro man. All three engaged in impassioned discourse over coffee. And this is what I always admired about Amy's mind. You see, the genitalia of the story made for a titillating detail, true. But, what she really wanted was the image of artists gesticulating wildly, brightly, in fact starkly overlit in the frame of the Automat's window. It was a little play. She stood outside at first and watched them, admiring their youth and enthusiasm. They were the stars of her own tiny theater, complete with millions of extras and the greatest set in the world. Of course I followed her in and sat across the adjacent table, facing her back, front stage. If ever she did happen to turn in my direction, I simply hunched over a bottomless cup of tea.

"Mrs. O'Dwyer," her pal exclaimed, registering actual friendship for the first few seconds before switching, unconsciously, to dollar signs for pupils. "Please join us."

She took her seat after investing a nickel in a cup of hot coffee and a slightly older roll with a pat of freshly cut butter floating in a bowl of ice. The cashier, of course, was matronly. Amy was slender. The cashier's hands were burned from ironing, cooking, lifting scalding pots for washing clothes. The cashier only had one reality. Amy had both.

"You know Emily," he said. "And this is Calvin Byfield, also a playwright. We're right in the middle of an impassioned discussion."

"Oh, don't let me stop you."

Playwright was open-faced, boyish, a bit too blond. He had wide lapels that were simply out of date. Emily, so that was the girl's name. She had a timeless bohemian veneer. But since she was a dresser, I knew it was distinctly chosen. Short-cut boyishly feminine hair, what flappers used to call a "bob." Streamlined stylishness, slightly male attire but with a soft cut at every turn that gave such a deeply womanly aura to her clothing that every man in a suit was implicated by comparison. Bright, mischievous brown eyes. Wells of mischief. Together, she and the playwright were just original and out of sync enough to be intelligently flamboyant.

"We're talking about the high unemployment among Broadway actors," the Negro told her. "Almost eighty percent."

Now this one was classic. He was extremely well dressed, but so conventionally that it was odd. And he had a high, chirpy voice. All of that affectation made him seem to be more of a dandy than an intellectual.

"Right," the playwright added. What was his first name?

"So, Chris, tell us about the meeting," said Emily the dresser, ever prompting him. Okay, Chris. That was his name.

"For the first time in Broadway's history," Chris said with an appropriately dramatic flourish, "an emergency meeting was called for all the unions and theater people. Folks had terrific ideas—making better use of the theater buildings by holding productions in the afternoons was one that I favor strongly. Or any evening when the houses are dark."

"Or before breakfast," Cal added. "On Sundays."

"Most important of all," Chris continued, "is the hope, of course, that the government will once again subsidize us like they do in Europe. But right now, the theater in New York is an organized calamity. Even the theater's mistakes have problems."

"Well, what are the actual costs involved?" Amy asked tentatively.

You see, that was the point of this story. It was the on-going question of how deeply she would get enmeshed in this theater business. How tempted she was and how much the personal charm of these characters brought her into it.

"A production is around fifty thousand dollars for a drama," Emily answered authoritatively, clearly the brains of the outfit. "Two hundred thousand for a high end musical. That's Broadway, of course. The smaller theaters do everything on a shoestring."

Amy sighed with relief. It was so completely out of her range that there was no danger of getting into this mess at all. Then she felt acutely disappointed. I could see her shoulders sway.

"What about the Negro theaters, Byfield?" Chris slimed.

On paper it was an innocuous question, but the Negro man twitched. He took it as a slight, and his humiliation was so obvious that Chris' question must have been a deliberately pointed dagger. Byfield wanted to be asked his opinion on the universe, not be the repository for only things Negro.

"The Negro theaters can do a show for five dollars," he said flatly. And then tried to save the moment by introducing a more general topic that he'd enjoy engaging. "After all, theater is not a product, shall we remember, fellow artists? It produces ideas and feelings. Not automobiles."

Now Amy had, in her travels, seen some Negro theater, and this fellow's comments clearly made her reconsider her theatrical future one more time. Perhaps that's where she should invest her imaginary patronage.

"I've seen *Deep Are The Roots* by Armand d'Usseau and

James Gow," she said. "It's about a Negro war hero who returns to the unchanged South and seeks to realize his love for a white girl."

Of course the subtext of her statement immediately took over and she realized the implication to the Black man across the table. On one hand, I'm sure she hoped the insinuation would drive Chris to take some action. On the other, the lady in her did not want any invitation to become too obvious.

"Oh, that drivel," Calvin said, unexpectedly strident. We, the white people, had anticipated a good-humored, appreciative acknowledgment. After all, it wasn't every white woman who took the time. But this man seemed capable of overreaction at the slightest opportunity.

"Why do you say that, Cal?" Emily asked.

"It's just so easy to be sentimental," he said. "And not connect these feelings to the news of the day. Like it all took place in one man's distorted fantasy instead of in the world in which we all live."

"What do you want, back to the *Living Newspaper*? This ain't the Depression, my friend." Chris snorted.

"It depends."

"Well, you're the writer, Cal," Emily said. She was the only one at the table who didn't seem to be afraid of him. "How would you set it up?"

"Yeah, the Negro war hero returns all right," Cal said. "But only to discover that all government promises to desegregate the army don't affect the vets. Why, it's right out of today's headlines, you've read about the strike at City College. The administration took Negro vets, coming to school on the GI Bill, and put them in segregated dormitories right on the campus."

"Okay so far," Emily soothed.

"Next scene: A. Philip Randolph testifying before the Senate. But his articulate call for justice falls, again, on deaf ears."

"No, no," moaned Chris. "Another courtroom scene."

"Paul Robeson, as Randolph, rises in the chair and faces his white opponents."

Then, the most extraordinary thing happened. The fellow took out a stack of papers, folded, anal-retentively into tiny squares, and picked out a monologue he had clearly been working on that day. Cal then rose from his seat and suddenly this little featherweight was a two-hundred-and-fifty-pound Shakespearean with enormous stature and that deep, resonant voice.

"*Negroes,*" he bellowed, and all the clattering of coffee cups and nervous late-night spoons stopped. The jury of hipsters and dopers and whores looked up from their cigarettes and worries to catch the show. "*Negroes will be serving a higher law than any passed by a national legislature in an era in which racism spells our doom. Negro youth have a moral obligation not to lend themselves as worldwide carriers of an evil and hellish doctrine.*"

He stopped, bowed his head, and then took his seat, glowing. He was absolutely radiant. I remember feeling immediately that I knew what Cal was getting at, but his character was flawed. There was a depth missing to him, and then I realized that he was being dishonest with the white people. Five minutes later, I couldn't remember what his face has been doing or what he was really thinking. Blacks don't tell whites the truth, but whites count on this. It allows us to achieve the sympathetic catharsis. He appeared to be a strange Black person, not seeming to appreciate Negro theater for what it was, a kick in the pants to the whites, a celebration. Then, I got it! He was more radical even than that. He had a picture in his mind that was so far beyond his time, none of us sitting around his performance, could begin to grasp it. He wanted to be our authority. He wanted to own what we have.

"That was quite a delivery," Chris said as Cal took his seat. "I didn't know you were such an actor."

"I'm not." He looked around, deflated. They still didn't get it. But he actually tried again. "Well, do you see what I mean? There are no issues in this so-called Negro Theater. Just sappy minstrel shows of false sentiment set in the old South filled with colored folk one step removed from pickaninnies."

"That's overstatement," Emily said, again the only one really willing to speak. "The Experimental Theater is staging a Negro version of Gorky's *Lower Depths.* I think it's called *A Long Way from Home,* or something like that. A girl I know is sewing the costumes."

"That is the only way America will integrate the Negro into their theatrical consciousness," Cal spat. "Black versions of white people's concepts. The *Carmen Jones* disease. The watering down of our themes for white people's consumption."

"Are you working with Negro theater companies then?" Amy asked, trying to fully understand what in the world this angry man wanted. The reason I understood him was because I listen very closely to my enemy, at every stage of his development. If you don't know him utterly, you can't co-opt him. The others were too arrogant, too assured of the permanence of their position to even try. Fools.

"No, no, not at all." He was exhausted. You can imagine his frustration at this point. "I want to write my plays, my Black man's plays for my Black actors about Black life, and then present them on the same stage as everyone else, for the same audience that goes to see *A Streetcar Named Desire.* I want to be called an *American* playwright with an *American* voice. None of you dream of having your life's blood on some second-rate stage. Why should I? Can any of you answer that? Can you?"

There was an uncomfortable silence, of course. White people were not used to being spoken to in that way. It was unheard of, actually.

"Well," Chris said, trying to smooth things over so that they would be over. "We'd better have cheesecakes all around, because this is going to be a long, long night."

But the two women wouldn't laugh, even though it might have diminished their discomfort.

CHAPTER FIFTEEN

N. Tammi Byfield

1

Despite his education, my grandfather was working as a cook at Cafe Society. It was the first club to have interracial audiences for the Black performers. But there was no integration going on over the hot stove.

Almost obsessively, he continued to seek out the company of whites in his free time. He was fucked up, but I understand. It's not pretty but a lot of different kinds of people have got to go through it. Then they realize and it's over, needing the approval. But, in those years, besides my Aunt Ide in Queens, the only Black person he bared his soul to on a regular basis was an older man named Joe Mackie who worked beside him on the grill. No wonder he was in a constant state of rage.

It was the middle of his Summer of Hate, and the Kitchen was a living hell. The cooks and dishwashers were eating salt to keep from passing out in the deathly heat. Plus, the food went bad faster than usual, and there managed to be revolting signs of rotting flesh or rancid fruits in most corners.

"Stupid asses," Cal complained to Joe, both men soaked through with sweat, hamburger grease, and the constant din of the kitchen. "So, this dumb ass, no more than twenty-five years old, crosses his arms, leans back and says, *Your play is just too . . . strident.* Strident! What does he think plays are? Neutral? That the colored neck he's scraping off the bottom of his shoe is objective? Dumb ass."

"That's a shame," the older man said.

"Then he goes, *I'm sure all producers are looking for the same thing—a good script. Color doesn't matter.* I could have smashed him right in those dumb blue eyes of his. How many horrible plays by white people with no talent are produced every day? Huh?"

"Hey, you sleeping back there?" snapped yet another blonde girl from the other side of the stove.

"What do you think I'm doing?" Cal snapped back, ready for another day of race war in the brutal kitchen heat.

"Give me three deluxes, well-done. Two cheeseburgers, medium."

"When will they ever put an all-Black waitress crew out on the floor so they can make some good tips?" Cal said loud enough for everyone to hear. "Or are we only fit to entertain?"

"There's plenty of mixed tables out there, Mr. Big Shot," the girl tossed back. "Nothing a Negro couple likes more than to be waited on by a white girl."

"You know they love it," Cal wiped the sweat off his forehead with a rag. It was already so filled with sweat it couldn't absorb another drop and just left oily streaks on his skin.

"The guys love it all right," she said. "But get some Negro ladies in here for lunch, and they suck their teeth, send me running around for extra that and extra this, and then don't leave no tips. I didn't do anything to them. Not my fault that they're ignorant and don't know how to act in a restaurant."

"Ain't it unjust," Mackie said, throwing some more chopped meat on the grill. "Come on now, everyone be friendly and let's get back to work."

"Pick up," Cal called out, hitting the bell and throwing some tomato slices on the plate. "So, Joe, this was after these jokers tell me to go to a Negro company to do my little plays. You know, in the backroom of a box somewhere underneath somebody's basement where nobody's ever gonna see it. They know they should be using their little white-ass connections to get my work on their stages. But no, they're too busy sucking up to lonely Miss Socialites and their white checking accounts. White people always have money somewhere. I never met one who didn't. Why, Caroline would have it too if her mamma didn't know she was married to a *Nigra*."

"I tell you, Cal," Joe Mackie said, throwing a basket of sliced potatoes into the boiling grease. "I am sixty years old, and some things never change. Those pale faces are stealing everything we've got, even our sense of humor. Last night my wife and I were watching Milton Berle on the television at her brother's bar. All of a sudden the guy is doing a minstrel act. But like he thought of it."

"Berle doing Jasper?"

"Naw, it was whitewashed. You know. The girl asks, *'Why don't you kiss the way you used to do?'* So Berle says, *'Why don't you wash your neck the way you used to do? You have the face of a saint.'* And then my wife, her brother, and I all yell out together, *'Yeah, a saint bernard.'*"

He pulled out the basin of peeled onions and started chopping them up.

"So, Florence's brother's wife says, *'What's up?'* And I said, *'That's some old Bert Williams routine.'*"

"Who's Bert Williams?" Cal asked, still thinking about his troubles, pulling out a new bag of rolls and slicing them in anticipation of future burgers.

"Who's Bert Williams?" Joe snorted. "You putting me on, man? You claim to be the big bad great Black hope, and you never heard of the most famous comedian, black or white, who ever graced the vaudeville stage?"

"Nope."

"Yes! He and his partner, George Walker, were billed in New York as *Two Real Coons.* Not white folks in blackface. The genuine article."

"Yuck, yuck, yuck."

"You know," Mackie said, throwing the onions on the grill and then some cheese, haphazardly, on top of the sizzling meat. *"Niggers hair am very short. White folks hair am longer. Niggers dey smell very strong. But white folks dey smell stronger."*

"Pickup," Cal yelled out, hitting the little bell.

121

"Hey, Mr. Jones?"

"No way." Cal looked right at Joe like he was the Devil. "I'm not going to play that game."

"Come on, Cal. It's that beat of the African drum so dear to your heart. Listen to the rhythm of your forefathers on the chitlin circuit because, any second now, Uncle Miltie's gonna use it to sell you a Chevrolet, a glass of soda pop, and a cigarette."

"Shut up, I'm tired."

"Hey, Mr. Jones."

"I'm not gonna do that."

The blonde girl came running in again, out of control and ready to blame it all on the kitchen as usual. "Goddamnit, where are my deluxes, lazy Nigger. You're screwing me up on purpose."

"Relax, Kemosabe," Mackie said through clenched teeth. "Here are your fucking deluxes, right under your pert little twa . . . nose."

"Coon," she said, grabbing the plates and tearing out of the kitchen. Cal and Joe stood there, deeply annoyed, steaming along to the soundtrack of fat sizzling on the grill.

"Hey, Mr. Jones."

Cal was still, his skin slick with grease. He stood quietly and let the cheeseburgers burn. Then he spoke very slowly and the meat withered and dried as the cheese bubbled up brown and flew off into black crispy flakes.

"Yawser, Mr. Bones."

"Does us Black folks go to hebbin? Do we go through dem golden gates?"

"Mister Bones," Cal said, completely flat. "You know the golden gates is only for white folks."

"Well, who gonna be there to open dem doors?"

Blondie came back into the kitchen.

"Look what you did to my cheeseburgers, you shit. I got a table of screaming customers crawling all over me."

Cal looked at her, his eyes bland and deceptive.

"Tell them to go eat some crackers."

2

That night it took three hours for both men to calm down. They went over to my grandfather's place, had showers, changed back into their civilian clothes. Then they sat around barefoot with cold beers and a cool breeze finally coming in through the window.

"Truth is, it's not that hot out."

"No," Joe said. "It's a beautiful night. There's just not any proper ventilation in that kitchen. Summer was one thing, the heat is nobody's fault."

"But the boss's," Cal added stretching out, cracking his neck and settling back into being human again. "That girl better not show up for work tomorrow."

"She won't. But you should be used to that kind of thing."

There wasn't a week that passed that my grandfather didn't have to defend his choice of a white wife. Joe Mackie managed to mention it once a day at least. To Joe, it was incomprehensible.

"Who wants the shit of the world in your own four walls? A wife is someone who should know where you come from and what you go through every single day, and no white woman can do that. No matter how different she is."

"Frederick Douglass had a white wife."

"Yeah, and where is he now?" Mackie tried to laugh it off. "Six feet under, which is where colored men with white women always go."

"You're not logical," Cal said, for the umpteenth time. He'd explained this over and over to everyone he'd ever met, and no one ever seemed to understand. Even his sister, my great-aunt Ide, couldn't sympathize. Every other time my grandfather went to his sister's for Sunday supper, he ended up trapped in the kitchen having to explain it all over again.

"Tell me again," Ide said, impatient, stubborn and sure.

"I love her. We understand each other. We're both crazy."

Yet, despite his protests, other anecdotes from his life with Caroline showed particular humiliations. Not between the two of them, necessarily, but certainly between them and the world. For example, whenever a new purchase went wrong, Caroline had to be the one to take it back to the store. There was a way that he had to go through a constant demotion, shouldering the humiliation of being one of the only men in America whose wife had more power than he did. But, on the other hand, he saw the ordeal as a personal testament. He felt that he was grounded enough in his Blackness to be able to meet a white woman as an equal. He didn't need to hide behind the safety of one race. I'd never really looked at it that way before. And I still wasn't entirely convinced. In fact, I wasn't convinced. But, not every man had the confidence to live with that kind of inequity on the other side of the bed.

Cal looked out the window.

"Must be a party going on at the Albert Hotel."

"Why do you say that?"

" 'Cause there's always a party going on over there. Hey," Cal said, grabbing a stack of papers off his desk, "I've got a new play underway and I think it's gonna be another good one. I've got to get the hell out of that kitchen before next summer. I did not go to Columbia University in order to be somebody's short order cook."

"Nothing wrong with working for a living."

"Whatever."

"Write me a good part this time, Cal," Joe asked, coming back to his favorite topic of conversation, his comeback. "You know I want to return to the stage. We'll take it around to the usual suspects and get a good solid run."

"On the chitlin circuit?"

"You gotta get a grip on reality, my friend. Watch my lips. *No white boy is ever going to rescue you.* If you don't settle for something else, you're not going to get anything at all."

"Something less, you mean."

"No, I don't. Look, Cal, even if a miracle occurs and the world changes overnight and some white guy or horny white moneybags society lady decided to put up the cash, you know you're gonna lose control from the beginning. They'll have a bunch of fools jumping around onstage and the whole point of your endeavor is going to be lost on the audience."

"I am not a second-rate Nigger and you will never convince me to become one."

Joe sat back in his chair. He started to say one thing and then said something else instead. "That's not what I meant."

"Joe, do you know how hard I'm writing? I've got five plays here, all have been through readings at the Black theaters. Some have even had productions, you know that. But you can't get your place in history on those out of the way stages. It's just a fact."

"You don't even know your own history, Mr. Columbia. For all of your education you are woefully misinformed about what the Black man has done. I take pride in the Black theater and I don't know why you're so negative about it."

"I'm not negative, I just want more."

"You have so much contempt for the Black man that you don't even know where he's been."

"Please." Cal poured another drink.

"You know I was a bit player for the greatest shows on the Black stage," Joe said. "And you owe us some respect."

"Not this again," Cal put his bare feet up on top of his manuscripts and leaned back in his chair, mimicking a good, long nap. Joe knew this routine. It was all cat and mouse between the two guys. But they took turns. Their whole friendship was a vaudeville act, could have taken that on the road, without even writing a script.

"I had a bit part in *Shoo-Fly Regiment* in 1906," Joe went on. "I had a bit part at the Pekin Theater, the Monogram, and the Grand. All on Chicago's Southside, all in the same year, 1908. I played the Regal in Baltimore, the 81 in Atlanta, the Booker T in Saint Louis. I put on blackface with Jackie Moms Mabley in the traveling tent shows. Performed Irving Jones's hit song *Saint Patrick's Day Is a Bad Day for Coons* all over the medicine show circuit. That's where I met Florence. We came to New York to be in Flournoy Miller and Aubrey Lyles's 1915 production of *Darkeydom*. More medicine shows. Worked side by side with Bessie Smith, Butterbeans and Susie, Kid and Coot.

125

Wilber Sweatman and his clarinet, Brown and Brown, S. H. Dudley and his mule, Mantree Harrington, Tom Fletcher, Sweet Mama Stringbean, whose real name was Ethel Waters. And then, the finale. Both me and Florence worked as chorus dancers in Eubie Blake's 1921 *Shuffle Along* before getting real jobs. That's not nothing, you know. That's nothing to sneeze at."

"Fine, Joe. But that's all in the past now."

Joe sat back, strategizing the situation.

"Look, Cal, you are never going to get anything but heartbreak from the white man. There's nothing shameful about being Black. It's just an inconvenience. But you can't make it go away. Look, why don't you write a show for me?"

"You still on that?"

"Yeah. A sarcastic song and dance musical with a vicious, vicious bite. Use your own ways to get the white man where he lives. Forget about his terms, do it on your own."

Cal just stared at the floor.

"Look," Joe said, standing up in the small apartment. "The orchestra starts up, curtains open, spotlight on yours truly and I do a George M. Cohan flag-waver with a knife in every line."

Then Joe started to sing.

"Every cafe has got to have a dancing jigaboo.
Pretty chocolate babies shake and shimmer everywhere.
Real darktown entertainers hold the stage.
Only the black man knows the latest rage.
Yes, the great white way is white no more.
It is just like a street on the Swanee shore.
Yes it's getting darker every day
On the great . . . white . . . waaayyyy."

"Joe, you're embarrassing me. Where is your dignity, man? I'm a good writer. I could be a Tennessee Williams if I could get any support. I need staged readings, workshops, out-of-town development so I can compete with those white people who have it all going for them. I'm writing Negro drama as important as anything by Odets or Miller or any of those suckers. Just calling it *Negro Drama* is part of the problem, this is *American*

Drama or nothing. All I need is the same support that they get. I'll never put a tap dancing nigger up there, Massa Lincom. Never."

There was a key in the lock then, and both men turned to face the door.

"Cal? You still up? Hi, Joe."

"Evening, ma'am."

Cal glared at Mackie, who pretended not to know what he possibly could have done wrong.

"Yes, babe," Cal said, turning away from both of them. "Just having some beers."

"Kind of late to be coming home, Miss . . . uh . . . Caroline," Joe offered, halfheartedly clearing the air that he didn't want to clear.

"Got a gig playing in a dive on Sixteenth Street," she said softly. That was her way of confronting Black rudeness. Go soft. I've noticed it myself around white people who hear a lot of truth. It's still the best approach. "And now I'm dead tired and going to bed. Come here, baby, you look so sad." She pulled my grandfather's skinny arms around her waist. She was taller than he was. Almost. "Gimme a goodnight kiss."

Cal kissed her to spite his world, just as she kissed him in defiance of hers. Thinking about that moment between them, *my grandparents* or whatever, reaffirms my values. That's why I don't believe in interracial relationships. It makes you break with your family, with your own people. I guess my grandfather thought he was being himself, it was his house. But I think, actually, he lost himself because every little act of normalcy, even kissing his own wife, was a statement to somebody watching from somewhere with something disapproving to say. Cal turned his back on his friend trying to unite with his wife. But really, I know he felt lonely from all sides. So, in the end, everyone in that tiny apartment also didn't know where they belonged. Every one of them felt alone.

3

After Joe went home my grandfather sat quietly in his armchair having a drink of whiskey. He wanted to apologize to Caroline for Joe's rudeness, but who was going to apologize to him? Finally he just walked into the bedroom, acting casual, hoping it had all passed.

"What are you reading, Caroline? Anything good?"

"No, just turning the pages. Listen, Cal. Hear the way she carries that song?"

"Yeah, it's fine. Who is that now?"

"Ruth Brown. Cal, you're silly. You're single-minded."

"I have to be," he said sitting on the edge of the bed. "Nothing's gonna be handed to me, you know that. I have to strategize."

"But you're so driven," she said, sitting up in her nightgown against two feather pillows. "Every second of the day and night. It's taking over your heart. Can't you relax?"

"No." Then he felt bad and leaned over to bite her.

"Ooh, you stink of whiskey. Pour me one, will you, Sugar?"

"So we can both stink?"

"Hear that? What a musician."

"She's a singer."

"Well, the voice is an instrument, Cal. You know that."

"Move over. You're hogging all the bed. Want a piece of candy?"

"What have you got?"

"I've got toffees." He dangled them near her lips. "I've got a Hershey's."

"Yum. But which is better? Chocolate and whiskey or chocolate and beer?"

"My mother used to have that ginger beer, heaven knows where she got it."

"Ask your sister."

"I'll ask Ide."

"Turn over the record, will you?"

"I'm resting."

"Come on, Cal. Be a hero."

"Okay. Who's that again?"

"Ruth Brown."

"She's all right. Caroline?"

"Yes."

"Am I ever gonna make it? What do you think?"

"Come here, little boy," she said, taking his head in hand, pulling him toward her, and rubbing his chest. "Come here, I want to tell you something." She looked him in the eye. "I don't know."

"I'm so afraid, Caroline. I fear that I'll knock down all their doors and then someone younger and less ornery will walk right on through. Without even tipping their hat."

"Could happen. Pour me a little whiskey, will you? It smells good. Any more chocolate over there?"

"Nothing sweet on the dresser."

"You're sweet."

"Ooh, that southern charm. It's deadly. You're the sweet one."

"Cal?"

"Yeah?"

"Come here and give me some sugar."

1950

BILLBOARD MAGAZINE'S TOP TEN HITS

1. The Tennessee Waltz.........................Patti Page
2. Goodnight Irene .... Gordon Jenkins & The Weavers
3. "The Third Man" Theme....................Anton Karas
4. The 3rd Man Theme........................Guy Lombardo
5. If I Knew You Were Comin' (I'd've Baked A Cake)
   .... Eileen Barton
   ....Nat "King" Cole
6. Mona Lisa ....Rod Foley
7. Chattanoogie Shoe Shine Boy..............Andrews Sisters
8. I Can Dream, Can't I? ....Andrews Sisters
9. All My Love (Bolero) ....Patti Page
10. The Thing.....................................Phil Harris

CHAPTER SIXTEEN

Austin Van Cleeve

1

Don't you just love to ruin someone's decade?

I waited until Jim had survived the round of punishing Christmas parties. Basted goose and glazed ham with his in-laws and endless igloos of potatoes with his own kind. Too much brandy. Fruitcake for breakfast. Minced pie, pecan pie with fresh cream and iced cream. A roast pig. Holiday punch on top of holiday punch. Eggnog for lunch, toddy before bed. Soufflés, cream sauces, and imported French cognac. Havana cigars and some chocolate cream cakes. Four or five Irish whiskeys, fois gras on the side. I waited until the New Year's champagne toasts, top hats and tails, chauffeurs and walking sticks had passed. Roaring fires, hopeful expectations, fearful predictions, and a desperate grab for renewal.

Then, when he walked back into the office on the freezing blue morning of January 2, 1950, there was a little handwritten message sitting directly on his desk. I'd changed the location of our dinner from 21 to Toots Shor's. He obsessively interpreted my action, particularly since the holiday confusion had allowed for a certain laxness in the area of Copy supervision and all of New York had woken up to an article by Hewitt that was deeply disturbing. The feature was supposed to be on the benign subject of U.S. celebrities with increasing presence abroad. But instead of the expected puff piece on the triumph of American entertainment as Europe rebuilds, Hewitt's focus was Paul Robeson. He reported HUAC's recent habit of asking unfriendly witnesses if they owned any Paul Robeson records. Saying yes had become a coded sign of Communist tendencies. When a journalist develops such a public taste for cornbread, it was clear that something had gone wrong at the *Star*. Jim was keenly aware that everyone knew. So, to have his first communication on the first working day of the new era be a little warning note from me was delightful. It was fun.

Let me admit, though, that while I love being very frightening, the facts are that the *Star* was supposed to be a newspaper for all New Yorkers, not just Negroes. And O'Dwyer was supposed to make the assignments, not Moscow. Hewitt was clearly out of hand, and if I could give Jim a good fright, it might shock him into taking some leadership. Ultimately my actions were for his own good, for the good of the paper and the city at large. It was my method that was questionable.

Toots Shor's was a disconcerting choice. After all, this was a Midtown hangout for sports' fiends. The loud children of immigrants displayed their newly acquired wealth by ordering slabs of beef and house wine. The only blue blood in that place could be found in the steaks. I could picture him pacing the office, asking over and over again, *Why would Austin want to be seen where no one he wanted to be seen by would be?*

Perfect.

"Hello, O'Dwyer, it's been much too long, hasn't it?"

"Where have you been?"

He seemed nominally composed, but when I flashed a particularly cruel star in my eye, he went on edge immediately. I could inhale his anxiety.

"While you've been tobogganing and singing 'Oh Christmas Tree,' I've spent the holidays in Washington making some new friends. Waiter, I'll have the New York strip and a Manhattan. Rah-rah for my hometown and all of that. O'Dwyer?"

"I don't care. The same."

"So, Jim, let's cut right to the chase."

"Thank God."

"What do you think of the Yankees this season?"

"In the middle of winter?"

"But surely you read your own sports page."

"Well," O'Dwyer said tentatively. "With Casey Stengel as their new manager I guess there will be some changes."

"Come on, Jim. You must have more to say about it than that."

A couple of greasy celebrities came in flashing their trashy girlfriends. He looked around nervously, even fearing the Guineas.

"The team's stars seem to be aging. Dimaggio's injuries and all of that."

"But he's still a mythical figure, isn't he? Whether he can continue to play or not."

He was clutching his bread like it was a weapon. That's how defenseless he was.

"I suppose so."

"I mean," I continued. "Dimaggio even looks good striking out."

"I guess so."

Jim was so tense that when the waiter arrived with our salads, he whelped in surprise.

"Nervous?"

"What are you getting at, Austin? Don't you want to go over the Hiss conviction? You know there'll be a second trial."

"That reminds me, Jim. Has that wife of yours dragged you to see *South Pacific* yet?"

"I think so."

And then I started singing. I started waving my hands and tapping my feet in place like a silly little chorus girl from Kansas.

" 'Bloody Mary is the girl I love. Her skin is as tender as Dimaggio's glove.' "

Suddenly Jim knew what I was doing. He knew me well enough to see it all awfully unfold. I wanted him to know that he had something to fear. That was why I had picked that dive, posh only for slummers. I didn't want to be seen anywhere with Jim, not anywhere that counted.

"It had something to do with being Italian, don't you think?"

He had to get his house in order.

"I don't know."

"You do know. Italians are bad at war and better suited for milder competition. But when I met Dimaggio in person, I found him to be far better groomed than one would imagine. He did not stink of garlic, and combs his hair back with water, not olive oil like the rest of them. This is his favorite restaurant, did you know that?"

Jim was paralyzed with fear.

"You haven't touched your food, O'Dwyer. Toots won't like that. There he is sitting at the bar, the big disgusting lug. Used to run Billy Lahiff's, a second-rate speakeasy. But I'm sure you remember it well from your youth."

He could not move. The red walls and garish decor of the place blinded him. This was torture, and I knew it. Whoever woke up each morning to decide who would rule and who would fall was sending Jim a very strong warning, and I was the happy messenger. He knew he should leave immediately and even clutched the edge of the table in one preparatory moment. But he did not move. After all, who did he have to run to?

"If only my son were alive."

"What then?"

"Then I'd be able to stand up to you like a man, Austin. I'd walk out on you and call my boy from the nearest pay phone. Then we'd meet at the office and develop our plan. But, as you know, I am all alone with no one to stand by me."

Well, it was interesting, really, to see him squirm. There are some people you have to make very comfortable before they can do anything for themselves. I took in a huge chunk of gristly meat and sucked it. I enjoy how predictable these people are. How responsive they are. How if you do this, they'll do that, etc.

"Well, that was fun. What? You haven't touched your steak. Are your tastes possibly improving?"

"I want a different life," he said. "Austin, I'd give anything for a regular day. Walk around on the long way to work, kick back with a sandwich on a stoop. Then come home to a walk-up with the landlady on the first floor. Go to the fights at Saint Nicholas Arena. Call my girl from the phone in the hall. My rival for her affections couldn't have any more clout than a college ring. Late-night black-and-white ice-cream soda at Romanoff's Soda Fountain on Tenth Street. I could talk my head off with my pals all night long and then forget about every word of it."

"Dear me," I said, patting my lips with a linen napkin. "You recite those clichés like it was the rosary. I'll get this one, O'-Dwyer. Better to save your pennies for your old age."

2

Jim would eventually get his revenge on me. But it wasn't through any act of brilliance or insight. He just stumbled along in his intrinsically bad judgment until he fell into a gold mine that would come in handy many months in the future.

When I left him in the restaurant, he was overcome by panic. He wanted nothing more than to get me on the phone blubbering for my forgiveness. Single-minded, he took off straight for the only place he thought sure to find me. And when, instead, he found the flashing lights of a sagging marquee, he didn't know what else to do but wait.

"Come in, fella. Feeling lonely tonight?"

"I'm looking for a friend."

"Walk on in, buddy. You'll find a friend inside. Dance to the haunting strains of some old records and come alive with forty lovely dancing girls."

He couldn't very well stand out in front loitering. Someone was sure to pass by. Convincing himself I was probably already inside, Jim started up the narrow stairs.

"That's one buck!" the hawker called.

"For what?"

"For tickets, fella. Don't give me a pain."

"Oh, I'm terribly sorry," he pulled the money out of his coat pocket. "This is my first time."

"Right!" the guy sneered. Couldn't be more than fifteen.

"Like every butcher, baker, and candlestick maker. I never saw so many innocents in my life."

The kid pressed the buzzer, and Jim walked into the dance hall.

The room wasn't very special. Sailors, some older men, some young lonely ones. He sat down on a folding chair by the bar. These guys had a bed, a job, and extra money on the side for liquor. That was their life. There was nothing exciting about it.

"What are ya drinking?" the bartender asked.

"Oh, I'm fine, thanks."

"Glad to hear it. Now, what are ya drinking? I don't hang around here for my health, you know. I get a cut."

"Oh, of course. Whiskey, I guess."

Standing at the bar he got a better look at the girls. They seemed to be trying to look cheaper than they actually were. This wasn't the syphilitic, drug-addicted crowd. Just the girls who couldn't pay the rent. Dresses were pulled tight in the seat and more makeup than necessary was mandatory. That's what signaled them as whores. Otherwise they seemed pretty plain. Pretty slow. Pretty bored.

"Wanna dance?" some blonde asked out of nowhere. Doing her job.

"No thanks," Jim said. "I'm gonna sit it out."

"But that's what you're here for," she said, distracted and annoyed in the half-light. "Guys don't come here to check their manicures."

He looked up to meet her challenge, at first seeing the ghastly pallor of her skin under the dim yellow. Then his eyes caught hers and he saw a look of recognition transform her face from utter disinterest to authentic fear.

"Oh God," she said, looking down and then turning away. One breath later she walked to the other side of the room and stood behind three rumbaing couples.

What in the hell was that? he wondered, somewhat intrigued. He was a newspaperman, after all. Nothing could shake him out of his stupor like a good lead. Jim figured this was worth pursuing since he had nothing else to do. Maybe the girl was the champion player at Hard to Get. Invigorated, he drank down his shot of whiskey and crossed the dance floor, after all.

Jim practically had to corner her against the wall before she'd stop running. And even then she turned away, eyes downcast, hand over her face.

"I'm sorry, sir, but you'll have to get another partner. I'm tired."

"But I just bought all these dance tickets."

The girl was so common that she looked absolutely familiar. Jim must have seen that face five times a day since he'd come to New York. Half the girls on the street had that face. That bad hair. Those tacky clothes. It wasn't her fault, of course. Why, hell. He'd grown up with girls like her.

"What's the trouble over here?" the floor manager asked. "Any problems?"

"No, Stanley," the girl said, pulling Jim onto the dance floor. She had no choice now. Her job was on the line. Finally, she dismissed whatever hesitations she'd had and went into her duty like a real professional. Like nothing had ever come between them. She put her hand on Jim's shoulder and placed his around her waist. She actually smelled of gardenia. A cheap girl on a cheap date.

"This is a cheap date," Jim said. He was feeling victorious. He wanted to flaunt it over her. How dare she turn him down.

"Yeah, this is the post office," the girl answered. "We only carry second-class matter here."

Okay, so she had a sarcastic sense of humor, which actually made Jim relax a little more. It didn't take much longer for him to admit he liked swinging around a dance hall with an okay-looking girl. In fact, he loved it.

"Why the initial brush-off?" he asked sweetly. Whispering in her ear. He loved that, the whisper. It was a younger version of himself at the parish ball, winter of 1914. Got his hand up Mary Margaret MaGuire's shirt and then went to church and confessed it the next morning.

"You look just like my dead brother," she said. "My brother was a belly gunner. We lost him in the Pacific."

"Oh my God," Jim thought he would crumple, so he held on tighter.

"What's the matter?"

"You," he spoke, barely breathing. "You know what that kind of grief is like."

"We're not the only ones," she said, looking around in case she needed help.

"The sacrifice is so . . . hidden. My son is always standing behind me, even in this room."

"Wear your Purple Heart," she offered, stroking his hair. "It'll let people know what you're going through."

"All right," he said. They danced a bit in silence. Her hand was on his neck. "So you have any others?"

"Other what?"

"Other brothers?"

"Yeah, one," she said. "He's a fat card player who's gonna die in the street some night. But you wouldn't know about that. What are you doing here anyway?"

"I don't know. Taking care of business."

"Well," she said. "For a guy like you to be up this late, the only business you'd be looking for is monkey business. Ain't that right?"

"No."

"I can be wrong," she said, smiling. "I could be wrong two times out of three. But you're the wrongest guy for this place that I've ever met. Why don't you just go home to your wife. Don't make a mistake."

"What kind of mistake?" It had been decades since Jim had flirted like this. He hadn't been so close to a mistake in way too long. He loved it. He loved her. He felt alive, like he was part of everything. Part of the secrets and the private pleasures that made it worth it to take a chance. When you've got the freedom of nothing to live for.

"Oh, you know. You're a honey, and this town is full of flies. Want another whiskey?"

"Sure, if I can have it with you."

"Oh, a smoothie, huh? From the old neighborhood. I know your type. Can't hide it in those customed suits."

"You like my suit?"

This time he held her a little closer. Found his hand a little tighter around her waist. Like gliding through a piece of glass.

"Night air goes to your head like dope, don't it, Mister?"

"I wouldn't know."

"You wouldn't? Are you telling me the truth?"

"Of course."

"Then, I don't get it. What are you after?"

"I'm after you," he said, breathless. "Won't you let me call you sometime?"

"Whoa, no. No way."

"Come on," he said, getting desperate. "Just tell me your name."

She looked at him like it was the end of the world. "My name is June, Mr. O'Dwyer. It rhymes with moon."

He stopped still, first out of authentic disappointment. Then he realized there wasn't going to be an easy way out.

"Oh my God, you're Austin's girl." Then he was scared. And finally, resigned. He stopped dancing at that point, just staring, like it was all so goddamn predictable. "And how the hell do you know who I am?" Austin pulled out every rug. Jesus Christ.

"Mr. O'Dwyer," she said softly. "There's something important you still don't seem to understand."

CHAPTER SEVENTEEN

Sylvia Golubowsky

1

In our office, each of the girls had her own wooden desk spaced two feet apart like cars in a parking lot. The fat ones had a terrible time getting through. Since we were so close together we started to look alike, follow the same trends. I remember that morning everyone came in with a ponytail, having systematically made the transition from the more ladylike bun. Now that we were growing up, girls my age didn't want to be ladies anymore. It seemed like a national craze. We wanted one last gasp at being girls. The intimacy put us all in a giddy mood, except for Theresa, who was her usual glum self. Lately she'd had lockjaw as far as I was concerned, and I'd given up trying to pry the story out of her. The only thing she wanted to talk about that day was anklets, and then Mr. O'Dwyer called her in. She came out directly to an early lunch, and then he called me in to take dictation. He seemed completely disoriented.

"There's something I need to do, Miss Ski. What was it?" He stared at me like I was supposed to know. "Oh yes, the messy business. Charlie! Send Hewitt in here."

In a few minutes Hewitt showed up, hat in hand. I was in my usual perch on the windowsill and Mr. O'Dwyer didn't ask me to leave. It was as though he'd forgotten I'd existed. I guess I had become a piece of furniture in his life.

"Yeah, Jim."

Hewitt was not a young man. He had those bags around his eyes that would no longer disappear with a good night's rest. His face was slightly jowly, that age when they really understand how things work. They understand all too well. That's what made him such a good reporter. He knew there was no such thing as objectivity, that it was a cruel joke pulled out every now and then to build up the security of those in power. He had an instinct for systems and could get to the bottom of any matter. You could see it at work when he talked politics. It was always about the mechanism and functions of things. But that was the point of this confrontation, I guessed. Hewitt did know. He understood consequences fully, and so any action on his part had to have been deliberate.

"Need a shoe shine?" O'Dwyer said, letting Hewitt know right away that he was going to let him have it.

"I don't know, Jim," the jerk answered, daring to look at his own shoes. That's when he lost me. If only Hewitt had stood there keeping his eye on O'Dwyer's eye, maintaining some dignity, I might have felt some compassion. But for all his big talk, I was surprised to find that Hewitt, whom I'd respected so thoroughly, was afraid. He was subservient enough to check his own shine.

"What would you do if you weren't working as a newshound anymore?" O'Dwyer asked, getting more sadistic.

"I don't know. Cryptanalysis?"

"Are you going to call the FBI to apply for that position? Or stand under a billboard at Columbus Circle with a sign around your neck?"

"You have no right . . ." Hewitt said but didn't finish the sentence.

"You could bus tables at the Mayfair Diner," O'Dwyer said. "Use a knife to dig out the crumbs from the old wooden booths. Or, how about cleaning up the Esso station?"

"Are you asking me to sign a loyalty oath?" Hewitt asked, ready to make his stand. Showing all his cards.

"No. I will never have loyalty oaths in this office. They go against everything I believe in."

"And what is that?"

"I stand for a free press," O'Dwyer said. "I am pro-liberal and anti-Communist, and you are free to be whatever you are because this is America. But, when you come to work for me you must leave your biases at home and turn in copy that is as objective as I am."

"No loyalty oath?"

"Nope. Disappointed? You could have made a big stink out of that one, right? Turned it into a moral issue like you try to do with the facts of the day. But, this has nothing to do with morality. This is about being a good reporter, which of late you have not been."

"I'm appealing to the union."

"Fine. But unless Josef Stalin heads the local, a guy with your record isn't gonna get many shoulders to cry on. You may be shop steward, Hewitt, but things are changing. Soon your kind won't be welcomed in any union hall."

"You sneak."

"Don't pull that girlie stuff with me, Hewitt. You had plenty of warnings. I'm no Father Coughlin, but this is not Party head-quarters either. It takes guts to make a stand for democracy, but that's exactly what I'm going to do."

Hewitt put his hat back on his head but didn't make a move to go. And then he did. I'd seen this happen many times before at work when people got fired, whether it was old Black janitors or inept stenographers. There is that last hesitation before they finally let go. Before they finally ask themselves, *Now what am I going to do?*

As soon as the man was out the door, O'Dwyer moved into action.

"Charlie, call everyone around. I have some announcements to make."

I followed him out to the newsroom. He seemed to feel proud of himself. He was bouncy and smiling.

"Tell you what, Miss Ski," he said joyfully. "Watch this. Now I'm going to stand in front of all my employees. Everyone will stop what they are doing to gather together in anticipation, waiting for me. I am their leader. And now they're going to remember why. Fuck Austin Van Cleeve. Excuse me, Miss Ski."

As for little me, I was processing the argument I had just witnessed. I saw two men whom I admired, both staking claim to moral ground. But which one was right? I didn't fully grasp what Hewitt's point was. He just seemed angry and sarcastic. But I knew that underneath he had firm beliefs about equality. But Mr. O'Dwyer claimed to be for the same things. So, why were they on different sides? One of them was not telling the truth.

"Ladies and gentlemen," Mr. O'Dwyer said, commanding a complete silence, a stillness, simply by raising his voice. "I have a few promotions to announce. Effective immediately, Sylvia Golubowsky will be promoted to the Research Department and Louis Golubowsky will be promoted to cub reporter. Lou, report to my office immediately for your first assignment. Sylvia, you can move your desk tomorrow. All the rest of you stenographers prepare to move up one step and be sure the shift is completed before you go home tonight. Thank you. That will be all."

2

If I had even mentioned that I had gotten Lou a job at the *Star,* you would have known immediately what was going to happen. It would seem inevitable. Nowadays we expect that sort of thing. Exposing the injustice didn't change the injustice, it just normalized it. I got him the job because I wanted him to put in a good word for me with my father. I wanted to show my father that I had accomplished something in the world, and I knew that the only way he would notice would be if I used my achievement to better his son's position. I desperately loved my brother and I wanted to secure his loyalty so that he would protect me from my father. But you—dear reader—have the advantage of history. Now you understand what we could never understand. The second Lou walked into that newsroom you

would have known he would get my job because you have col-
lectively learned that merit has no strength against caste. You've
learned it so well, it has become a benign cliché. But, in 1950
we did not know. It never occurred to me. You, in the future,
you get to look back now and watch us squirm.

3

I automatically followed O'Dwyer back into the office and then
stood, silently, against the wall. By this time I had no property
beyond silence. I was the wall.

"Sir?"

"What? Oh yes, son, come in and take a seat."

Lou entered the office slowly, tussled hair falling over his
visor. Fresh from the print room, his hands were stained with
ink. He had all the attributes required of promising Jewish masculinity, the acceptable kind. He had eager enthusiasm, an inof-
fensive curiosity, a soft gait. He had thick, curly hair, but it was
light enough. An aura of kindness. The potential for fair play.

"Now, son, we have to do something about that last name
of yours. Sounds like a prison in Upper Silesia. Won't fit under
a headline."

"What do you suggest?"

"I don't know," he said. "How about Gibson?"

O'Dwyer was really happy. He was doing something right for
a nice young man.

"All right."

"Proud of yourself, son?"

"No, sir."

"Why not?"

"My sister deserves this promotion, Mr. O'Dwyer."

Oh.

How can I convey what I felt at that moment? That all my
life had been right and true. That I had been on the right road
after all and going in the right direction. That the sky was blue.

147

Never had I felt so honored. The love that came from my brother transformed me, and I was reconstituted as a new being, one who was justly and deeply loved. It was the revelation that every person comes to in which they are changed, for the first time, permanently, forever. For better or for worse, and I was one of those for whom the change was for the best. An elevation. My brother could have so easily betrayed me, all the rewards were laid out on the table. But instead, he was the man I'd hoped he'd be. He refused any prize he hadn't earned and instead he stood up for me, which was what I deserved. I was stunned by justice.

"You're kidding. I mean, let's discuss this. Lou, this is very honorable of you. I admire that about you. That's why I've had my eye on you ever since you came to work here. You're a very easygoing good-natured fellow. You're a good boy. That's why you're perfect for the job. Have a seat, Lou."

Cautiously, my brother tread deeper into the office. His back was to me at this point, and since O'Dwyer made no move to get up from the single chair, Lou just stood awkwardly in the middle of the room. O'Dwyer before him, and me far behind.

"You see, my sister really deserves it."

"Look, Lou, Sylvia and I know each other. She knows that she works hard. She is a very, very bright girl. But Sylvia also understands that sometimes being bright and hardworking is not enough to make a great reporter. You have to have other characteristics."

"Like what?" he asked.

"Like . . . flexibility. You have to be . . . easygoing so that people can trust you and so that you can be . . . flexible in difficult situations. Your sister, here," he gestured toward me. "She is very bright and strong-willed, isn't she?"

"Yes."

"Of course she is, otherwise she wouldn't have gotten this far, would she?"

"No, sir."

Then O'Dwyer addressed me directly for the first time that afternoon. He faced me, but I couldn't catch his eye. It was like he was noticing something right over my shoulder.

"Strength is an excellent attribute for someone who works in Research. But it is not the best for a reporter."

The moment of confrontation over, he turned back toward Lou.

"I mean, Lou," he continued. "The fact that Sylvia is a contender at all is evidence of exactly why she wouldn't be right for this spot. Don't you see?"

"I don't know," Lou said, very disturbed. "But she did all this work for two years and then I get the job. That's what's not right."

"Exactly," O'Dwyer said, leaning across the desk. He didn't have much more time for this. "She had to struggle, and so she is too bitter. But it was easier for you, and so you'll fit in a lot better. Believe me, I know what I'm talking about. Right, Miss Ski? Look, Lou, I know that you love your sister and she knows it too, and you and I both agree that this is an admirable thing. But she just would not be the best person for the job, and you would. If you turn down the job, it will not go to her. Those are the facts of the matter." O'Dwyer opened his palms and reached out across the table. "Lou, have you ever been the best at anything?"

"No, sir, I have not."

"Well, now you are. Now you can call up your father and tell him that for once in your life you are the best qualified. Think of how proud he will be of you. Sylvia's been the best many times I'm sure." He looked at me. "I'm sure of it." He turned back to my brother. "But you never have. This is your chance."

"Thank you, sir," he said, his back stiffening. "But . . ." he stammered in that dislocating transitional phase when a person suddenly realizes that they have no support. That whatever position they're taking is not the favored position and cannot ultimately win. When they start to see this inevitability, often they simultaneously start to calculate exactly how much loss will be involved in sticking with that increasingly improbable position, and how they are going to shake the responsibility of it.

"And, son," Mr. O'Dwyer added, smiling with grateful satisfaction that this scenario was coming to a close. "I'd like you to start off your first evening as a reporter by doing me a favor."

"Yes, sir."

"I'd like you to take my place at the theater tonight. Just show up at curtain time and tell my wife I couldn't make it. Tell her that you're the new reporter and that I want her to make you comfortable. Ever been to a Broadway show before, Lou?"

"No."

"Good. Well, you'll love it. It's part of being a man-about-town, here in New York City. Let me tell you something, Lou. Take a seat, son."

There was still no chair.

"Lou. For the people who make things tick, New York is a small town. Sylvia, you'll be interested in this too. Once you make a name for yourself here, you will never be able to walk down a street in this city without meeting someone you know. A good reporter knows everyone. They know the bum in the pokey, the cop on the take, the guys chasing runaway beer wagons on Bleecker Street. Tonight you'll be on Broadway, to-morrow, in the back of a windowless police van. Everywhere you walk some Negro in Harlem or some Dago on Mulberry Street will yell out, Hey Lou. And they'll call you over with some information, some gossip, some behind-the-scenes dope. This will be your town. Once you've got it in your pocket, no one will ever be able to take it away from you. Right, Lou?"

He half nodded.

"Right, Lou?"

"Right."

"You treat everyone who has ever trusted you with dignity and respect, like I do, and they'll give you the information that you need. Don't ever forget that, son."

"No, sir."

"Okay then, here's the address of the theater. Have a good time. And report back for work tomorrow morning, first thing."

"Yes, sir," my brother said, turning his back to me as he left the room.

"And as for you, Miss Ski. Let's take one last piece of dictation. Just for old time's sake."

4

"I just can't get that play out of my mind," Lou told me first thing the next morning. "I keep saying the actors' names over and over again, checking and rechecking the Playbill. Here." He pulled it out of his jacket pocket. "Mildred Dunnock, Arthur Kennedy, Cameron Mitchell, but especially Lee J. Cobb, that weary plodding Willy, and Dunnock, his tired gallant wife. But it was Kennedy as the glib son who stuck with me the longest. You see, Syl, the whole play takes place in the front rooms of tired neighborhoods, like the ones we've always lived in. 'Attention must be paid,' said Dunnock. 'He's not to be allowed to fall into his grave like an old dog.' See, the trouble with Willy Loman, Syl, from my point of view, is that he felt sorry for himself. And I do sympathize because there are a million trod-upons out there. But why can't Willy just do something about it? I mean, what the hell is wrong with Willy Loman?"

We had met, accidentally, in Copy, and he followed me, continuing to talk all through the print shop and newsroom. It was as though he had become a new man. His body, somehow, had risen above all the others around him. As we passed, these others patted him on the back in congratulations with some sense of comradely appreciation. But it was clear from the way he received their physicality that he had left them all behind forever. As soon as we walked past he forgot their good wishes.

"Broadway is incredible, Syl. I must have seen it all with new eyes yesterday. It started in the afternoon when I took the trolley across Forty-second Street. Even though it was just a couple of blocks from the office, I knew I could splurge. The streets were packed with black sedans and green and white cabs. That's how I want to travel from now on, by cab. Soon I'll have enough for my own car. *Buy That Automobile Now* said one neon sign flashing on Times Square. It was strange, but like, for the first time in my life, I noticed all the advertising slogans. *Planters Peanuts: A Bag a Day for More Pep.* I've got to remember to buy a bag. *Coco Cola: The Pause That Refreshes.* I stared at the Camel's billboard and then bought a pack. The neon was no longer overpowering. I could make out every word, like it was being whispered in my ear by a good-looking woman. *Kinsey Blended Whiskey.* Or how about *Make Mine Ruppert: Slow Aged for Fine Flavor.* That's what I want to find out. Which things are finer.

"But the real deal, Syl, is that this morning, when I walked into work, I knew that I was having the moment that every man dreams of. I've seen it in the movies, read it in the books, the man whose dream comes true. And here I am, not even twenty years old and already set right on the path to success. It's so strange. Like everything's going to be perfect. Like the whole world is set up just for me."

5

"I am the man," he said as I shook, embarrassingly, before him on the building's back stair. It was so pathetic in his eyes, my bereavement.

"You know it's because girls don't stand a chance."

Lou started for a moment and then stopped himself. Normally he would have engaged me, but from now on he didn't have to anymore. He didn't have to consider my demands or listen to my complaints. This time he could just put his foot down. It was his right. As far as he was concerned, he'd earned it. He wasn't my baby brother anymore, and he never, ever would be again.

"I am the best person for the job," I shimmered. "And you took it away from me."

"Don't be such a bad sport," he said, still nervous about

standing up to me. "You can't have everything your way all the time."

"Shut up, you fucking liar," I said. "You know it is totally unfair. It's not fair. It's not fair. Who are you to do this to me? You've never done anything in the world but roll ink."

"Okay, Sylvia," he said, adapting permanently, the fake calmness, that condescending stability by which men like that always rule. "Maybe some things aren't as fair as you would like, but the world isn't fair. And you have to take responsibility too. I mean, you heard him. Mr. O'Dwyer knows you and he knows me, and he prefers me. That's not my fault. Why don't you look at yourself? You go blaming everything on being a girl, but you're never going to be a man no matter how hard you try. And that's what Mr. O'Dwyer wants."

I could see Lou feeling sorry for himself. A crying, furious woman yelling at him, pointing her finger. He hoped that none of the guys in Copy would walk by or they might think he couldn't handle some dame.

"You should march right into his office and tell him that you know you don't deserve this job. You have to. Tell him right now."

"You know very well what I've already done for you," he said, turning to granite. "He doesn't want you. Get it? You're crazy."

"You don't deserve it," I screamed, a dog. "How can you sail through life at other people's expense? You talentless creep. You're a creep, Lou. You're shit. You know you wouldn't have that job if you were a girl."

"Shut up, you bitch," he said, in the final phases of his transition to power. "Someone's gonna hear you. That's the last thing I need now. According to your screwed-up logic, anything I get in this world is because I'm not a girl. And anything you don't get is because you are. Jesus."

"I'm your sister," I said. "Don't violate me for a job you don't deserve and haven't earned."

"Shut up."

My teeth were clenched so hard I thought they had cut through my face.

"You go to his office now and turn down the job."

Lou took a step back. "Pop was right," he said, filled with the absolution from responsibility that condescension always implies. "You're an animal. You tried to get me in trouble with Pop, and now you want to take my job away."

"Tell him," I screamed. "Tell him now."

Lou turned and walked away from me. I followed him silently through all the labor and production, through the teamwork and sea of individual desire and resolution that every vibrant workplace generates. When we got to O'Dwyer's office, Lou turned back toward me with a calm finality.

"I've made it now," he said. "I've got all the connections. And I'm going straight to the top where bitches like you can't come near me."

O'Dwyer's door opened as Charlie came out with a stack of instructions. Mr. O'Dwyer looked up from his desk and waved.

"Lou, come in son. Have a seat."

I stood in the hallway, staring through the threshold of recognition. O'Dwyer made no effort to get up from the only chair so Lou leaned, casually, against the wall.

6

After I smoked a cigarette, I went back to my desk and started packing up for the move to Research. For the next month I stayed every evening, reading through the files and catching up on the fine points of international news. It was, in the end, a better job than typing, but that was no consolation for a heart turned to rancid butter.

"Happy Washington's Birthday," Irving Podolsky, the chief of Research, greeted me one morning. As a professional collector of small facts, Irving precisely noted every commonplace and obscure holiday.

"What's in the news, Irv?"

It was just the two of us, every day, in that breezy room.

He was entertainingly sad without being morbid, an older man with thick glasses who never combed his few remaining hairs. He didn't have a college education either, being from the old guard, and seemed to know at least something about everything.

"They always send the Jews to Research," he told me the first day. "Unless you change your name, Jews can't get ahead in newspapers owned by goyim. That's why we have to have our own papers."

"Mr. Gibson seems to be doing fine."

I was incapable of keeping Lou out of my daily banter. His name came up with bitterness so many times it came to define my bitterness. In truth I liked my new job. I found it interesting. I had never spent my whole day being interested before, most people don't get that chance. I knew I could warm up to it if I tried. Make it palatable. Irv was a nice old man. He wasn't the coziest person in the world. But he was curious. He asked questions, tried out different ideas. He wasn't afraid to discuss. I did not have the habit of that kind of respect. But was my whole life going to be a process of making peace with defeat? That's what they always try to get you to do, accept the ways that you've been cheated.

"What's on the agenda this morning?"

"Well," he said, adjusting his glasses. "I've been perusing the Joe McCarthy files for an article in tomorrow's morning edition. Too bad Hewitt's not around, this is his kind of story. Snake comes out of nowhere and ruins lives. Hewitt would have loved it."

"What's he doing?"

"McCarthy?"

"No, Hewitt."

"Claims he's taking it to court, poor guy. But, frankly, I don't see how he can win. You got to ask yourself, what is a fellow with three children doing taking chances like that? I mean, principle is one thing, but when it comes to making a living, well some things are just more important."

"You sound like my brother."

"I'm putting together this month's McCarthy events on a

155

briefing sheet," he said, cleaning his glasses. "I'll read it through, and you compare it to the clips."

"Okay," I said, reaching for the bulging folder.

"On February 9, 1950," Irv read, "McCarthy told a Republican Women's Club in Wheeling, West Virginia, that he had a list of two hundred and five names of members of the Communist Party who are still working in the State Department."

"Check."

"On February 10 in Salt Lake City, he said that he had fifty-seven names."

"Where did he get those figures? Heinz Varieties?"

"February 20, he testifies before the Senate for six hours clutching a suitcase bursting at the seams with what he claims are eighty-one names. Spends the whole session shuffling the papers but never shows one of them."

"I hate people like that," I said. "Coward."

The blatant fact was that I had been transformed by my strong feelings. Every day there were moments when I felt overcome by hate. I woke up in the morning with hate, and it returned to me as a possibility seven to ten times during the day. I wanted to be a reporter. Then, at night, it sat with me in the dark, keeping me from sleep. That hate was grief. How could my brother do this to me?

"Shameful," Irv said. "This is 1950. A whole new decade. Time is running forward, but morality is running back."

I looked out the window over the city. It was nice to work in an airy place for a change. Ever since the move upstairs I hadn't been back in the steno pool once. I didn't have any real friends there except Theresa, who had become more distant as time passed. She straggled in exhausted every morning with no explanation and absolutely nothing to say.

"They're all a bunch of anti-Semites, those thugs on the Committee. Did I ever show you . . . ?" Irving rolled his chair over to the wall of filing cabinets and, after some expert rummaging, pulled out a well-thumbed clipping. "Did I ever show you this one from Congressman Rankin of Mississippi? He was on the Committee in '47 before McCarthy even saw the opportunity."

"Okay, Irving, set the scene."

"It is November 14 and Shmuck is on top of the world. He gets a petition on behalf of the Hollywood Ten and decides to read the names of the signers into the Congressional Record. 'One of the names is June Havoc,' he says. 'Her real name is June Hovick. Another was Danny Kaye and his real name was David Daniel Kaminski. Another is Eddie Cantor, whose real name is Edward Iskowitz. There is one who calls himself Edward G. Robinson. His real name is Emanuel Goldberg. There is another who calls himself Melvyn Douglas, whose real name is Melvyn Hesselberg. There are others too numerous to mention. They are attacking the Committee for doing its duty in trying to protect this country and save the American people from the horrible fate the Communists have meted out to the unfortunate Christian people of Europe.' "

"But is it good for the Jews?"

"The thing is," Irving said, enjoying the pleasure of a bright idea. "None of these people would have been famous in the first place if they hadn't changed their names. So what good is their success? Make it in Hollywood and keep your name—now that's something to be proud of."

"I never thought of that."

"Which, Miss Golubowsky, leads me to two conclusions. First, I wonder how many beautiful Jewish names are going to fall off the face of the earth. And second, I bet if you did a study you'd find that the ones who changed their names did a lot better in America than the ones who didn't. Once again proving that this country loves you more if you sell your soul."

"How do you sell your soul, Irving? I don't understand exactly how to turn it in."

"Speaking of which," Irving went on in his own reverie of idea, idea, idea. "I thought I'd better tell you that Lou is stopping by the office this afternoon. Needs this background sheet on McCarthy. You know, I don't care about the boy one way or the other, but people should not change their names to get ahead. Then their whole lives they have something to hide. And it makes the goyim feel too safe. They get a false sense of security that all the accomplishments in the society are theirs. They take the credit."

Immediately I was furious. "Lou couldn't tell Joe McCarthy from a shop girl at Woolworth's."

"Well," Irv said, strategically turning back to his desk. "He'd better figure out the difference, because O'Dwyer is putting him on Hewitt's old beat, and if the boy can avoid any Marxist innuendo—which Lou wouldn't know if it got in bed with him—he'll get sent down to Washington in the spring to interview the senator in person. And he'd better not come back with a handful of nickel lipsticks."

"Lou is interviewing Joe McCarthy? The waitress at Schraft's would know better what to say."

"Well, he's coming over in twenty minutes."

"Then I'm going home early," I said, already packing up my purse. "I wouldn't help that boy dig his own grave." Filled with grief for the eighth time that day, I grabbed my stuff and ran down into the street.

7

The best suggestion Caroline could come up with was to go out for a drink. For the first time in my life I tasted hard liquor in the middle of the afternoon.

"You know I've never seen my parents drunk," I said as we stepped out of the first saloon.

"I have," Caroline said. "Every night at the dinner table."

"I guess Jews really don't drink."

"Well, southerners do." She laughed. "Helps you sit still on a hot day."

"But it's not hot," I pointed out, seriously. "We're running around in the middle of February."

"It's late February," she reassured me. "That's almost spring. Look, a bird. Well, a pigeon."

"It might get hot," I said, looking up at the clear blue sky. "And you know we want to be prepared."

Maybe drinks were the official motivation, but the two of us ended up walking all the way down around the Bowery, swinging our arms freely and closely watching the goings-on. Groups of men in old, hopeful suits gathered in front of employment agencies, answering ads for a dishwasher. Thirty dollars a week. Or, a counterman's job for forty. Their outfits were an amalgam of styles, especially their hats. Old boaters, white straw, beat-up fedoras, and checkered caps. Not one had a warm-enough coat. We could see the newspaper sticking out of the torn soles of their shoes. Those hats didn't go anywhere but in their hands. Hats were the most evocative and necessary prop for any disorganized man with a long history of failure. Especially when he's making the forty-seventh bid for a real job. Even the old cranky-faced Irishman, wasting the afternoon in front of his flophouse, was wearing a suit. The place costs twenty cents a night, but he never paid it in shirtsleeves.

"It's a sea of men," I said. "But it's not threatening because it is so obvious that this is where these men belong. Where are all the girls who can't make ends meet?"

"Don't kid yourself," Caroline told me. "The city is full of Jane Does that no one ever reports missing."

"How do they get that way?"

"You know, anything. Five years ago there were half a million marines, two girls apiece. Nowadays they're just regular Joes, and the girls are wised up or knocked up or both. There are a lot of people wandering around lost."

"How do you know so much about it?"

"How come you don't know," she snapped. "I don't mean to be stuffy, but I guess that being so far away from my birthplace, I know how easily a girl can slip through the cracks."

We peeked into a run-down beanery lined with greasy tile and old timers dying behind their glasses of beer.

"Jeez, look at those faces. The whole city is built out of granite from Grand Central to Grant's Tomb," she said grandly.

"Some of it is still wood," I said. "When I was born we lived in an old wooden house on Pike Street. Shopped off of pushcarts. There were flags of beat-up, worn-down laundry flying high over the rooftops. Families sleep out on them on summer nights, and others would go up to sneak a little romance. The roof was a place in your life, not just some flat thing on top of a building. It was a place to go for a smoke, a cry, a secret drink, a peek at the thundering iron cascade that was the city."

"Oh my, how prosaic."

"Then we moved to Brooklyn where Lou was born and everything became so safe and benign. It's like he and I grew up in two different worlds, in two different classes, in two different families."

"It's funny," she said dreamily. "Everybody has their own neighborhood in New York. Even the people that no one else wants have a place to go. The bums have a place to go. The Negroes have a place to go. The Chinks and every little group. But I feel like I belong nowhere."

"What about the South?"

"Oh, no."

"You are different."

"Hard to say how, though, isn't it. Sylvia?"

"I feel something like that too," I said as I realized it. "But I don't know what. I feel like I also have a group somewhere, someplace where I'm not strange. But I don't know where the others live, and I've never met them. You know, people who will understand. And, if you explain it a little further they'll understand even more."

"Jewish people?"

"Well, when I'm with them, I do know them. But there is something they do not know about me. And . . ."

"What?"

"They don't want to."

We walked under the shadow of the Third Avenue El. The light through the rails crashed onto the cobblestoned street. In turn, it was sliced again by the trolley tracks. This was the geometry of destruction. Too many systems on top of each other. Too much movement, more than any one street could bare. All along the sidelines, watching the travelers, were men who had run out of luck and couldn't go anywhere. They were the only ones sitting still and staring.

"Girls like us," Caroline said. "We don't know where we belong but we gotta keep on tiptoeing through the tulips until we get there."

"That's the thing about Lou that is so devastating. It's different for you, Caroline. You've got Cal. But I'm never gonna have a man to support me. I'm gonna earn my own way."

"Cal barely supports himself," Caroline said stiffly. "And he certainly doesn't support me. I bring more in from piano lessons than he does on the grill."

"Okay, but you know what I mean. Most girls at least believe that some man is going to help them along. But that's not true for me. And it's harsh for a girl alone, harder than I ever imagined. People want to defeat you at every turn. They try it every day. That's why I believed that Lou was going to stand by me. Stand up with me. But the second he had a chance—"

"I know, honey," she said. "Kiss me. Didn't your mother warn you? Never let a man know how smart you really are."

"That is down-home North Carolina advice. They don't tell you that in Brooklyn. What did you say?"

"Look," she said, stopping to examine a tiny storefront. *"Body tattoos picturesque, painless, and permanent."*

"I want a tattoo," I said.

"What?" Caroline laughed and laughed.

"No, I do."

"Honey, you already feel like a freak, why advertise it?"

"No, I want it."

The place had clearly been an old barbershop. The red, white, and blue pole still turned in front. But the black letters on the white glass bulb spelled out *tattoos*. The proprietor was a skinny little man, somewhat resembling Joseph Goebbels. He sat impressive and sallow-faced in suit jacket, vest, and tie.

"Black eyes made natural," he said.

"I don't have a black eye," I said.

"I don't either," Caroline cracked. "And I won't have one in the future because I am never getting a tattoo."

"You can get it anywhere," he said with an expert assessment. "Arms, chest, back. Or, I can place it high on your rump so that no one will ever see it unless you want them to."

"But I want to see it."

"High on your hip then. No one will see it, even if you're in a bathing suit. But you'll know it is there every morning when you get up and every evening when you go back to bed."

I looked over the designs advertised in the window.

"Eagles were big during the war," the fellow croaked. "Especially if your old man was a swabbie or even a merchant sailor."

"No eagles," I said.

There were naked women, Uncle Sams and death heads, Gay Nineties bathing beauties, Jesus on the cross, and endless hearts with *Mildred* embroidered in blue and red.

"Your girl named Mildred?" Caroline asked.

"My ship," he said, spitting into the gutter.

"Maybe I'll get a word."

"You're really going through with this? Baby, you are a lot tougher and wilder than I thought when we first met."

"I've changed," I said, my voice like cement pouring out of the mixer. It would only get harder.

"Well," the man said, finishing off his spiel. "It should be a word that has great meaning for you. A word that you'll never forget. A word that will set your juices flowing and keep you going on toward your goal. A word that will make you never give up, no matter how painful and long the journey. A word that you want to carry with you to the grave."

"I know that word," I said, reaching into my purse and stepping into the shop. "That word is *Lou*."

CHAPTER EIGHTEEN

N. Tammi Byfield

1

Yesterday was my nineteenth birthday. It started out good, me and my cousin Sheryl just goofing, walking up and down Atlantic Avenue looking at all the Arab pastries and breads. Selecting. I love that, going in and out of stores, looking at fabric or whatnot. Then I got home and Steve gave me the worst present of my life. A membership at The Health and Racquet Club. He thinks I'm fat. This is so depressing and frustrating. I like myself the way I am, but everyone around me, except my mother, is trying to tell me otherwise. Then I felt bad that no boys like me, no one finds me attractive. And I got the message loud and clear that Steve agrees. I hate him. When I started crying he looked so stupid. Like, *hey, what did I do?* Chump. *Lightly, slightly, and politely.* That's how I tread in class today. I still felt sensitive from my messed up birthday and was not in the mood for one of those racialized classroom moments that is mind-twisting and soul-searching for everyone else. It did nothing for me. Why do I always feel like these white students should be paying me a salary for their daily tutorial in race relations? Someone mentions Toni Morrison, and all the heads turn my way.

"Don't look at me," I snap.

Or the other day when someone mentioned something about Africa, they all turned toward me.

"Don't even try," I said calmly. "Look it up in the encyclopedia." My limits are overestimated. My purpose here is to get an education, not to be a walking, talking *National Geographic*. I know from experience that if I start explaining, soon I'll be snapping, stomping, and telling someone off in a way that does no good to me. Me. I am my own best cause, and so I keep quiet. Even when one of those look-alikes actually said, "Everyone knows white men can't get jobs in academia these days."

I'm not going there.

Everyone.

I'm not going there.

In all my years of higher education I have had one brown-skinned professor and that was in Spanish.

I have a photograph of my grandfather and my great-aunt Ide, young. They're all dressed up to go out dancing or something. She's in a butt-spring skirt and he must be wearing forty-three inches of trousers. Drapes, shags, and righteous rags. Zoot suit.

That's what I said to my cousin Sheryl, "It's my birthday, let's go dancing." So we went out to the clubs and it was Drum and Base. Just like my grandfather, put on a nice pair of glasses, shoes from Giraudon.

There's a new Black girl in my program. The professor wanted her to also write about the Harlem Renaissance. Unless the professor thought the girl was me. Either he can't tell us apart or there is a conspiracy for all Black students at Columbia University to write about the Harlem Renaissance. It keeps us out of Midtown.

Poor powerful Black face, intruding into the holy places of the whites. How like a spectator you haunt the pale devils.
Claude McKay

"I know Harlem," the girl said back to him. "I was born in Harlem. It does not hold the same thrill and glamour for me as it does for you."

That's what provoked the uproar among the look-alikes. She started it. She finished it. I kept my mouth shut.

Back to my current identity issues.

Now, assuming that this Caroline could have been my real grandmother, that would not be good news. From everything my grandfather painstakingly recorded about this woman, she was one of the rebellious caucasians. I know them well. There are a couple thousand of them on this campus alone. They have pierced foreheads, take heroin, and work as strippers. They are so tired. They have ugly tattoos all over their arms that makes them look perpetually dirty. But they're still white bread. Caroline was a 1940's version of this animal. She loved everything her family hated, including herself. She was a freak, and she loved freaks. But the problem I have with this type of white person is that colored folks are not freaks. We're regular.

The professor gave me a reading list for this fantasy HR (Harlem Renaissance) report that he dreams I'm writing. *Cane, There Is Confusion. Home to Harlem, Passing, The Big Sea, Black Manhattan, Infants of the Spring, One Way to Heaven.* I told him I'm still writing about my grandfather. There were more Black people who did something in this country besides HR. The other Black girl is comparing Sun Ra to George Clinton. I've got to tell her about the similarity I've noticed between Prince and the Bar-Kays.

2

According to Cal's memoirs, one night in early May 1950, my grandparents, I mean my grandfather and Caroline, were getting ready to go out on the town. It was a date long in the planning.

"Don't you stand me up again," she'd threatened the night before. "I'm beginning to feel like Tess Trueheart."

My grandfather was candid and extremely detailed in his recollections of his own life. And, from the day-to-day chronicling of his and Caroline's existence together it was obvious that she never had time for him either. Night after night they would meet back at the apartment, exhausted after having given everything they'd got away to other people. It seemed like months since they'd done anything together. So, this one night my grandfather knew he had to get home on time to take his lady out for some music.

My grandfather wrote a lot about that night. Almost thirty pages. A texture was emerging of my encounter with his life story. I became more and more absorbed, identifying with increasing dedication. At first his writing style had put me off. It was stiff, almost British, and felt pretentious. But as his world's view unfolded I started to see him as a gentleman. An old-fashioned one, styling himself in the tradition of the great Black intellectuals with bifocals and gold pocket watches. But there was also this very modern, psychological side to Cal. He wrote about his feelings and speculated on the feelings of others. Then one day I realized that these memoirs had not been written for publication. They were too true. I realized that they had been written for me.

Basically, he acknowledged that, for all his busyness, he actually spent his time with only a handful of people. Days were cooked away with Joe Mackie on the job. Evenings he tried to work or went out schmoozing with the white theater crowd, hating them more and more. He was getting more desperate for anything. An inch.

My grandfather had basically given up trying to convince Black show people about his views. He thought he was just too far ahead. There was nothing for him to get there, they offered him nothing. So, he'd stayed away from his own people and now he felt really isolated. Like he had no people. If it wasn't for Ide he'd have no one to talk to.

Here's what he said about that night.

For the first time in months it was not too cold to open the windows on the IND. By the time we got off at 125th Street and started walking uptown, the sun had disappeared into that moment of calm that leaves the work world behind. Two quiet young men were sitting on wooden crates, engaged in the spring season's first serious game of night checkers. Their friends, young and old, stood around in jackets chatting, offering commentary. Kids drank from a leaky fire hydrant. One girl's hair hadn't been combed out. My mother would never have let me go out on the street that way. That was it, really, I wanted to see my mother. That must be why I was feeling so alone. It had been years since my great-grandparents had returned to die in our homeland, Jamaica, and had managed to live on healthily ever since. I was thinking that maybe I should go back too. Become the director of the national theater. Things would be easier. But, as soon as I pictured it I saw a leisure of defeat. I saw those fools at the Automat gloating. "Oh, Byfield? He went back where he belongs." *I would never give the ofays that satisfaction.*

My parents had waved good-bye to Ide and I from the pier and it wasn't till a few months later that I fully felt the impact of their absence. Oh, my sister took over the Sunday dinner, handing out advice, the pat on the back. But, when we were little, my mother, Nathalie, waved us onto buses, sent off from Harlem to the country by the First Presbyterian, always promising us a better life. Now it was my parents who mastered their own nation while I was free to argue with inferior whites. My people were free to drink from colored water fountains and waste their lives playing checkers. I was too polite. Not sassy like those American Negroes. I'd been brought up to have a stake in the order of things, and now it was killing me.

"There's the grocer," I pointed to my wife. "That's where I used to run errands. Six cents for milk. Half a pound of bacon for a dime."

I'd watch other children stand in line for bags of food all through the Depression while my father still managed to earn a living as a presser. Kids would be crying for lack of bread, but we always had two cents for some shaved ice and cherry syrup.

Nineteen thirty-five, the year I started at Columbia. That was also the year of the riot at Kress's Department Store after the Jew shopkeeper beat up a colored child. I ran home the next morning to see the smashed windows, the dressmakers' dummies lying stripped in the shards of glass. Then came the Ethiopian War protest. Lots of brothers signed up to go over to Africa and fight Mussolini, but I decided to stay in school. A couple of my white classmates joined up and shipped out to Spain. But none of them ever mentioned thinking about Ethiopia. That was the first time that I'd really lived in two worlds. One that had clout and one that only existed by collective agreement. Black men's needs were like a strip of film that never got out of the can. If a white man even saw that piece of celluloid he never thought about what it contained and didn't notice that it never got projected.

Nineteen Thirty-Seven, Father Divine went on parade. My daddy was a proud Garveyite and stood, sneering by the side of the avenue as mixed race columns of women in white paraded by with their signs.

Father Divine is the Supplier and the Satisfier of Every Good Desire.

Then Father Divine himself came by. A little man riding in an open car. He waved at his followers who were screaming, crying, reaching out, and doing everything they could just to touch him. Father Divine said there was no black, no white, no female, no male. But these women's passions were at such a high pitch. I wondered out loud what kind of satisfying they were referring to. My father, the Puritan, didn't say a word. But I took the sexual message to heart and saw it as private permission to stop being so isolated on campus. I started socializing across the color bar from that day forward.

Ironically, it was Caroline who followed Black music. She was devoted to it. I just went along making minimal efforts to stay informed. At least those jazz musicians had a mixed audience, that's why they eventually had an impact, got treated with respect by all. But, I also knew, even then, that Black music had always pleased the white man. A Negro with a horn in his mouth can't talk, after all. Except in the coded language of music, and white people didn't have to translate if they didn't want to. They could sit back and have a catharsis without doing any of the work. Typical. In fact, they could be soothed by the entire pain of the Black race issuing from the sensual lips of a good-looking jazz king.

I guess that's why white people don't like rap. They can't understand the words, but they know there are words and it irks them. I mean, there are things I can get from my grandfather's ideas, but in those days things were not the way that they are now. I know it may sound like my grandfather's life was a lot like mine, but the lack of dark faces among the look-alikes at Columbia had an entirely different meaning to him than it does to me. In the thirties, his presence on campus was a sign of transformation and the promise of a better future. Nowadays it's a sign of failure. He needed to cross that color line because he thought that was the way the world was going to go. Integration, both spiritual and, I guess, genetic. For me, I'm at Columbia to retain some minuscule territory, get my credentials and go out for myself. I have no interest in bettering the opposite race, or letting them affect my shimmering presence.

It was 1941 when I got drafted and had my first real taste of segregation. At Columbia I was treated as something special, after all. Of course, it was something strange and special, something mysterious to all those butterballs who knew the ropes. Though I was lonely at Hartley House, I was used to being lonely and took some comfort in knowing that it was Langston Hughes himself who'd integrated that dorm ten years before.

I think the army was the most humiliating experience of my life. Not only did I have to take orders from stupid country boys with vulgar habits, black and white. But I had to take these orders in a second-rate unit. The army let Nigger soldiers know that they were inferior in every way, didn't even get a chance to be a hero. At least at Columbia I'd had the chance to excel. But few Negroes ever got out of the latrines to do anything special in battle be-

sides die. And when they did succeed, no one else ever seemed to notice or else the whiteys took the credit for themselves.

I spent the war at Fort Huchuca doing administrative work for colored foot soldiers who came through for combat training. It had been an outpost against the Apaches in the 1870's and "out" was an understatement. Boredom and the desire for an assignment that matched my education got me transferred to Virginia where I had to use the "colored" entrance for the first time. I sat in the colored balcony at the movies and ate the colored slop.

That's why, of all my works, I was most determined to see my Black soldier play get a production. And it had to be a good production where white people could watch it and face what they'd done. I owed himself that much. Why put it on only for a bunch of Negroes? They already know it's true.

Caroline and I walked by the fresh-killed-chicken store, the Negro cop on the corner, a kid sitting on a stoop reading comics. Teenagers sipped Cokes through straws at an overflowing soda fountain, and some straggly kids looking dusty and hungry stood on the street lost. It was like a sight from my time in the South. Urban sharecroppers' children at the end of a long, hard day.

"Cal? Cal?"

"What?"

I looked up to see Caroline fuming.

"You never listen when I'm talking. The only thing you ever think about is yourself."

While reading my grandfather's account of that night he and Caroline went out on the town, one thing really struck me. It amazes me today, years later, how bad Harlem in 1950 looked to my grandfather. And how good it sounds to me now. Businesses, checkers. No white gentrifiers.

CHAPTER NINETEEN

S y l v i a   G o l u b o w s k y

I suppose that I've always idealized Caroline and Cal's marriage. In fact, for many years after all these events had passed I fashioned my own version of a marriage fundamentally on theirs. Freedom and interest. Unfortunately, I grew up to discover that I needed an obligation in my marriage to anchor me. I needed someone insisting on a level of participation that I would have been very happy to elude. But until that adjustment to my fantasy became inevitable, I thought of Caroline as a projection of myself that transcended geography, temperament, and even experience. I suppose that means she was my hero.

When Caroline Hall got off the Greyhound bus from Flat Rock to attend Barnard College, she spent the first night studying in her dormitory room. The second night she was at Small's Paradise on 135th Street with her terrified roommate, and after that with anyone who would go along. She was always reckless about companionship.

Her parents had sent her off to be a classical pianist. However, one long exciting conversation on the bus with an old white musician between Atlanta and Baltimore had her mind completely changed before she crossed the George Washington Bridge. But then, Caroline had never been a person who did what was expected, often to the degree of scandal. At least by Flat Rock standards. She was sure that her parents had sent her out of town so that, in case she couldn't return a proper

171

lady, she could at least get lost in New York and never come home to shame them again. Caroline had learned from a young age to keep her most important secrets to herself, and that she had done all her life long. There wasn't a soul on this earth who knew the whole story. In her case, having a husband didn't mean the usual investment of confidences. The one habit she had firmly retained from her mother was that if other people don't bring it up, there is no need to ever bring it up. Caroline relied on the unspoken.

She had days of great anxiety. Anxiety in the mornings and later on in the day. Following her granddaddy's tradition, Caroline took the edge off with a little whiskey, usually poured into a glass of tea and followed by an orange or a spoonful of jam. That was before three o'clock. It made her lips numb and helped her keep them shut. It kept her throat tighter and took attention off of her demons. Without careful surveillance, those devils dove into her mind and spirit and occupied her body like an army of invading Huns. If she wasn't careful they would take over her world.

Whiskey and jazz had always gone together. If you drink with people you end up in bed with them, she'd learned that one right away. And if you drink alone you end up dead. Better to drink with people. Drinking in a nightclub let her into the music. She didn't have to sloshily reveal anything too personal, just sit back and let the music do all the seducing. Then she could save her own soul for the blast of the horn.

The fact is Caroline had long ago accepted that she would never be a great jazz pianist. Never. She was, in many ways, too earthy. Jazz, after all, is a galactic endeavor. But because she had accepted this, she was not envious of the greats. In fact, she could appreciate them more. Oh, she would gladly play for other people's pleasures and riff on a couple of measures before the crowd sang along again. But she knew what was great about the great ones. For herself, she could only excel at what bored her, or be second-rate at what she loved best.

Small's Paradise had long been a safe place for whites to go, with downtown couples dancing in the cellar to the Negro bands. A big room with a narrow marquee, Small's had fifteen hundred people crowded in for the 1925 grand opening. From the first,

Charles Johnson's group featured a violin and banjo in addition to all the brass and reeds. In the '30s, they built a larger Negro following. And throughout Caroline's college years, the house band was led by Earl Bostic. She used to try to catch his eye, hoping for an audition, but could never communicate her desire past the level of flirtation.

It did not take long for her to branch out to other clubs, other music, and to buy and devour records religiously. But it was bebop that she first connected to as a practitioner and not just as a consumer. To Caroline, bebop was the manifestation of a revolt. And, in her own little way, in comparison to the expectations of her background, she too was revolutionary. There was a lurid and rococo atmosphere growing up around jazz in the late '30s, a delight in the music's origins in whorehouses and its transformation through the minds of conservatory-trained Black men.

Then the day came when she heard Thelonious Monk at Minton's Playhouse on 108th Street. Only twenty-one, with a little beard, he played the piano like it was a monsoon. It all made sense to Caroline who, over her handful of whiskeys, came consistently to the same conclusion. That modern life is fast and complicated, and modern music should be the same. That was the ethic she tried to emulate in her playing, even if it was just late nights in special dives for people with other reasons to congregate beyond their love of jazz.

The thing she concluded at the bottom of every bottle was that Caroline Hall desperately needed the world to change quickly, immediately. Otherwise her life would be one absurd limitation imposed upon another. She embraced every forward-thinking, crazy, disruptive instinct in music because she hoped it would bring the rest of the world along with it, or else make everything come crashing down at once. She was an enemy of Western Civilization. She hated it. And she knew it hated her. When the Black man ruled the world, the white man would not. That could only work in the best interest of someone like her. So, she listened and learned and practiced and played and tried to live the daily ethic of organized chaos, emotive gyrations, and haphazard manipulations on the universal and personal plane.

173

CHAPTER TWENTY

N. Tammi Byfield

It must have been really hard on my grandfather to have to walk around Harlem with a white woman. Everyone would look. But at some point, he just stopped mentioning it. Reading his memoirs is like watching a windup train run down. Whole subjects just drop off. But I'm starting to understand a little bit more each day about how he looked at things. It's like he had his own sense of Blackness and it wasn't the same as anyone else's. I mean, being Black—well you can't get out of it and no one can take it away from you. Unless you're very light skinned. All I'm trying to say is that maybe my grandfather thought he had higher hopes for Black people than they did for themselves. And despite all the pain it caused him, that fact alone makes him into kind of a hero.

Like this one night I was just discussing. He and Caroline went to a club uptown called Small's. When he walked into the place, it was packed, and he was not happy about running right into Burt Heath, an older playwright who thought of himself as one of Cal's mentors, even though he'd never actually done him a damn thing.

"Cal!" Burt leeched onto him as soon as he could grab his arm. "Hello, Caroline, how are you?" This was a gray old man, one of those old-fashioned patriarchs. Formal manners, sad eyes, and a brand-new suit, at all times. "Sit down, sit down. I've been stood up by my son and his date, I'm afraid. When he was young he was irresponsible and now that he's a big man at CBS, he is only irresponsible to me. Here, children, I've been saving these seats for an hour. Now everyone standing in this club is going to envy you. Think you're something special. Keep me company, Cal. What is going on with your work? I haven't heard of or seen any notices for your plays for a long, long time."

"I'm working hard," Cal said, not wanting to get into it.

"I know it's a long, hard path," Burt said as they all took their seats. "But a writer is a writer, nothing can keep him from it. I started out as an actor, myself. But I discovered that I wanted to write for the theater before too long. Did you know that about me, Caroline?"

"You were an actor," she affirmed politely while channeling her real excitement into searching out the waiter for a drink.

"I was an actor during the Depression of all things. Always had terrible timing. I had four lines in *Green Pastures*. That was a very famous show in its day."

"Oh, I didn't know."

"Directed and produced by whites," Cal said instructively under his breath.

"For Negro actors, Cal," Burt said, even more instructively. "That's not a small thing."

I was beginning to understand that my grandfather could not talk to another Black person for more than five minutes without getting into this argument. And I still don't know which side I'm on. When white people accepted his expectations, they did it because of their own entitlement. They expected the privilege of neutrality and could understand why he did too. But Black people from all sides thought it was a trap, for a wide variety of reasons. And there must have been a way that my grandfather and Caroline were sick of the whole dynamic, having to sit through it over and over again.

"No fighting, let's have a drink," Caroline said, temporarily wifely. "We just walked along Seventh Avenue. It's buzzing."

So was Small's. Black men with Black women, Black men with white women, white men with white women and all combinations of friends. The Black woman, white man thing wasn't in full swing yet. At that time lonely sisters would stay at home rather than subject themselves to that mess. If men like my grandfather had gone for their own kind, those sisters would have been out dancing that evening too. I can see why Cal couldn't listen to Burt go on. Who wants to have to look in the eye of a defeated version of your future rationalizing self? Cal was wriggling in his seat, listening to Burt, being respectful like he was raised to be. But he didn't want to listen to it. Not one word of it. He knew the whole rap by heart, and if he felt like hearing it, he could recite it himself.

"Now, I remember the star," Burt went on. "Richard B. Harrison. He spent his career as an elocutionist reciting Shakespeare in colored schools. Being a complete stranger to dialect, he had to be coached by a white actor who once played darkey roles. 'Gangway for de Lawd Gawd Jehovah' was his entrance line. That's when I decided to start writing plays."

"Burt was in the Federal Theater," Cal said. Then he too started looking around for a good strong drink.

"Which was a godsend for colored actors but didn't do much for the playwrights. The Negro Macbeth syndrome, you know. Although you can't blame Roosevelt or the WPA."

"Who do you blame?" Caroline asked absentmindedly.

"The white stagehands' unions. Those racist so and so's. Even a colored movie house had to have a white man running the projector. But the Harlem unit did put on a couple of our plays."

"Waiter," Cal exploded. "We want some drinks. Two whiskeys here neat and a water on the side. Burt?"

"I'll have another scotch. As I was saying, Cal, that's why you have to do for your own kind. Thank God for the Lafayette Theater where we colored writers at least had a chance. They had that Negro Folk Theater in residence there for a while. *Black Salome* and some originals. You remember Ted Ward's Negro Playwrights' Company, don't you? Had one production in 1940. Opening night was closing night. Shut down by those racist unions. The play was called *Big White Fog*."

Good title.

"Then there was the Suitcase Theater."

"Yeah," Cal said, unable to contain himself any longer. "One hundred and thirty-five performances of Langston's *Do You Want to Be Free,* and no white people saw it as part of the American theater season."

"I'll tell you what's on right now that is really good."

"What?"

"Robert McFerrin singing Langston's libretto at City Center. Too bad the leads are all whites in blackface."

"Still?"

"Caroline, don't be naïve," Cal snapped.

"That Ossie Davis play ran one week."

"Burt, you are depressing me more than I already am, which is a lot."

"Why are you so depressed, Cal?"

"Because every time some black bodies get onstage they stuff their mouths with white words. I want to be the man. I want to put the words in the mouths of Black actors. And in the mouths of whites. Of blonde white women like the one whose hand Paul Robeson kissed onstage in *All God's Chillin Have Wings.*"

"And how are you going to do that?"

"Someone has to be the first."

"What makes you so special?"

"I am special."

"Cal," Burt said, his face creased with concern, eyes brimming with worry. "Do you know how many Negro playwrights have had their work on the Broadway stage in the history of this country?"

"Ah . . . no."

"Nine." And Burt started counting automatically, like he took inventory every morning. "Nineteen twenty-five, *Appearances* by Garland Anderson; 1928, *Meek Mose* by Frank Wilson; 1929, *Harlem* by Wallace Thurman; 1933, *Louisiana* by Augustus Smith; 1933, *Run Little Chillun* by Hal Johnson; 1934, *Legal Murder* by Denis Dennis Donoghue; 1935, *Mulatto* by Langston; 1941, *Native Son* by Richard Wright; 1947, *Our Lan'* by Theodore Ward."

Cal sat silently.

"Do you know, Cal, how many Negro playwrights have had

full commercial productions in non-Negro off-Broadway houses?" Burt continued, unstoppable.

"Tell me," Cal whispered.

"1937, *Don't You Want to Be Free* by Langston; 1938, *Joy Exceeding Glory* by George Norford; 1940, *Big White Fog* by Theodore Ward—one night only; 1945, *On Strivers Row* by Abram Hill. Four. That's it. Now you tell me your plan, Cal. You tell me exactly how you're gonna do it."

CHAPTER TWENTY-ONE

Sylvia Golubowsky

1

I got off the subway in Brownsville and raced to my parents' home in a state of rage. I was possessed. I know that it may seem, officially, as though enough time should have passed, but each day was so consumed by my experience of betrayal that a month could have been an afternoon or a year. In public life there is a pretense that time is the great salve, but times does not heal for me. The only thing that has ever healed me is resolution. I've never discovered the existence of redemption. It seems to be a strategic imposition intended to function as a colonial panacea. Jews still gather to remember the wrongs of five thousand years past. And that, I believe, is why we have continued to exist as a people, despite being so few. You don't need numbers to survive. You don't need an army to survive. In fact, as the last fifty years of Jewish aberration make clear, if you have an army, you ultimately cannot survive. You just need a critical mass of consciousness. It is when one switches to the precipice that requires protecting your dominance that one becomes invested in the forgiveness of the powerful by the weak. For those of us in perpetual danger, forgiveness can be suicidal.

And so desperation taught me to seek new allies. I had never asked my parents for help. But now I needed them desperately.

I needed someone to step in and lay down the law with Lou. I did not yet understand that the law would never advocate for me. After all, Lou was just enforcing, finally, my father's value system. His whole life he'd seen my father put me down, and then he did it too. Easy. So the key to changing Lou was to get my father to recant. Lou, clearly, had no mind of his own.

I practiced and practiced in my apartment until I knew exactly what I was going to say to appeal to my father for help. He had always wanted to exert some kind of leadership, some kind of guidance and protection. But he never knew how to go about it. I would give him that opportunity. That was my plan. I would explain to him exactly what needed to get done.

By the time I arrived on the front stoop I felt much calmer. I'd made this decision out of desperation. There was nothing else I could think of to do. But walking from the subway I saw how, in the long run, it might turn out to be a wonderful thing. This could give my father the chance he'd always wanted to stand up for me. Maybe, after all of this, I would have a father. I would have his attention.

Most important, my goal was to get Lou back. He might still be just a dumb kid, not permanently transformed. Once Pop set him straight, he could understand how much he had hurt me. How he had devastated me. He would realize that a sister is forever. A sister is more important than any business connection. All he had to do was apologize, talk to Mr. O'Dwyer, and that would be that. Then we could get back to our plans, maybe run that newspaper together someday. Go to McCarthy together and write it all up. After all, this whole thing still didn't make any sense. Why would my brother do this to me? Could he really be that weak?

One thing I knew for sure, even if a girl couldn't get that job, Lou still had to give it up. You don't eat the bread out of your own sister's mouth. That's what they'd believed at City College during the strike of 1949. The Jewish students demonstrated because the Black students were being treated badly. That's the way things should go. People don't benefit from others' oppression. Not in City College and not in a family. How come Lou didn't know this? How could that be?

I'd come into the house and kiss my father and kiss my mother. My mother would protest the flowers, of course, but she would love them.

"Pop, I know that for years you have been trying to help me and I wouldn't let you help me."

"You wouldn't let me," he would say.

"But now I really need you. I need you by my side."

"Anything. You're my kid. You tell me what you need and I will do it."

"Pop, listen," I'd say sitting down beside him at the kitchen table. "You know how hard I've been working at the paper."

"No one works harder than you. I worry about you, you work too much."

"Well, I was up for a promotion that I deserve but the boss is prejudiced."

"An anti-Semite?"

"No. He doesn't like girls. He gave the job to a fella at work who doesn't know anything about it."

"That's not right," Mina would say, coming in with some coffee. "The best worker should win the promotion."

"And that fella is, of all people, Lou."

"Lou?" Pop would say. "But he just started there a few months ago. You got him the job. He's not ready to be a reporter. He's just a boy."

"Don't worry," Mama would say. "We'll talk to him. I'll tell him, *Lou, there is no job in the world worth more than your sister. She has loved you all of your life and helped you. Now you have to do right by her.* Don't worry, Sylvia, we'll make him understand. Won't we, Joe?"

"Of course. What is more important than family? Nothing. Sylvia, I'm so glad you came to me for help. I'll be there for you, you'll see. And . . ." he'd get shy here. "I hope that this is the beginning of a better relationship between you and me, Sylvia. I hope that from now on we can be a real family. Each one of us standing up for the other, no matter what."

I stopped at the front step and turned to walk back down the avenue where I bought a bouquet of flowers from Mrs. Rubenstein. That was an indulgence. No one in our family ever had flowers. My mother loved them; she'd stop and admire every passing window box. But to spend hard-earned money on flowers? That was foolishness. That was only for special occasions. When I graduated from Thomas Jefferson High School my mother wore a corsage. My mother looked like a little girl in the countryside of Poland making headdresses out of wild flowers. Would she ever see wildflowers again?

"What did you do to your brother?" my father demanded as I stepped through the front door.

"Here, Pop," I said. "I brought Mama some flowers."

"What did you do to your brother?"

How many times can the world cave in?

"What are you talking about, Pop? He's the one who did it to me. How do you know about this, anyway?"

My father came at me with all his disgust.

"Your brother tells us everything, not like you with all your secrets. He told us what you did to him."

"What I did to him?"

Where was my mother? Where was she hiding?

"You told Lou he had no talent? You said such a horrible thing to your brother? I shouldn't even let you in the house."

"That is not what happened," I yelled. Yelling confirmed, of course, my monstrosity. That I could be annihilated by their hate proved that it was true. The only way out would be to hang myself and thereby physically manifest what they were spiritually demanding—that I forfeit my life. That was, ultimately, the only solution they would have found acceptable. "Lou violated our relationship just to get ahead on the job, and it's not going to get him anywhere anyway because he's not even qualified and can't pull it off. Then he went running to you to cover it up."

"He's got a right to make a living," my father yelled.

"I thought family was more important than money."

"That's right," my father said, clutching the newspaper like it was a lifeline. "And he needs money because he's gonna have a family."

"Anything your brother does," Mama said flatly, "is all right with us."

"I told your brother you were troubled," my father said, winding up. "But he didn't listen. Now he's finally listening. It's better that way."

"Why is it better?"

"Because your brother's relationship with you was not healthy," my father sneered. I could see the tops of his dentures. "I'm glad it's finished. A boy's hero shouldn't be his sister. He shouldn't be talking back to his father for his sister. A boy's relationship should be with his sweetheart and then with his father. Now everything is finally going to be all right around here."

2

I won't be ruining any of the suspense to tell you right off that my brother and I never reconciled. Soon I'll let you know his fate. The details of his participation in many of the events involved in this story were actually quite mysterious to me for many years. But I was patient. After all, my mother didn't find out until 1955 that her sisters had been killed at Auschwitz.

I got a crucial piece of information about my brother one night at the New School for Social Research in the Village. This must have been in the '70s, the interim period when Eighth Street was empty and filled with drug addicts snarling over their Orange Julius. Bleecker Street was deserted and somewhat boarded up. I remember at that point the San Remo had become a Blimpies and later reopened at an inauthentic spot. The Eighth Street Bookshop had closed. Balducci's had not yet opened so Villagers still couldn't buy a twelve-dollar onion. The terrain was a free-for-all of dreariness. I believe that Djuna Barnes passed away around that time. It was a strange moment.

At any rate, the New School was having a series on the McCarthy era and the Media. I went to hear Elizabeth Merz give a public interview. At that time people didn't talk about it much anymore, and frankly they still don't today. Vietnam was a hell of a lot easier to face. What you do to someone else is far easier to confess than what you do to your own kind. But the interviewer was brash and young and took quite a few chances. I had always been interested in Mrs. Merz's career and had followed it as closely as one can by reading the daily paper. She had been one of the original people in public broadcasting and became an early pioneer of children's television. I believe she was a producer on the Charity Bailey Show. At the time of this lecture she had just cohosted a talk show on new issues in urban architecture and then, briefly, one on mass transit. That's what we talked about before bulimia. So, I went to hear her. After all, her father had been a very important person in my life.

After about an hour of chitchat about many aspects of the whole thing, the talk got around to a representative anecdote that she offered about young reporters and the McCarthy era. She started to tell a long story, and suddenly I realized that she was talking about Lou.

What I had already known was that the same week I was being emotionally evacuated by my father and mother in his name, my dear baby brother had just stepped off the train into Penn Station in deep trouble.

He had interviewed McCarthy, all right. But they had never really gotten down to it. The whole conversation was a collection of missed opportunities. Lou had spent every second of the train ride home trying to decipher his scrawls and scratch out his first big assignment. But it wasn't going anywhere. Back at the station Lou felt around in his pocket for a nickel and then went to a phone booth. Pulling the wooden door tightly shut, he pushed his newsroom fedora to the back of his head and dialed my phone number, which at that time was Canal 8-0151. It rang and rang, but no one picked up. I was still at work. Feeling both panicked and relieved, he headed toward the office. He thought I might be working late, and he actually thought that we could go over the article together before he handed it in to the boss.

Walking underneath the Ninth Avenue El, Lou stopped in a drugstore to buy a handful of penny candies. He picked out a couple of cigars from under the front glass counter. Then he purchased one shiny red one off the top of a bushel of apples from a street stand, popped into the *Star* building, sat down at his desk, and turned on his dictaphone. I know this because Theresa was supposed to type it for him. She got the apple and the sour balls. Charlie got a cigar.

"McCarthy sits at his desk like a . . . like a . . . like a bulldog. No, like a big dog. Like a dog. McCarthy sits at his desk, papers like falling leaves, on his desk. Like falling autumn leaves twisting and falling from the trunk of his tree . . . er . . . desk."

Lou stopped.

"Jesus Christ."

He picked up the phone and called over to Research.

"Hey, Irv? It's Lou. Is my sister there? Still out to lunch? Where did she go? Chop Suey or pancakes at Child's, you're not sure? Did you give her my other messages? Okay, well I've got to try to find her, I really need some help."

Of course I was standing right there by Irving's side.

That is what I knew.

But Elizabeth Merz recalled meeting a young reporter, Louis Gibson, who had just interviewed McCarthy. He was coming out of the *Star*'s lobby muttering to himself.

"The sun reflected off McCarthy's scalp like leaves falling from the trunk of his maple desk."

"If I were you," Elizabeth interrupted him. "I would get rid of that tree imagery right now."

"Yeah, that's right. Hey, I know you."

"Sure you do," she said. "We met at the Arthur Miller play, remember?"

A look of great relief washed over his face.

"Yeah, sure. What are you doing here?"

"I was supposed to meet Father for something to eat," she said. "But I guess he forgot, so I was on my way back home."

"To your mother's?"

"Oh no, I've got my own apartment now. On Twenty-third Street. Things have really worked out since I saw you last."

"No kidding; that's swell." He still couldn't remember her name. "Well, I've got nothing to do. Why don't you let me take you out somewhere. One man's mistake is another man's . . . uh . . . duty. No, I'd say . . ."

"Privilege?"

"Yeah, that's it. So, you have a way with words?"

An hour later they were sitting in her living room, paper and pencil spread out over the coffee table.

"Okay," she told him. "This is the way we do it in television. You pitch me the story and then we figure out the tone. It's like a science."

"Okay," he said. "Well, there's McCarthy, bald like falling leaves."

"No, okay." She went into a work trance, one I know very well from my own writing, where she was so deeply immersed in the interior sounds of putting words together that he could literally see her think. She noticed nothing else. Not even him. He was just a part of the thing she was thinking. Then, like a timer had rung, she came out of it and the thought was complete.

"Okay," she said, writing as she spoke. "We set it up with a sinister surrounding. Like the reader doesn't know what to expect."

"Where did you learn this?"

"Radcliffe."

"I tell you, Elizabeth. I didn't even know that O'Dwyer had a daughter. I mean, I saw the pictures in his office . . ."

"I know. Just poor Teddy. Imagine what my life would have been like if he had lived. Okay, listen. *'A visit to the McCarthy lair on Capitol Hill is rather like being transported to the set of one of Hollywood's minor thrillers. The waiting room is generally . . .'* Were there a lot of people in the waiting room?"

"Yeah, I guess."

" *'The waiting room is generally full of furtive-looking characters who seem to be suborned State Department men. McCarthy himself . . .'* What does he look like?"

"Balding. DT's.

'Balding. DT's.' "

" *'McCarthy himself, despite a creeping baldness and a continual tremor that makes his head shake in a disconcerting fashion, is reasonably well cast as the silver screen version of a strong-jawed private eye. A visitor is likely to find him with his heavy shoulders hunched forward, a telephone in his huge hand, shouting cryptic instructions to some mysterious ally.'* "

"Elizabeth, you're the greatest," Lou said. "I'm so happy I could kiss you."

"Let's finish the story first," she said going back to work. "Then you can kiss me after."

The audience at the New School was very entertained. But I sat frozen at the spectacle of my personal tragedy conflating with history. And I knew that I would be denied the justice of resolution because my country would never take responsibility for its own acts.

3

" *'The drama is heightened by a significant bit of stage business. For, as Senator McCarthy talks, he sometimes strikes the mouthpiece of his telephone with a pencil. As Washington folklore has it, this is supposed to jar the needle of any concealed listening device.'* "

I crumpled up the newspaper for the fifth time that night.

"There is no way that he wrote that," I said. "No way. This guy, maybe he could imitate an ad for Burma Shave off of the radio, but he could never compose something like this. What the hell is going on?"

"Wouldn't you love to know."

We were sitting in my apartment this time. And it was later than usual. Caroline had been drinking for hours, and even I had three or four.

"God, between you and Cal I feel like climbing into a secret hiding place in the abandoned hayloft of an old firehouse," Caroline said, halfway between slurring drunk and jester. Her images were starting to get fuzzy.

"All alone in Flat Rock?"

"No, a hayloft in Brooklyn watching the elevated go by."

"That must be Brooklyn, North Carolina."

"You're always teasing me," she said. "Sourpuss."

"It's just," I got up from my chair and paced around the apartment. We'd developed an easy coexistence by that point, and the apartment seemed to be half hers. She was in there every night. "I know everything about that guy. I've loved him, so I know him. I know the way he plays stickball. I know how much Fox's U-Bet Chocolate syrup he likes in his egg cream. I know him, and there is no way that he wrote this. Period."

Caroline put "I'm in the Mood for Love" on the phonograph and started slow dancing around the room.

"Baby, what would you do if you had a lot of money?"

"I don't know. Travel. What would you do?" Distracted, I walked to the window.

"Spend all my dough on oysters and good lookers. Marble hallways, big clocks, and clean shirts. A butler named Hamilton, after Chico of course. Winding my gold watch. Come on, fella."

Caroline sailed over to me and took my arms, half dancing, half dragging me around the living room.

"Would you drive me to La Guardia Field?" she asked. "And book us two tickets on the next flight to Europe?"

"When?" I asked, dancing, but awkwardly.

"When you're rich. Another glass of sherry?" She poured two more shots of rye. "Baby, why don't you take me to dinner some night?"

"Okay."

I stood still now and stared at Caroline, holding my glass of whiskey, wondering what was going to happen. She had my full attention now. My fascination.

"You know why men take women to dinner?"

"No."

"Because they need someone to talk to about themselves. I want to talk about *myself*, so you take me to dinner."

"I swear to you, I would kill him," I said. "I would kill him for taking my family away."

"Oh, pull yourself together and face the facts," Caroline said, dreamy no more. It was a sudden way she had of turning ugly that I had only recently begun to notice. "Lou trashed you, and when he did it he held a gun dangling in front of your face.

Now it's your turn to get back. You use that gun, Sylvia, and then you'll have a gun in your hands for the rest of your life. Every poor girl who tries to be her own king manages to get herself jammed in the end. Shhh."

"What?"

"Listen," Caroline whispered. "Can you hear it?"

"What?"

"The foreigners next door are making atom bombs."

"You're crazy," I said sitting back in my chair and reached for the newspaper, smoothing out its pages.

"You never come to the club where I work," Caroline said, pouting again.

"On Friday nights? You never invited me."

"Don't you want to hear me play the piano?"

"Sure, I love it. I hear you almost every night as it is."

"Well," she said, almost scared, "I'm inviting you."

"Okay," I said. "West Sixteenth Street, right?"

"Oh, I'm gonna piss," she said walking toward the bathroom.

I went back to the window. There was a horse and a buggy filled with flowers rolling in the night. What on earth could that be? Behind it were two cops on motorcycles. When they came to a stop, I raised up the window. The streets were silent. It must have been three in the morning.

"Can't you say 'yes sir' without making it sound like an insult?" one cop was saying to the other. That business complete, they continued on their way. All over town there were people in tiny moments. Little seconds of intimacy where they let each other know what they really felt.

Caroline staggered back into the room, wiping her face dry with a towel.

"Did you throw up?"

"I guess so."

"How can a thing like that happen in New York City?"

"Piss off," then she smiled. "I've got a question for you, madame."

"Yes?"

"Is that a real mink?"

"No," I said, gathering the curtains around my shoulders. "It's just dyed squirrel, after all."

191

1951

BILLBOARD MAGAZINE'S TOP TEN HITS

1. Cry......................Johnnie Ray & The Four Lads
2. Because of You.............................Tony Bennett
3. How High The Moon ......Les Paul & Mary Ford
4. Sin...Eddy Howard
5. If..Perry Como
6. Come On a My House............Rosemary Clooney
7. Cold, Cold Heart............................Tony Bennett
8. Too Young.............................Nat "King" Cole
9. Be My Love...............................Mario Lanza
10. On Top Of Old Smoky..............................
.......................The Weavers & Terry Gilkyson

CHAPTER TWENTY-TWO

Sylvia Golubowsky

1

I did run into Elizabeth Merz again. In the late 1980s. Only, by this time her first husband, Christopher, a playwright, had died of AIDS and she was remarried to Mitchell Gornick, a broker. Her name was now Elizabeth Gornick. Ironic that an Irish girl should end up with a Jewish name. In the '60s someone might have wondered if she were the daughter of Jim O'Dwyer, but by the '80s no one remembered him anymore. She could have kept her own name.

Elizabeth had been forced to quit public television after a major controversy. She'd produced a series of town meetings around the country on abortion rights that half of the local stations refused to air. Now, transformed, she was in real estate. This is how we met. I had finally decided to give up my apartment, which I'd bought at an insider's price of $12,000 on a thirty-year mortgage when the building first went co-op. It sold for $300,000. Do you hate me? My little building. When I'd lived there it was across from the Albert Hotel, over Romanoff's Soda Fountain, catty-corner from Joe's Fish Market and facing Rubin's Deli. Now it's called the Gold Coast. That's what happens when you're a real New Yorker. You're never out of each other's lives for good. New Yorkers are expansive people. We constantly interact.

So, after all those years Elizabeth and I finally got together. When I sat down across the desk from her, it was quite amazing. She didn't resemble her father, but she had his hair. It's not often in my life that I've been across a desk from a real Irish redhead, and it evoked a lot of feelings, memories of being obstructed. I didn't hold it against her because she was very professional. But it was the kind of memory where the original emotion reemerges as fresh and lethal as the first time around. It is not a reminiscence, it is an event. She told me the names of all the famous people she had sold properties for. I had never heard of most of them but I remembered two because their names were so rhythmic. Keith Haring and Leonard Nimoy.

She made a good commission on the deal, and I was able to buy a house here in Plainfield instead of renting. It all worked out. I also got more information about my brother. Interestingly, Elizabeth did not remember me very well. She recalled that Lou and I did not get along the whole time that they were dating, but she could not remember why. And she had no idea that I was the one at the center of events. In fact, much of her memory of that time had faded. I understand her ambivalence. After all, there was so much pain involved. If I was her I wouldn't want to think about it either. But what was so strange was how automatically I could fit in the details. I still knew Lou so well. I mean, I have been a writer all my life, and I can visualize naturally. But, she'd say one little fact and suddenly I saw everything he did and felt as if I had been there doing it with him. Interestingly, I saw how little she understood him. She'd tell me something and completely misinterpret it. She had no idea of the kind of life we'd had. She didn't know what anything meant. I must admit, with all the bitterness I still feel and will always feel, the details were of great interest to me. They provoked anger, but they also provoked pleasure. I still want to get back at him, after all this time. After all these years I have come to the conclusion that what my brother did was unforgivable.

2

Lou had been nervous all afternoon about this dinner. He'd found it impossible to stay in his office. Stepping out for lunch, he'd ended up at the penny arcade at Playland playing Jumbo Skeeball—nine balls for eight cents. Buy your tickets from the girl cashier and then take your chances. Every move in life involved some degree of risk, that much was certain and worth a diversion. He went to the news dealer next to the taxi stand and bought a copy of *Movietone News.*

He needed two yards—two hundred dollars. Moving out of Mama and Pop's was the right thing to do, but these bachelor digs were costing a lot more than he'd expected. And he missed home cooking, giving in to the diner around the corner when he just couldn't face the stove himself. Besides, having a rich girlfriend was expensive. She wanted to go to nice places, and he had to keep his wardrobe in order. Especially this night, when it came to impressing the folks.

I'm sure that Lou was well aware that dating the boss's daughter was a dangerous spot, one you could never get out of. Courting her was digging his own grave, one more step forward and he'd be in it. The grave of marriage, that is. What's wrong with marriage to a rich girl? She'd been showing him the ropes anyway. And, frankly, her little hints and encouragements had been turning his head around. Giving him a more strategic look at how to get breaks and take initiative. Someone was going to have to take over this newspaper someday, and it wasn't going to be the old lady.

I'm living behind the eight ball, he thought, stepping into Hamm 'N Egg and ordering at the counter, radio blaring.

"Those new songs all sound alike," said the lifer working lunch. "But it's the old songs that really stick. What's the matter, kid? Got the blues?"

Lou didn't think that he looked sad. He thought that he looked fine.

"I'm fine," he said, trying out one of his tussled smiles. "How about you?"

"Eh, I'm a Third Avenue girl," she said, wiping up. "And I like my Third Avenue spots. Broadway, there are too many strangers."

"Miss the old days?"

"Yeah," she said. "There's nothing I'd like more than to have an old Prohibition beer while the rain is splashing through the tracks."

"Oh, don't be that way, old-timer," Lou teased her. "The war's over, the whole world is opening up. Everyone's walking around with their dreams on their sleeves, and they're all gonna come true. There has never been so much opportunity in one place at one time in the history of the world. So what are you grousing about?"

"Easy for you to say," she sneered, lighting a cigarette. "What about us working slobs who are never going to get a break? If I could see into the future and look back at the two of us I would see a couple of swells like you walking on a red carpet and the rest of us on the mat before the bell even rings."

"So, okay, don't crowd me. I haven't got the answers." He sipped on his Orange Drink, feeling like a kid. "Let me have one of those Tastycakes." Why do dames always make him feel like a kid? Lou fell into that New York–style lingo of chewing the fat, those special attitudes, pronunciations, and expressions. No one but the steno girls used them around the office. Once he'd left Brownsville, he hardly had a real conversation.

"Jeez, lady. So it don't all add up. What do you want me to do, call the Quiz Kids?"

"It's not your fault," she said, backing down instead of going for the jugular like he'd hoped she would. "The short order cook here jumped off the thirty-first floor of the Grant Building last week. Couldn't make ends meet. Couldn't get a piece of that opportunity you're waving around."

"Your friend jumped off the Grant Building?" Lou perked up. This might be the kind of story Mr. O'Dwyer had been pushing him to find. 'Talk to the common people,' O'Dwyer had said. 'Then you'll start to get some interesting ideas for stories.'

"Yeah, he wanted to move into management, high school diploma and everything. But he couldn't get no jobs because he was colored."

"Oh, he was colored," Lou said, deflated.

"Yeah, I feel so bad, but how'd I know he was gonna take a Brady?"

By the time he got to Elizabeth's apartment, Lou had come up with a great idea for a story, which he'd pitch to the old man after dinner.

"How do you do, Mr. Gibson?" the doorman said, holding open the front gates.

"Just fine, Bobby," Lou said, getting back into his front of entitlement. He felt like he spoke three languages and owned three sets of skin. Know-it-all New Yorker, Young Buck on the Rise, Innocent Kid. It was all natural.

"Hi, Toots," he said, kissing her hello, handing over the requisite flowers and wine. "How was work?"

"You know who came into my office today? The guy who produced the Texaco Hour. He talked to me for almost thirty minutes. I think he was really interested and maybe he could get me a job on that show. Then I sent a note to the director I told you about. The one who did *Portia Faces Life*. They might need some writers for the new project over there. I knew his son in Cambridge, and he also knows that director at *Henry Aldrich* that Daddy knows."

Lou mixed a highball and sat in the living room waiting for his future in-laws. There, he'd said it. That decided it, he guessed.

"I hope you didn't go to too much trouble," he called into the kitchen. "Like I said, I could have treated your folks to a restaurant."

"Daddy would never have let you pay," Elizabeth said, in her crisp black evening dress. "Besides, he's so paranoid about other newspaper people at this point, he won't speak freely in public."

"Well, don't tell him about my two-way wrist radio," Lou said.

"Oh, I don't think he's afraid of Dick Tracy, at least not yet. Not until Dick has his own television series, and then Daddy will view him as stiff competition."

CHAPTER TWENTY-THREE

N . T a m m i   B y f i e l d

1

I had lunch with the other security guard this time. Thomas.
He's from Belize, it turns out, which is exactly where I would
like to go. He lives in Brooklyn with his mother, who makes his
lunch every day. She even made lunch for me. I guess he told
her about our date. Patties, yum. And coco bread. He's going to
Manhattan Community at night to become an accountant.
Works hard, *hard*. He hates American women, thinks they're
too skinny. I can't wait to see Steve's face when he hears that.
Thomas is motivated which is exactly what I have not been.
I've been sad. But I think he really likes me and it makes me
feel so sweet. Like no one else matters. Sheryl says to watch
out for that feeling because then you give up all your friends
and if your man disappears, you've got no one. She says she
hates those girls who just call you when they had a fight with
their man. But, I can see the temptation. When Thomas smiles
as I come through the library door, it means that he is the
person who I am meant for, seeing as my pure existence lights
him up. I love that. It does make you want to say so long to
everyone else.

I was wondering on the subway home if maybe the islands
are for Black people of my generation what Africa was for my
mother. I must admit, Africa doesn't hold much sway for me.

Dictators, European pretensions, killing each other. I like the islands. Thomas came over here in high school and was so far ahead he didn't even have to study for two years. He just waited for those undereducated Americans to catch up.

The promise of a boyfriend and thinking about my grandfather has brought up to me how truly lonely I have been. I sit in class thinking about that and resenting this whole institution. Most of my classmates can't come to me as an equal. They either want to be above or below. It did not take me long to realize that having them below was the best possible option, so I walk that walk. The one of public heightened awareness. Most of them have nothing to say. They're not grappling with anything. The greatest contribution they could make to the society is to be quiet.

The truth is that I am a very tribal person. I know who my people are. My people are the ones who had to fight for everything themselves. They have original thought. The others are the enemy, I have to disarm them. The best way to do so is to be far, far above. My grandfather's loneliness is so pungent it penetrates the years between us. I can feel it like it was me back there with everybody up in my face always saying NO. It puts history right in my lap. Now I know what they mean by *the pain of our ancestors.* I'm talking beyond the drama of ball and chain.

I finally talked to the other Black girl in my program, Elaine. She has a boyfriend at Harvard. They're engaged. Their fathers went to Morehouse together. She's having an affair with a Black professor in Sociology. He's married to a white woman.

That's what I like about Thomas. He has never been the only Black person in the room. He lives in a black neighborhood, he went to a black high school, he comes from a Black country, goes to a Black college and works in a Black profession. When he becomes a CPA he'll have Caribbean clients. How did he work it out so well? It's the curse of my family, my grandfather, and me. We are wanderers in the other world, which thinks it is The World but is really Their World. Will they ever know what it is that we see?

2

Burt Heath's lack of faith really did a job on my grandfather. He was starting to feel defeated. In other words, starting to be defeated. New Year's Eve came and went, and all his resolutions were the same. To not implode.

Some idiot caucasoid in class complained today that all the books by Black people were depressing. They don't have happy endings. The Black people don't win. Gee, I wonder why.

Since my grandfather was the only source of energy for his mission, defeat was the death knell. He'd always counted on getting by on the merit of his work. But now, sinking fast, he entered a new phase, which was all about a desperate grab for any way to get some help. Staying at point zero was the new definition of winning. And there was no way to tread water without some kind of encouragement, interest, recognition, some kind of progress. After a horrible week of self-loathing morning, noon, and night, my grandfather decided to take the step that really was the most vile option of all.

I sat, freezing, on a bench against the wall that enclosed Central Park, waiting for my prey to return to her nest. It took a few days of standing still in the brutal January weather until I managed to catch her stepping out of a cab with shopping bags from Bendel's, accompanied by that fool, Chris Merz. I had decided that the guy really just was a fairy. I'd seen Chris look longingly into women's eyes, but his coffee shop and barroom dialogue revealed all his dates to be side-by-side strolls with some attractive female talking about fashion or art. That sounded like a punk to me. Sure enough, Chris gave her some faggoty pecks on the cheek and skipped off back to fairyland. But he got a couple of shirts out of it, I noticed, seeing how many Bendel's bags he took home. I looked down at the newspaper I'd been clutching.

Inquiry by Senate on Perverts Asked.
Yeah, I wanted an inquiry on them too. Especially on the

young blond ones who want their plays produced by juicy old monied sophisticates. I had a lot of questions I'd love to ask. In those freezing hours of premeditation, I had to face some very unpleasant truths about myself. I had to come to terms with the fact that beneath every fair-minded, progressive-thinking playwright there lurked a man desperate for glory. I'd had to accept that I was no different. If there was anything I'd learned from the theater it was this. A man dreaming of glory will never settle for normalcy without losing his soul. Without losing everything he'd ever believed in, himself.

In America it was much less dangerous to be a Communist than to be a Negro, that was for sure. I was sick of all this complaining about Hollywood figures getting called before the Committee. All white. A Black man in this country couldn't even get to the level where he could be noticed enough to even be called by the Committee. He was too invisible to be a threat. He couldn't even get to Hollywood where he could be officially repressed. He was just repressed as a matter of course. The Negroes were the real Blacklist. There didn't need to be a list, we just had to be Black. We were so kept down that nobody noticed, it was just the normal state of things. Now people whispered that some blacklisted writers were getting their movies made using fronts. They wrote the scripts and then hid behind other people's names. Even a blacklisted white writer got his work out there in the way that the most upstanding, meritorious Negro could not. I was the one who needed a front. I needed an ofay to hide behind.

Snapping out of my trance, I got back to business. I had to get a hold of Amy before she disappeared into the fortress of her apartment building. There was no way the doorman would let me in so, running in front of a bus, I got to her at the last possible moment.

"Mrs. O'Dwyer?"

"Here," she said giving me her bags. "Take these upstairs."

I gathered all her packages and then followed her

through the dark, cool hallway, into the elevator, run by another Negro man. Then we got out at the ninth floor. Amy opened her front door with the key.

"Put them on the table."

I laid down all her newly acquired possessions and then stood there awkwardly.

"That's all," she said.

"Mrs. O'Dwyer . . ."

"Oh, all right," she said, reaching into her purse and taking out a dime. "Here."

"No, I am not the porter," I said. "I am a playwright, Calvin Byfield. Do you remember me? I believe you asked me to call you Amy."

"Oh my God," she said with mock horror. "I'm so sorry, please come in. Have a chair, right here in the living room. Please excuse me, Cal, I didn't recognize you. You look very well. Can I get you a cup of coffee? May I take your coat?"

"No, thank you, Amy," I said, calm for the both of us. Absolutely still. Fierce, ironic, vicious, dangerous, and implicating in my complete lack of response.

She took off her winter coat and sat across the coffee table on the big sofa with striped silk upholstery. Then, she gave me that look, like she knew I must be a real buck underneath those careful clothes. After all, what else could a Black man be?

"What brings you to Central Park West, Cal? It's a long way from Harlem."

"Not too long," I said. "But I don't live in Harlem. I live in Greenwich Village. We have a nice apartment on Tenth Street and University Place. Forty dollars a month. Lots of families, old Italians sitting outside on folding chairs in the summer. Artists. Young children with lemonade stands on the sidewalks. A mixture of old and new New York."

"Well, you speak about your neighborhood with great passion," she cooed. "You're a man who knows what he wants."

"Amy," I said, sticking to my plan. "I've taken the lib-

erty of coming here to talk to you about financing my new play."

"Oh, I see."

"Yes, I'm sure you are aware of the long tradition of white patrons who support Negro artists. Our best Negro artists all had generous encouragement, and I admire your interest in the Negro participating fully in the production of American art."

"Yes," she said, fluffing out her hair with a false casualness. "I am very interested in elevating the colored man. I've always had a special love for your people. Perhaps it started with my wet nurse Sophronia, who raised me in Connecticut. It's hard to be prejudiced when you've experienced a mammy's love."

"Oh," I said, adjusting my jaw. "You grew up in Connecticut?"

"Yes, but I don't miss it. Sophronia was a wonderful woman who stayed on with us for years. She was part of our family. She made a point of showing me the plight of poor Blacks, and when that understanding drove me to tears, she took me to the other side of town to see the plight of poor whites whom I never knew existed."

"That was very Christian of her," I said, repulsed. "Those experiences should make you an ideal patron for my new play. It is about the punishment of the segregated soldier and how his lack of reward becomes the Negro's rage. It is a subject that I feel should be of vast interest to every theatergoer."

Amy looked me over, making her decision.

"Leave me a copy of your play, Cal. I see you have it under your arm. When I read it and review my funds I will be happy to get together with you, perhaps for drinks or dinner, to discuss the details."

"You would?" I asked, somehow shocked that this was all working out.

"After all," she said, rising from the sofa, "we must all take chances in life, mustn't we?"

"Oh yes, Amy," I said, jumping to my feet.

"And chance," she said, extending her hand, "and the-ater make for strange bedfellows, don't they?"

"Yes ma'am," I said in spite of myself as she held my hand five beats too long. "Yes, yes, ma'am."

CHAPTER TWENTY-FOUR

Sylvia:

The whole time that Elizabeth was recounting her story she had a very calm demeanor. Like it didn't faze her. I believe she told me everything she knew, no matter what it implied about her and her family. I was very impressed. I guess she'd come to terms with it all.

Her father was dominating the discussion at this fated dinner with Lou and her mother, going on and on about politics so that nothing personal could ever come up.

"Nixon thought the whole show was a disaster," he said, gesticulating wildly. "The Commies were very lucky the day McCarthy cast himself as the next Jesus Christ. Now he's made a mockery of anti-communism. But that doesn't diminish the fact that those stables do need cleaning."

"Are you shifting your position, Daddy?"

"Elizabeth," her mother said sharply. "Don't oppose your father."

"No, no," O'Dwyer answered. "There is some merit there, although I think, Elizabeth, you could have been a bit smarter about the way you phrased it. I would say that as times change, the moral man must be flexible in order to keep reapproaching his opponent at every turn. Isn't that right, Lou?"

"It's absolutely possible," my brother said, stuffing more salad into his face. The level of hostility Elizabeth reported between herself and her father was, I'm sure, not what Lou had expected of a good family. It was just like being at home, except for the filet mignon instead of boiled chicken.

"After all, young lady. I have always been one hundred percent American. Don't forget that I gave my son for this country."

"What branch of service was he in again?" Lou asked, trying to change the subject.

"Navy. Marshalls. Marianas. Iwo Jima," O'Dwyer answered gruffly.

"I'm sorry."

"He got the Silver Star," Amy said on automatic. "See, now Jim wears it on his lapel."

"And Amy worked in a Defense plant in Newark. We all did our part."

"You're a great American, Mr. O'Dwyer, going by the book."

"Funny, Lou," Elizabeth said. "You don't seem like the bookish type."

Oh no, Lou must have thought. Another girl with opinions.

"So, Mr. O'Dwyer, I followed your advice today, talking to the common man and all of that. And I came up with a great idea for a feature story for the *Star.*"

"A feature? Are you itching to get out of News already?"

"Oh no. No, sir," Lou said, worrying that he had stepped on a land mine. "Trying out both, sir."

"Good boy."

"So, I was thinking," Lou said, putting down his silverware and looking O'Dwyer eye to eye, trying to summon up the feeling of *man to man.* "I was thinking, how about a feature on white jazz musicians?"

"White jazz musicians? Are there any?"

"Oh sure, and they must have a hell of a time."

O'Dwyer didn't even bother in give Lou a dismissive look. He just dismissed him.

A u s t i n :

I'd gotten Jim into a state of high paranoia. Amy related the
whole story to me, when we were married, as a preamble to her
confession of marital indiscretion. With a Black man! But, of
course, I was far more titillated by the effects of my intimidation
than by her infidelity. I never let on, though. Pretending to be
shocked, empathetic, and then enthralled. The perfect
gentleman.

"Watch the events of the day," O'Dwyer said to no one in
particular. "February, the Senate votes unanimously to conduct
a complete investigation into disloyal persons. McCarthy starts
naming names. First a judge from New York, Dorothy Kenyon.
Then, a professor from Johns Hopkins, Owen Lattimore. Starts
with the society's most distinguished figures. But before you
know it they're mixing in the real gutter sleaze and then set up
a subcommittee to focus on sexual deviants. McCarthy reports
on a Russian scheme to entrap female employees at the State
Department by enticing them into lesbianism. So the District
Police, at McCarthy's beck and call, set up a special detail of
the vice squad to investigate links between homosexuality and
communism. Next thing you know, it will be lawyers from Harvard and perverts from the school yard thrown into the same
cell."

"Daddy, are you done?" Elizabeth asked, rising to take his
plate.

"What? Oh, yes."

"That was delicious, dear. You must tell me how you made
that sauce."

"Thank you, Mother. Coffee?"

"Last night," O'Dwyer said, "we were at a cocktail party
given for McCarthy by Frederick Wolman of the Scripps-Howard
newspapers."

"You went to a party in his honor?" Elizabeth gasped. But
actually Amy knew that she wasn't at all surprised. The extra
breath was for emphasis. It enabled her to turn, dramatically,
and carry the plates into the kitchen.

"A shapely young lady was commanding his attention and she asked, rather seductively over her martini, 'Senator, when did you first discover communism?' The old pig grunted, never taking his eyes off her bosom. And can you guess what he said?"

"No, sir," the daughter's boyfriend, that Jew, whispered.

"He said," Amy piped up from nowhere, "he said, '*two and a half months ago.*'"

"Amy," Jim whined. "Now you've spoiled it. But anyway, that's the point you see. He said it with a swagger and then looked around to be sure that the lot of us had noticed how fearless he was of exposing his own falsity. The bully's bravado is a lot harder to face than someone who thinks they have something to hide."

"Coffee?" Amy asked, bringing in the tray.

"No, no," her father jumped up from the table. "I have got to stop by the Stork to catch up on the latest gossip."

"Are you still trying to run into Austin? Obviously he's dumped you."

That's my girl. You see, I think Amy liked me even then.

"Amy!" He looked around, truly afraid. The whole facade melted and his family stared, openmouthed, at this unexpected exhibition of weakness.

"Yes?"

He hated her.

"Amy, dear, thank you so much for the dinner, but I'm afraid I have to go."

"You mean Elizabeth," Amy spooled. "We're in her apartment now, and she cooked the dinner."

"You have no idea of what you're talking about, Amy." He bared his teeth. "I have a plan up my sleeve, and for your information, I can play it just as tough as anyone. I'm not some farm boy, you know. I can play hard ball. Just you wait and see, Amy. Wait and see."

He was gone without a retort, leaving a room of three quiet people, each one deciding not to articulate their own private thoughts as he fruitlessly searched for me, me, me.

N . T a m m i :

My grandfather's fate could have gone either way, I suppose. But even if he hadn't fucked her, the end result probably would have been the same. Oblivion. I don't know what he imagined she would do for him, explode the world? But the sick extra layer of temptation was clearly the devil's labor, although Amy passed it off to him as a "crazy coincidence" no one could have possibly foreseen. But I know that humiliation, no matter how elaborate, is never an accident.

Amy sat there naked on her chenille spread recounting the story of the "crazy coincidence" of her family dinner conversation the evening before. It was surreal and yet it was real. As each phase of this event, seduction followed by subordination, unfolded I realized with alarming clarity and increasing fear that I should have left well enough alone. I should have loved my defeat and wallowed in it instead of trying to defy it. For now she was plunging me into a drama so meaningful it had the weight of a historical event in a time warp. Like Lincoln crossing the Delaware to hear Marian Anderson sing at Ebbets Field. It was everything at once, every force that had plagued me, convulsing on the same sickening moment. All this was unraveling inside of me as she repeated her family's conversation.

"So," Amy said "I asked my daughter to catch me up on that television job of hers. She was very grandiose, claiming they were doing something that is going to be enormously important, and we have to think about its consequences at every turn. I warned her not to exaggerate, but her boyfriend piped in at her defense. He went on and on quoting her, of all things, about how Television is like an automobile, the programs need to be built on reliable patterns. But they need just enough design variation to be resold as a new product each installment. 'Right, Liz?' he kept asking like he didn't have a thought of his own."

At this point Amy interrupted herself to tell me how much

she hated her daughter because the girl's hair was long and messy. The girl's face was even more crooked than her mother's, but too much so, out of the range of interest. That's why she hated her.

"Then Elizabeth went on about her theories about television, how the TV program format is small, intimate. It's a friendly thing that people want to let into their homes. Something comforting to watch with your family so you don't have to listen to Father's bombast or the parents fighting, or stare your lonely defeated children in the eye for hours every evening. Its repetition is part of its charm. Well, I wished we had one on at that very moment, she was unbearable."

She had strange mannerisms, this wealthy powerful woman. Not the kind of drawing room gestures you'd see in movies but it was very coarse, crass, filled with contempt.

"So," Amy continued. "I asked her if television was really any better than radio? I do still listen to the radio, a bit. The news, some music and Fred Allen. But I do remember all the great shows, of course."

As she spoke I remembered sitting by the radio as a young boy listening to all the adventure shows. I resented being drawn into her nostalgia but unfortunately we were both Americans, and Blacks and whites picked up the same radio frequency. Anything having to do with cowboys or space travel. My mother would be sewing, reading the bible while my father read Black Star and other political tracts. Then the news would come on and he'd object to its slant. His large hands, bald head, suspenders. If my father could have seen me buck naked in that lady's boudoir he would have been deeply ashamed. And yet, at the same time, while listening to her, I came to understand that I was forced into this spot because of his failures. If he had stayed and fought instead of running back to Jamaica, then I would have had an easier field to plow. The more alone you are, the harder the labor, the more disadvantaged the greater the debasement. And yet I was prostituting myself for a play, not a pair of shoes or a piece of bread. My goal was something special and that would never be achieved without the highest level of risk.

"Then Elizabeth asked me which shows I remember because right now they happen to be deciding which radio shows should become television programs and, of course, she wanted to know what I think. I told her I remembered listening to 'The Smith Family.' Oh, but this is back in the twenties now. They were an Irish family, a couple trying to marry off their two daughters. And . . . oh well, of course the best was Sam 'n Henry."

"Sam N. Henry?" I asked.

"Not N., like the middle initial," Amy said. "You know 'n,' like the way that colored people say 'and.' "

She looked up at me and raised her eyebrows to signify my agreement that colored people cannot pronounce the word 'and.' I said nothing, signifying that agreement.

"Sam 'n Henry was a hysterically funny show about two colored country bumpkins. But that was the early version of Amos 'n Andy, I realized as I spoke. How could I not have put that together before? Then Elizabeth started asking me about Amos 'n Andy, if I liked it. What I remembered. Actually, Jim and I listened to it religiously when we first got married, on the radio we'd received for our wedding. You remember, they were owners of the Fresh Air Taxi Company, so named because the cab didn't have a windshield. And they belonged to a kind of club called, what was it? Mystic Knights of the Sea Lodge. It was a sham outfit run by a fool named Kingfish. And Kingfish was always being told what to do by his big, fat mammy of a wife named Sapphire."

"How did you know she was fat?" I asked.

"What?"

"Well, it was on the radio."

Then Amy did what they always do in those moments, talked faster and louder and more broadly instead of being quiet and thinking.

"Of course it was on the radio, but everything was so vivid. And many mammies in those days were fat with *soft warm bosoms and tongues of steel for their no-good husbands. 'I'se regusted,' they used to say. You see, they did not know how to speak English. I'm not just saying that about uneducated colored people, not ones like you. We also listened to* The Goldbergs, *but that was later. They couldn't speak English either. Molly Goldberg. 'Give me a swallow, the glass,' she used to say. It was hysterical."*

"What is all this about?" I asked, pulling on my drawers.

"Well, Elizabeth says that The Goldbergs are going on television."

"And?"

"And so are Amos 'n Andy."

"They are?"

And then it all became so clear to me. I knew exactly which way things would go. I knew that it was beyond my ability to resist.

"And the thing is, Cal," she said, putting on her dressing gown. "Amos 'n Andy, well, they haven't hired all their writers."

CHAPTER TWENTY-FIVE

A u s t i n V a n C l e e v e

It was mid-March 1951. It had been almost a year since I'd made
Jim stammer at Toots Shor's. He hadn't followed my advice
and continued to publish semihostile mush about the House
Committee. Since he would not listen to my suggestions, and
at the same time was incapable of putting up a real fight, I
simply stayed clear of him until there was something in it for
me. I knew that inevitably there would be. Life is long. Life is
very long. If you wait and strategize, it all comes back to you.
When I look at a man having his moment of success, all I see
is his impending disgrace. When I watch a man at the bottom of
the heap, I see his hateful vengeance upon returning to power. I
have always considered my enemies to be future friends and
my friends as future enemies. It's like living with an emotional
X ray, I see right through the artifice of the moment. And then
I wait.

Jim did not disappoint me. Oh, no. He was quite splendid
in his comeback, after all. He actually caught me by surprise.
He was quite entertaining.

"How dare you?" I said, having appropriately stormed into
his office, dramatically clutching the typed article his messenger
had delivered to my office that morning. I knew he'd been
watching the clock, waiting for my reaction, so I gave it to him
immediately, as a gift.

" 'Society Journalist Was My Pimp' by Theresa Calabrase,

special to the New York *Star*. Jim, be reasonable. How was I supposed to know that Junie Moon, my little taxi dancer, was a moonlighting tart from your steno pool? It could have happened to anyone."

Jim crossed his arms, stupidly victorious. He smiled up from behind his newly disorganized desk.

"Jimmy, you must have known. You were there when she came to our table with that cigarette tray."

O'Dwyer stood up from his desk like he was Gary Cooper and stroked his imagined jaw.

"All the girls look the same to me," he said.

And then we both burst out laughing. It was absolutely true. Who could blame him?

"There she was," he said, "waiting on us at the Stork Club, but I didn't recognize her. I even got stupid with the girl at the Rhumba Palace after passing her in Stenography every day for two years. You know how it is, Austin. They all look the same."

"Yes, I know," I said, feeling forgiveness. "But you're still slime, O'Dwyer. You print this piece, and I'll sue and send you up the river. I've been telling you for years that scandal was the future of the newspaper business, but I'll make sure you never work in it. You'll be twiddling your thumbs in Sing-Sing, you scum. You shit."

"Well, I got you here," he said. "And that's all I really wanted."

Oh goody-goody. He was going to tell me what he needed. I love a good game of hide and hide.

"Austin," he said, losing all his bravado, lower lip actually quivering. "I got a subpoena."

"Well, you dug your own grave, you fool." I snapped, getting immediately down to this very serious business. I lit a cigarette and perched on his desk. "Those mediocre falsely heroic editorials. 'Just what is Un-American activity? Is it un-American to hold unpopular opinions?' Yes, O'Dwyer, as I have been telling you over and over again. It is, you pompous ass."

"Don't wave your flag at me. What could the Committee possibly have? I've done nothing."

He'd aged, this O'Dwyer. There was finally some of that gray he'd long desired popping up through the orange bristles. His head now looked like a big plate of carrot salad with too much mayonnaise.

"Give me the original," I said. "I want that girl fired and then I'll help you."

"If we fire her and don't murder her, she'll take it to another paper."

"Well then, keep her working in perpetuity, for God's sake. Whatever it takes to shut her up. And don't make jokes about crimes punishable by the electric chair. You never know where a whore like that can end up."

"All right," Jim said soberly.

"All right," I sneered. "Now let's take care of your little problem. And get up out of the chair so that I can sit down for Christ's sake. Get some furniture in here you half-wit."

I think that was the first time that Jim had ever noticed there really wasn't another chair in the place. He just never could see anything from anyone else's point of view. Fatal. Perplexed, he stood awkwardly for a moment, and then, like everyone else whom he'd ever placed in the same position, Jim leaned back against the windowsill.

"Look," I said. "The ultimate test of credibility for a witness is the extent to which he gives other people's names. It was one thing in '47 to take the moral high road. But there have been marked changes in civilization since then."

"But why would they call me?"

"Because it's 1951 and they can. Even the old Commies themselves are turning yellow. Dmytryk, big shot of the Hollywood Ten. The creep changed his stance after only six months in prison. Twenty-six names."

I looked over his shoulder through the window. It really was an extraordinary view. I could see everything from Macy's to the clay brick sidewalks of Central Park West, part of the Camel sign over Times Square, and I could imagine the rest. The big clock in Grand Central Station, the locker where travelers store their goods. The lonely dresser drawers in old tenement buildings. Drinking Pabst Blue Ribbon on a wooden bench with iron arms. Looking up from that bench a man could see the Empire

State Building with a bar 1,050 feet above the city. The Chrysler looming over all the rest. The dial on the pay phone at Playland, open twenty-four hours. The Rhumba Palace. Lindy's wire wastebaskets and their cheesecake on a plate.

"Herman Greenspan called today," Jim said. "Do you know him?"

"Of course, that pig. There's no swine I don't know. Former lawyer, former press agent for a Las Vegas gambling house, and former gun runner for the state of Israel."

"Right," Jim said. "Kike mobster, lawyer, gambler. The last creature on earth you would trust. Told me he's got proof that McCarthy's a poof. A member of the senator's staff was picked up for sodomy in Lafayette Park. Greenspan's got a story from a Marquette coed about Joe's reluctance in the sack. Claims he's got an affidavit about some sick account with another man, if that's what you would call him. Go with it?"

"Of course he's a queer," I said. "All the pawing of everything with boobs only when the camera's on. But try proving it. He'll haul you into libel court, and you'll produce the Jew? I wouldn't recommend it. No, it's going to take more than scandal to bring McCarthy down."

"Like what?"

"Something mundane like the pendulum of history or even, yawn, principle."

"In the meantime, I'm being called because of my principled editorials."

"And because you have an office filled with Reds."

"I do?"

I reached into my breast pocket.

"I have here," I said. Imagine my pleasure. "I have here, a copy of a petition against loyalty oaths provoked by one Harry Hewitt, a hard-core Party member who has been named six times already this year, and it's only March."

"I fired him."

"Yes, Jimmy, you did fire him. But you did not fire all the people on the staff who signed."

"How many?"

"Thirteen who are still on your payroll, including your entire

Research Department. What do you expect with an office full of Hymies?"

"What about Gibson?"

"No," I said. "He didn't sign. Believe me, I looked. And thank you for the announcement of your daughter's engagement."

O'Dwyer fingered his lapels.

"Maybe I could survive the stand."

"Oh, please. Now your ego is completely out of control. What are you going to do, sit up there like Pete Seeger and, when they ask for names, sing them some songs?"

"Well," Jim said, almost completely deluded. "Some people put them off with great humor."

"Right," I spat. "Zero Mostel. 'My name is Zero Mostel. Zero, for my financial standing in the community.' It's great for one big laugh, but it's the last one that pig will ever get."

"I need some time."

"Don't take too much time or you'll *do* time."

"Perhaps we can go out and talk it over."

"Out of the question. Look, O'Dwyer, if you do decide to cooperate, I can help you. Just send me a blank piece of paper in the mail and you will hear from McCarthy's attorneys forthwith."

"Why a blank piece of . . . oh."

And slowly, deliciously, I saw reality crawl across his face. For the first time that afternoon, Jim understood what was at stake.

"You see, O'Dwyer. You're at risk of becoming untouchable. You are about to lose your cachet. Try to imagine what that would be like. No one will ever return your phone calls. No one will ever take your phone calls. Your invitations will be ignored and never reciprocated. Imagine inviting someone to dinner at your own home and having them never respond. Imagine leaving unrequited messages for longtime friends. You will endure passing familiar faces daily with no sign of recognition from them. You'll be the object of gossip, then pity, then amnesia. Derision of you will be the bond between others. You will not be able to participate. You will have no influence. You will have no expression. You will be excluded from everything."

"Call him," Jim said. "Call him today. I'm ready."

"Good boy," I said, tearing Miss Calabrase's article into tiny bits of nothing. "After all, these days it pays to be one hundred and ten percent American."

CHAPTER TWENTY-SIX

N . Tammi Byfield

And now the truth be known. My upstanding grandfather violated his marriage vows in order to get his play produced. They brought him in from the field to the house and he did Miss Anne.

And then it was conveniently after *all* the fireworks that he got his reward. And guess what? It was not exactly what he had imagined. It's not that she offered him nothing for his body. That would have been too modern. No, she simply offered him something he really did not want and could not use. She gave him equal opportunity, all right. An opportunity to become exactly what she wanted him to be. Another opportunity to never have the life he deserved. It was an option that, in his wildest moments of hate, my grandfather never could have fathomed.

Glen Heath was well-dressed and slick. Brooks Brothers from head to toe. I was thanking God that I had settled on a flash restaurant for lunch. It would cost me my week's salary but this connection was worth it. After all, how many Negroes worked inside television? And of those two, how many were "family" friends?

"My father speaks very highly of you," Heath Jr. said, sipping his Rob Roy. "He thinks you're one of the great hopes for the Negro stage."

"Hopefully for the American stage." I winced. I still

hadn't let go. "The Negro stage should be a thing of the past along with Negro drinking fountains."

"Soon, perhaps," Heath said, his face professionally flat. "But not today."

We were, of course, the only brown people in the restaurant. Caroline had come in earlier and gotten the table. Then I joined her. After a respectable five minutes, she disappeared so that I was casually waiting in the center of the room when Heath walked in. This was not the afternoon for lost reservations, tables by the kitchen, and all full up in an empty room.

"So, as I explained on the phone," I began tentatively, "I've been recommended for a job on the Amos and Andy Show, and I wanted to fully understand what's involved. I was hoping you could give me a little background."

"Ah, yes," Heath said, smiling for the first time that day. "You have come to the right person. I've been hearing about this project on a daily basis, and I can give you a good overview." He adjusted his cuff links in such a way as to ensure that I saw them. "Cigarette?" Heath smiled, offering yet another beautiful piece of precious metal. Then he looked at his expensive watch.

"No, thank you."

"Let me level with you, Cal. I am not my father's son. I believe that the only way to secure power for Negro men is one fellow at a time. Yet, each of us who are that chosen one are dependent on the good will of the entire people to help us get that foot up. So, in the name of the future dissolution of Negro Theater, I will tell you exactly what I know. But, only once, understood? As soon as you step on board at CBS, I am your superior and will never offer you a single helpful hint. I will not pal around with you in the hallways. We will not socialize privately until you reach an acceptable stature within the company. I'm willing to help you now but with no obligation for the future. Understood?"

"Yes," I said, a bit taken aback. Even though dishonest conversations are filed with land mines, it is only in truth telling that they constantly explode.

"Okay," Heath nodded, content. "Let us begin."

"Are Freeman Gosden and Charles Correll still oversee-ing the project?"

"Only in the background. The higher-ups figured out right away that they needed an all-Black cast and so reas-signed the white radio actors to advisory roles. We've got the first all-Negro cast in television. This is a big step for-ward for Negro actors, and believe me, they appreciate it."

"Who is in the cast?"

"We held eight hundred auditions." He then broke off a piece of bread and perfectly performed Buttering in Upscale Places. "Fifty screen tests with excellent results. Spencer Williams, a vet of race films from the '30s will play Andy. Alvin Childress . . ."

"The stage actor?"

"Will play Amos."

"Those are both good choices," I admitted, impressed. I had a lightbulb suddenly about how wonderful it must be for these actors. After lifetimes of humiliation and defeat, they could finally make something of themselves. Finally have some recognition. I felt desirous and envious of their justice.

"Tim Moore, from vaudeville, is Kingfish and Ernestine Wade will continue on from radio as Sapphire."

"All-Negro cast. All the writers white?"

"Unless you join. Scripts will be supervised by Bob Mosher and Joe Connally, the radio staff."

Our lobster bisques were served.

"So," I said, noticing his own interest growing, "do you think . . . well, is there really a place for Negroes in television?"

"Absolutely," Heath said, as sure as he'd ever been about anything. His confidence was refreshing. A sure thing. "As far back as 1939 Julius Adams, the critic for the Amsterdam News called television our new hope and I readily agree. I tell you, Cal," Heath leaned over in lowered tones to share a real secret in that white room. "I tell you, it is an amazing new weapon that can be all powerful in

225

blasting America's bigotry to bits. But we've got to hold in there. Even Variety ran a headline last year, Negro Talent Coming Into Own On TV. It's no secret. But the potential impact of equity on television on the rest of an unequitable America is mind-boggling. It is a joy to imagine."

"How do we do it?" I panted, feeling like Einstein looking at his first split atom.

"CBS is the most liberal network. That's why I'm there. Bill Paley was a good pal of F.D.R. and Ed Murrow's See It Now is the most forward-thinking program on the whole dial."

"But what does Amos and Andy look like?" I asked, still not able to bring myself to say 'n."

"Well," Heath said, backing off. "Baggy pants, plug hats, cheap cigars, pushy wives, naive plans, and illiterate sentences."

"Oh."

"But they do have a consultant on racial matters, Flournoy Miller. Know the name?"

This time I had to smile, thinking of Joe Mackie's kitchen routines.

"Oh yes. A . . . colleague of mine shuffled in the chorus of his play called Darkeydom, I believe."

"Well, Blatz Beer has come on as corporate sponsor. The premiere is in June."

"Could go either way," I said, thinking out loud.

"I should tell you," Heath said, wiping his lips daintily with the corner of his linen napkin. "The NAACP is furious. Walter White and his crew. They're ready to fire off a boxcar full of telegrams the day after the show airs."

"Do you think they're right?"

"Look, Cal, now we're at the heart of the matter. I tell you what I believe, deeply believe to be true. The interests of the race are greatly served merely by the ability of Blacks to look at people of their own color performing for people of every color. That holds true to your beliefs about theater, doesn't it?"

"But not with white scripts."

"Look," Heath said with determination. "I'll tell you what Ernestine Wade believes. She says that the agitation from officials of Negro organizations in the past jeopardized the progress of Negro shows. The Coordinating Council of Negro Performers is threatening a picket of the NAACP. Are you so for Black people that you would stop any of them from earning a living?"

"But you know actors."

"CBS is paying forty thousand dollars a week to employ an all-Negro cast. This may not be the best we can ever dream of, but it is the best we can get right now. And if you don't let Nature take its course, we will never make it to the next step."

"Step 'n Fetch it," I said.

"There is an excellent example," Heath said. "Stepin Fetchit earned millions of dollars on the silver screen and he showed thousands of Negro children that they could have a place in the entertainment of the country. Do you think that Lena Horne could have done Cabin in the Sky if Stepin Fetchit hadn't been there first? I don't think so, sir."

At first I didn't know what to think. There was a lot of truth to what Heath was saying. You could not have everything at once. Perhaps TV was the place to reach that great American audience that I had always dreamed of. Certainly, both Black and white could watch my television scripts in numbers far exceeding anything on the Broadway stage. It turned the limitations of playwriting into a cruel joke. Maybe I could work something in about Amos being a veteran. For once, was I going to make the right move and walk in through the door?

"Did you bring the sample script?" I asked.

"Of course," Heath said taking it out of his monogrammed leather briefcase. "Here it is."

I took my glasses out of my breast pocket and reached for the folder.

"Let's see," Heath said. "Okay. I'll read Sapphire, and you read Kingfish."

Then we began to read.

SAPPHIRE: *Well, George, did 'ya have any luck finding a job today?*

KINGFISH: *No, honey. It just seems like dere ain't no employment aroun' for mens. I hunted high an' low, but I ain't give up. I gunna try again in tree-foah months.*

SAPPHIRE: *Well, George, you don't have to look no moah. I got me some wunnerful news for 'ya.*

KINGFISH: *Ahhh . . . wassat?*

SAPPHIRE: *I got a job for 'ya at Superfine Brush Company as a door-to-door salesman.*

KINGFISH: *You done what? Now look here, Sapphire, you cain't do dat. Issa violation of da Atlantic Charter, da Constitution, da Monroe Doctrine, an' not only dat, issa violation of one of duh foah freedoms, duh freedom of speech.*

SAPPHIRE: *Freedom of speech?*

KINGFISH: *Yessum, you didn' give me a chance to say no.*

I lowered the script and looked over the top of my glasses at Heath.

"Well," I said slowly. "At least after this episode, more white people will have heard of The Monroe Doctrine."

He took a moment to stare at me. Now I was revealed to be the enemy. The short-sighted fool that was obstructing his way. The one best left by the way-side.

"The problem with Negroes like you," Heath said with barely maintained control, "is that you want to be in the future, but you don't want to have to do any of the things that are necessary to take us there. You want people like myself to do all the dirty work, so that you can step in later on the road to glory with clean hands."

"There might be some truth to that, Mr. Heath." I had never felt clearer in my life. "And if your efforts today lead logically to freedom for the Black man tomorrow, then I would like to be the first to say thank you."

Heath didn't know what to say, a sensation that rarely occurred to him. But I was entirely relaxed. My career was over. That was clear. I did not have the stomach for any of this. I could not do it. I would never do it. And so I could never be what I wanted to be, because what I wanted to be could not exist in that historic moment. I understood very clearly that if the historic moment is larger than one person's will, even if they have a will of steel, that is a fact that person needs to know. And accept. Then, all the humiliations and insults and put-downs, all the underestimations and lies, false promises, snubs, manipulations, and rudeness that I had endured over those last ten years descended and lay before me on that china plate. All those attacks that I had deflected, one after the other in order to move on. I let them all come in. I took them in. I felt it. That's why I had not felt anything for years. Because if I had let in any emotion, it would have been humiliation first. But now, finally, I could notice my own broken heart and cry over it.

"Are you all right, Byfield? You seem a little ashy. Was it something you ate?"

"Oh, no," I said, sighing the deepest sigh of my life. "So, tell me Mr. Heath. What do you do at CBS?"

"Assistant Deputy Secretary of Consumer Development."

"What's that?"

"Advertising. It is the tribal drum of the future."

"Selling white products to Black people?"

"Selling all products to all people." Heath laughed. "But selling them directly to Black people is not such a bad idea. There might be a place for you in the future, Cal. Even if it is against your will."

CHAPTER TWENTY-SEVEN

S y l v i a   G o l u b o w s k y

1

Lou had gotten the message loud and clear. After more than a year of avoiding me every day at work, he got direct orders from Mr. O'Dwyer to track me down for a talk. But the boss wasn't motivated by a belief in family unity or even concerns about the upcoming wedding. This was about politics, and for O'Dwyer, politics meant business.

Of course I have no way of knowing exactly what he did that night, what went through his mind. But over the years I have created a Lou inside me that I know better than I know myself. I easily step into his shoes and see where he goes. That's the thing about dominance—we know them so well, and they can't even bother to imagine us.

At first Lou was terrified by the assignment. He was to find me alone, in a place far from the office, where we would not be overheard. He was to tell me that the government had a copy of a pro-Communist petition with my name on it. He was to present me with the *Star's* all new in-house loyalty oath and assure me that, if I signed, my job would be secure.

Of course my little brother was most frightened by my anger. But because he had never really come to terms with it, he believed that deep, deep inside I still loved him more than anyone on earth. In his mind I was just jealous. I simply had to get over it. He thought I would welcome him coming to my rescue and all that. He had a colonizer's fantasy. He did not know what he was seeing. I was a woman transformed by betrayal. I had loved one person unconditionally for twenty years of my life, and then he had become a man. I had already determined that, based on that experience, I could never have children. Having lived through such a long committed love, I could never give that way again. But Lou was cocksure that by the end of the afternoon everything would work out to his advantage. He had his wedding day approaching and, of course, he expected me to be nice about it. To dance and give him presents.

Finding me outside the job was not as easy as he had hoped. Even though it was Friday afternoon and everyone rushed to get home, I had stayed in the office until well past eight. He kept having to look for the light through the venetian blinds on the glass door of Research. I'm sure he felt like a spy for the FBI. After all, he was a spy for the FBI.

Finally, at almost nine o'clock, I straightened out my desk, shut off the office lights, and headed toward the elevators.

Shadowing me was, I'm sure, quite amusing. He raced down the stairs, arriving just in time for my elevator to arrive. Then he stayed lost in the crowd as he followed about half a block behind for the trip to the subway station. The whole time he was watching me, Lou was thinking about all the ways that I had loved him. He felt more and more sure that this love would resurface if he just asked for it. He never considered making restitution. It hadn't really been that long, as far as he was concerned. How much could a person change in such a short time?

Lou put his nickel in the turnstile and sat down behind the curtain in the photo booth, watching me wait for the train. Hiding behind the *Tribune,* he pushed past the other passengers to get as close to me as possible, without being seen. Lou imagined himself as a first-rate grifter working the subways, thinking he could have been a good canon if he had been a thug. If you ask me, pickpocketing was more along his line than loan-sharking. He wasn't the violent type. He violated you by pretending to be sweet. He was the kind to take a little microfilm camera like they have in the movies, follow the broad to her apartment, and then hide out in the dumbwaiter, feeling angelic.

I got off two stations early.

My brother followed me down Sixth Avenue, and then he followed me onto a side street. We both passed a bum advertising *Men's Suits* for fourteen dollars on a sandwich board. The guy with the signs had never even seen fourteen dollars. He had a lousy pair of pants and a sandwich. It seemed ridiculous for this guy to be working on a Friday night. There weren't any customers.

I walked in through the entrance to a blacked-out storefront, the windows were painted black and there was no sign. The place could have been anything, and Lou was supremely confused. Was it a hock shop for stolen goods? Was I a courier of some kind? A croupier? A counterfeiter? It had to be some kind of criminal outpost.

And then, all of a sudden, Lou realized what the deal was. It dawned on him that his sister really was a Commie. That was it. Here I was on a Friday night delivering all the secrets I'd gotten from working at the newspaper during the day. And I was clearly delivering them to this little spy shack on a deserted westside street. God, he never would have come to this realization on his own, but now, confronted with the evidence, it all clicked into perfect place. I was, of course, all the things that Communists were. I was sullen, antisocial, negative. I was just the type to want a Communist takeover of the world.

Lou pulled back in shock and stood against the equally dark building across the street. After a while, he remembered to light a cigarette as a way to try to get back his nerve. Even two cigarettes didn't calm him. He just stood there, sweating, wondering what in the hell he should do. The whole thing was big. Really big. It was a lot bigger than a little favor for Mr. O'Dwyer. Maybe he should call the cops. The newspapers. Then he remembered that he worked for a newspaper and that this was the golden opportunity he had long been waiting for. If he could bust open a Commie spy ring he'd be such a big shot no one could ever take it away from him. Why, he'd end up the next editor in chief for certain. In fact, he'd be more than that. He'd be a big hero.

"Hey, buddy."

Lou almost jumped through his skin.

"Waddya want?"

"Hey, buddy." It was the guy with the men's pants on his chest. "My cousin Mickey was a war hero in Italy."

"Oh, don't give me that old pitch. That one went out with the windup Victrola."

"Just help me out with two bits, fella. Have some sympathy for your fellow man."

"Ah, get lost," Lou said, and then had a change of heart. "Wait a minute. Boy, you sure look beat."

"Sure am."

"Why are you advertising on an empty street?"

"Oh, I'm not working," the guy said. "Just found these underneath a pushcart. Hoping to sell them for ninety-five cents to buy a hot sandwich with french fries."

"Tell you what," Lou said. "I'll buy your signs for a buck. But first, you gotta do me a favor."

"First pay up, then you'll get your favor."

"Okay," Lou said, reaching into his pocket. "You see that storefront over there?"

"You mean the dyke place?"

"What?"

"You want me to go rough them up?"

"You're kidding," Lou said.

"You want me to throw a few of them animals around? Five bucks it'll cost you."

"What?"

"Five bucks."

"This is just too much," Lou said.

"Okay," the guy said. "I'll do it for four."

2

When I walked in I knew every woman in the place but one.

"Hey, Spin."

Spin had *my* scotch waiting for me on the bar.

I took *my* seat and only then turned to smile at my lover at her piano. Tonight was our first anniversary. It was one year before that I had naively stopped off after work, at her prodding, to come see my dear, dear friend. Even with the address in hand, I had gone in and out of every storefront on Sixteenth Street until finding the right place.

I did not even realize that it was queer at first, with Jimmy, the bouncer, seated at the door and Danny, the owner, walking back and forth across the floor. Besides, I'd thought that Spin was a boy. And when I saw Caroline at the old honky-tonk upright, I felt an overwhelming happiness in its perfect context. There was nothing about the official world that provoked any allegiance in me. I was not a good citizen. And so this offering was gratefully accepted. It inspired a very deep loyalty for which I thought I had lost the potential.

I drank and laughed. I talked to her friends, and they flirted with me, they teased me. They saw all the ways that I could be beautiful. Ways I'd personally appreciated but the girls at the office had never understood. And this time when I looked at Caroline I saw her strong white arms, the hair and burns on her skin, the rough spots. The muscles in her forearms and those veiny pornographic hands. Her lips like steak. I heard the sounds that she made as she kissed my neck, and I recognized all that I was capable of, physically. How silenced I had been. How terribly alone. How still and closed against my own nature.

This is, dear reader, how I understood my own condition. Others require more of an explanation. They are fixated on that process of understanding. And why not? It has no parallel in heterosexual life. It is exotic. And the curiosity of others is imperial. It gives them a cage in which to contain us. This coming to a self-acceptance and a permission for a passion of our own invention is the part of the story that others most like for us to tell. For that reason, I hate this part of the story. It is so palatable because others pretend that it is about romance when it is really about savagery. What I feel about women is animal. There is no separation between my desire, my capacity, and my self.

I am much more interested in the other story, the story of what was done to us. All the ways that we have paid even though we've never done anything wrong. The punishment without crime. And all the ways that the others have profited. But when I turn on the television in my old age, to absorb the lies of the new tolerance, I never see a single sign of their guilt. Their complicity. I never see a character like Lou in those stories. He always turns out to be the savior. There is a lie followed by a resolution and then a happy ending. It's all marketing. And it's all false. They want us to tell about our moment of awakening because they don't have one, and they don't want us to say what we know to be true about them. It is a diversion. The truth is still forbidden.

It was in that bar that we'd had our first kiss. Our first stark confession of attraction. Of physical need. It was there that Caroline confirmed her many past indiscretions. And, so, it was in that bar that we had our first fight. Our first negotiation. A lot of the girls who came there were married, of course. Although most did not have husbands like Cal, who turned a blind eye to everything as he pursued his own particular needs, his own need for glory. And so living next door had its mercies and punishments. I understood, of course, the necessity of keeping everything between us a secret from her husband. And that required her leaving my bed abruptly every time. His disinterest had left much space for the two of us over the course of our year of love. Yet, having an internal sense of order, I had begun to experience a sad longing to spend a complete night together with the woman I loved. I wanted to wake with her in the morning instead of separating at two and joining back together, fully dressed, the following day. I wanted to see her naked in the luminous morning light.

"Can I buy you a drink?" one stranger asked.

"I've got a tab," I said. "Give me another one, Spin." That

was my practiced brush-off for first timers who didn't know the score. "My lover is the piano player."

"What a day at work. I never thought I'd make it to Friday," the girl answered. She was a young one. Hair brushed back, wearing a white button-down shirt and snaky black trousers. Couldn't have been a day over nineteen. "What do you do?"

"I'm a researcher for a newspaper," I said, wanting to be a snob.

"Well, I'm a carhop at a drive-in in Jersey. Got a problem with it?"

"A drunk is a drunk, and a pass is a pass," I said, giving the message loud and clear.

"Yeah, and I bet you're a nice clean girl in a nice clean world."

"Boy, the customers here get meaner every day." I lit a cigarette, enjoying this match of wills. Caroline smiled at me and started playing 'I'm in the Mood for Love.' That was our song.

"I'm a good waitress," the girl said. "It's something I can do better than other people. Makes me feel like somebody." She rubbed a smudge off the shine of her pants. "Hey, bartender, how often do you clean this place? Every Decoration Day?"

"Shut up or they'll hear you in Newark." Spin got a big laugh from the regulars with that one.

"Ah," the girl said. "I've had that dialogue from you poolroom hotshots my whole life."

"Look," Spin said. "Don't come in here and get tough, or Jimmy'll have to bounce you and then you can sit home on Friday nights and memorize the dial tone."

"For the love of Pete," the girl said, backing off. "It's only eleven o'clock. Give me a break."

"Sweating?" Spin asked, wiping down the bottles.

"Yeah," the girl answered. "I'm trying to reduce."

That cracked everybody up, so the peanut gallery at the bar relaxed again.

"Give me another one, Spin," I said.

"What about you?" Spin said to the new girl.

"I'm not in a hurry."

"Well, this is a bar, not a waiting room."

"Okay, okay."

I watched Caroline play the piano. I loved it. There was nothing that woman loved more than music. Not even making love. She'd stop in the middle of a moment of passion to say something about the latest Gerry Mulligan cut. But Caroline was a queen, a real belle. She was dainty as a tiger.

She was coy. She was, I well knew, as seductive as honey on an apple. I loved that girl. I loved her. All these years later I can still say that with feeling.

There had never been this kind of love in my life. I hadn't had someone I could really count on. All my life I'd been let down by people who were weak. Rita was weak. My father was too weak to understand what I had to offer. He was too scared to think for himself. My mother was too cowardly to defend her only daughter. She just shuffled through her life, kowtowing to the men in the family. And my brother was the biggest sadness of them all. The biggest liar. He had pretended to be my friend, but it was just a holdover until his first opportunity to stab me. And then he sealed the door shut between my parents and myself to justify what he must have known was wrong. He broke my heart.

But now, all these people turned to sawdust. They didn't matter anymore because there was someone on earth who would stand up for me. There was someone who was on my side.

"You from Jersey?" the girl was at it again.

"Why?"

"I'm from Jersey."

"Pretty quiet over there."

"Not the parts I'm from." If anyone could swagger on a barstool, this chick could do it. "I got a second job too."

"What's that?"

"I'm a masseuse."

"Oh, really?" I had to smile at that one.

"Yeah. I'll show you my license and everything. You should try the modeling game. All you need are some good connections." She looked around. Caroline was still playing. "You know, you're a good looker," the girl said. "I have a friend who could get you started in an acting career."

"Don't give me that," I said. "I've been handed lines all my life." *But no more,* I added silently.

3

I'd had four whiskeys and the girl at the bar had never let up. Finally Caroline was able to take her break.

"Hi, baby," she said, coming to stand by at the bar. "Spin, put all my girl's drinks on my tab."

"You got a tin box?" That's one of the things that fascinated me about my sweet, she was so courtly. "Your music does something to me."

Now that I am older I've learned to love the one night of love, the one thought of love, the furtive hand on thigh, the only kiss. Ah bliss. Moments such as these. A good person doing a good thing. What could be sexier than that? But then, I was a fresh furnace. When Caroline gave me truly dirty thoughts, I went into her debt. *You put your hands down my pants and you won't be in for a surprise. You'll find out how sexy you are, which you already know.* Now I understand that the quietest woman has the most shapely, girlish back. She has a long, slender body and a tomboyish veneer. Now, I savor such ideas privately, until the last shudder of erotic recall can no longer be turned to. It takes a while for the memory of her mannish shoes to cool down. But it does.

"Sweeter than home cooking," Caroline drawled. She had a surprisingly tentative mouth. Those shy lips. But I looked at them again after I'd tasted the preliminaries and knew she was a beast.

"Hey, blue eyes," I reached up to kiss her.

"You know the rules," Danny said, watching all the girls and the fluctuations of our hunger. "No funny business."

"Oh, relax," I said, slightly drunk. "There are no cops in here." I pointed to the now dark, red warning light waiting over the door. "Give me a break."

"I'll give you a break," Danny said. He would break my arm as casually as ban me from the bar.

I kissed Caroline's hand. "I'm just checking her manicure," I said, and Spin started to laugh. "Baby," I pulled my darling over to a corner away from the friendly, voracious, understanding, knowing, insistent eyes of the girls at the bar. "I'm so sad at home staring at my lonely piles of laundry. You know I want to be with you all the time."

But Caroline did not warm up the way I had expected. She did not move to comfort me.

"What do you want from me?" she snapped. "Did I personally raise the price on pork and beans?"

I was surprised, but I had seen that mean streak many times before. I had not made peace with it, in fact, I was disappointed by it. But I had the love of my life in hand, and so I had to accept it.

"I know you don't like it either," I said. "But I want us to be together. Every time we're torn apart I feel like an old windup Victrola running out of speed."

She was silent.

"I want us to move in together," I said romantically. Cinematically. "We can get a different apartment, of course. Maybe even move to a different town. Listen, Caroline, I've been thinking it over a lot. Every day. I don't mind leaving my job. I'll never get anywhere there, anyway. No matter how well I do. There's nothing more important for me than to be with you. I'd go anywhere you want to go. We could move to Europe or to Chicago. I don't care if I have to roll cigars in a factory as long as I can come home to you."

Caroline turned to face me directly. She was not an avoider. Her brown hair was swinging, slightly unkempt, and she had those superior blue eyes that were the center of her face.

"It doesn't work that way." She was quiet, staring at me, dumbfounded. How could I be so stupid? Like everything was so obvious she couldn't even begin to explain it.

"What is it?"

"Look," Caroline said. "Girls don't move in together and get the milk delivered every morning. We can't just go to some quiet neighborhood and rent a house. That's ridiculous."

"Why can't we?"

"Because what are the neighbors gonna say every time your freaky friends come over to play a game of poker? Who is gonna rent to a couple of freaks with nothing in their baby carriage but a bottle of rye?"

"What are you saying?"

There was a terror coming over me. It was closing in on my life like an increasingly obvious deprivation of oxygen. I knew the details of my disaster and only one word could come out of my mouth.

"No."

"What the hell?" Jimmy said, getting up slowly from his seat by the entrance and waddling over to where we two were engaged. "Okay, that's it. Take it outside to another city."

Everyone in the dive shut up immediately. The girls at the bar sat and stared. They were all watching what they knew would be a great cat fight.

"It's okay, Jimmy," Caroline said, trying to wave him away with all her other annoyances.

"It is not okay," I said, waving my hands frantically at the wrist. I didn't know what to do so I just flapped my hands back and forth like a trained seal.

"Look," Caroline said. "Cal is going back to school. He quit his job at the club, and he's out of the theater permanently. We need to move in with his sister in Queens."

"But I don't want you to."

"In fact," Caroline said. "It's already decided. We're moving out tomorrow."

"But," I was panicking now. "What about us?"

"We can still see each other here on Fridays."

"What?"

"That's it. We're moving out tomorrow."

I screamed for blood this time and threw myself at Caroline. Scratching her face, grabbing her arms and pulling them toward me.

"No, you can't do this. What am I going to do? Don't do this. Don't. I can't take it."

"You're crazy," Caroline said. "Don't get me fired."

Jimmy lumbered back to our corner.

"Okay, that's it," he said.

He pulled me off my love like I was an empty cardboard box and hauled me past the bar, just the way he'd hauled a hundred drunken girls before. My people.

"I'm gonna get you," I said. "I'm gonna get you for this."

And then I was out on the street.

CHAPTER TWENTY-EIGHT

A u s t i n   V a n   C l e e v e

1

I watched James O'Dwyer squirm on a bed in a cheesy hotel room in Midtown on a dreary Friday with two lawyers from the House Committee on Un-American Activities. All thanks to me. This time they'd sent over a poker-faced Jew and an Irish dandy for the occasion. As Jim spoke, his words were echoed by the tapping of a lemon-lipped stenographer recording all for a dubious posterity.

"I want you to understand clearly that I am doing this under protest," Jim squealed, and then rolled in the mud with his hooves in the air looking for a reaction. Of course there was none.

"Just give us the names," the Jew said. "There are no newsreel cameras here to put a show on for."

The dandy was combing his hair and glancing at himself, repeatedly, in the mirror.

"Well, I just want you to make it clear to the senator," O'-Dwyer continued, getting more nervous. "That I believe that the most effective opponents of communism in the United States of America have been the liberals associated with a belief in progress."

"The letter," I hissed.

"Oh, yes." O'Dwyer was really losing it now. He should try

to stick to the scenario. "I have here a letter from Richard Nixon praising my editorial endorsing the second guilty verdict of Alger Hiss."

"What do you want me to do about it?" the Jew asked. He was obviously in charge. An ice cube wouldn't melt in his pants.

"Pass it on to the senator."

Silence.

"I don't want you to think I am intimidated," Jim whimpered.

I almost laughed out loud at that one. He was an obvious wreck and a complete coward. He smelled of garlic. He had stains from lunch and breakfast and the previous night's supper on his suit. His skin was oily, filthy.

"Of course not," the Irish one said, brushing his bangs back the other way.

"Of course your questioning of my opposition to communism was the greatest affront an American can endure."

"Yeah, yeah."

"But I could not further jeopardize the fragile life of the free press," O'Dwyer whined, reaching for his handkerchief and mopping the sweat off his face. "I mean, if there was any trouble, advertisers would punish the paper. It's a real danger."

"The names."

O'Dwyer took the envelope out of his breast pocket.

"There are so many ways to do it. I can stand, humbly, hat in hand and thank the Committee for the honorable opportunity to serve my country. I can be vague, forgetful. I can lecture the Committee on the true nature of freedom and defile my soul. I can answer and be led away in handcuffs—my career and family shamed for all eternity. I can hesitate and then return six months later in a state of thoughtful reconsideration. I can . . . I ca . . . Oh America, land of choice and opportunity. There are so many detergents to choose from on the shelf. Do I want All or do I want Tide?"

The lawyer raised his eyebrows at me. "What is this, Van Cleeve?"

"Do I want notoriety?" O'Dwyer continued. "Dignity? Do I want shame in the present and security in the future? I've always hated Stalin. I didn't even like him at Yalta. Should I treat Richard Nixon to three martinis at Le Cirque and listen politely to his bad French. Gentlemen's agreement?"

He looked around at four stony, silent faces.

"Honor the informer," O'Dwyer dribbled. "It takes guts to be one."

"Has this come to an end?" the Jew said.

"Just one more point." O'Dwyer squirmed.

"Five more minutes. I know, you want to be able to brag to your boy that you told us off."

"I lost my boy in the war."

"Rough deal." He looked around at the rest of us, sitting back against the greasy wallpaper and airshaft view. "All right, five minutes."

"Men identify with the people who protect them. To step out of the umbrella of evil protection is the rarest step. Everyone else carries on in their own filth. This whole McCarthy thing, my brothers. This is a flight from reality. It elevates the ridiculous and ridicules the most important bonds between people, like loyalty and love, more crucial than . . . than . . . than . . ."

"Than what, for God's sake?" the Jew gasped in desperation.

"Shut up, O'Dwyer," I snapped. "Hand over the list." O'-Dwyer did shut up and dropped the envelope in the other big Mick's lap. The two lawyers immediately stood up and walked out the door without another word. Not even another look. Only the secretary shifted her eyes my way as she packed up her machine.

"This one was really pathetic," she said.

2

I followed a silent O'Dwyer to the *Star*'s offices, haranguing him mercilessly. Pressuring him to take care of things my way. Suggesting, threatening, convincing, and filling his mind so thoroughly that no ideas could thrive there but mine.

I knew I had made a big mistake. After toying with someone for so many years you get attached to them. There is something about manipulating someone that makes the two of you very intimate. But it is an illusion. I had to face that I had been weak. I'd confused pulling his strings with thinking I owed him something. Oh, my God, I had actually stooped so low as to do something out of loyalty. Well, now I was in over my head. I'd gone to bat for Jim by going directly to the really big cheeses. They paid me my favor and the moron had embarrassed me completely. I knew the word would get back to Winchell and Chambers, and I'd lose some of my best connections. My credibility. There is nothing that reflects so strongly upon a man as the fact that he stands up for fools.

How to recover?

I sat back in his chair, smoking a cigarette, staring at the man. I'd spent many hundreds of hours watching him closely, testing his reactions to understand how to best force his hand. And all along my instincts had been excellent. But now I needed something very new and large that would finish off this whole mess and let me out scot-free. To begin again.

"Charlie," Jim called out. "Get Gibson in here. And bring in two more chairs."

Good sign, I thought. He's changing. He had accepted that I was the real authority in that room and that my seizure of the chair was permanent. He'd responded to it practically by leaving me in the regal position behind the desk and finally conceding to bring in some wooden ones from the hallway. At least I knew that I was still in charge.

"Lou," O'Dwyer said, sitting awkwardly opposite the younger man. No furniture between them. "We're going to be making some changes around here."

Gibson started to panic. He almost burst into tears. It was fascinating to watch. Here was someone whose sense of strategy was absolutely primitive. I could tell immediately that he had never taken the long view in his life.

"Please don't fire me, Mr. O'Dwyer," he pleaded, showing all his cards. "I know you wanted to see Sylvia's signed loyalty oath this morning, and I know I don't have it. But I'm working on it. I'm doing the best I can."

"We're changing the whole direction of the paper," O'Dwyer continued, as though this kid hadn't said a word.

"We are?" Gibson asked, hoping for a last-minute save.

"Yes, have a seat, my boy."

Oh, my God. The kid was already sitting.

"I've been thinking," O'Dwyer continued. The smell of stale garlic wafted my way.

"Yes, sir."

"You know, Lou," O'Dwyer said. "It's a new world now. Everything is changing. Americans are tired of politics. That's left over from the gloomy days of the war. Right?"

Good boy. He was following my instructions.

"Right," Lou said, not quite getting it.

"Young people like you, they want to have a good time. They want to drive around in cars, go dancing. Right?"

"Right."

I'm sure that kid had never gone dancing in his life. And he certainly did not know how to drive a car.

"And the New York *Star* should not be left behind," O'Dwyer droned on.

"No, it shouldn't."

"Good, I'm glad you agree."

Then O'Dwyer belched. After a minute of silence he reached for his handkerchief. It was filthy.

"There is a new technique in reporting out there, Lou. And it is sweeping America. There is a new style of journalism, and the American people love it. Do you know what that is?"

"Uh, no, sir."

"Good, because I'm going to tell you. It is all about . . . about . . . What's that again, Van Cleeve?"

"Sensation."

"Yes," O'Dwyer continued. "Sensation."

At this point I faced the truth. Even though my first-rung emergency plan was unfolding beautifully, I had to accept that it would not be enough. This man was dangerous. His incompetence made him entirely unreliable. I had to act and act quickly to take care of all of this once and for all.

"Sensation?" Gibson squeaked. "Like girlie magazines?"

"No, you idiot." Suddenly O'Dwyer stood up and stretched out over his desktop, a man prostrate on the operating table waiting for his anesthesia to kick in. But he was not passed out, he was digging into his bottom drawer with his head practically in my lap, and then he pulled out a bottle of bicarbonate of soda. Sliding back into his chair, he poured it enthusiastically into a tiny paper cup. The foamy powder overflowed all over the floor, but O'Dwyer did not seem to notice. He just stirred it with his finger. "Yes, sensation, drama, and scandal are not just for housewives anymore. Now they influence the direction of political discourse. The world is a melodrama, Lou. All that falls outside the extreme is dead, stale stuff that interests no one and is of no significance."

A phrase directly from my mouth.

"That's true."

Gibson started to relax now. He was off the hook. All he had to do was nod his head.

"So, Lou, here is where you come in. We need to dream up some gooey, delicious story. Some scintillating, shocking tale designed to stimulate and provoke our readership. But, in an entertaining way. A 1951 kind of way."

"Yes, sir."

"Got any ideas?"

"Well," Lou said. "There is always murder. People love murder."

"Yes," O'Dwyer said, wagging his finger. "Murder is exactly what I'm talking about."

"Everybody wants to be a detective," Lou said, taking his hands out of his pockets. "I think it's all those radio serials we grew up on."

"Yes, but there is more to it than that. There's the tension of modern life. Don't you feel it, Lou?"

"Yes, I feel it."

"It's that tension that could drive any New Yorker to murder. Don't you think?"

"Well, with everybody always yapping at everybody, blowing off steam, a murder could happen easily."

"Do you know of any murders for the next issue?"

"Ah, not offhand."

"I'm counting on you, Lou. In fact, I'm depending on you," O'Dwyer said. And Lou could see a flame of panic in the guy's eyes. "We've got to make these changes right away. By . . . by today. And you've got to get a good juicy story for the front pages of Monday's edition."

"You want me to commit a murder?"

"Sure, that would be a great story. No, you idiot. I want you to find a good, soggy, splashy, dirty tale, or that is the end of your job. No job. No marriage. No nothing. You can go back to Flatbush Avenue and bake bialys for all I care, you little half-wit. Find me that story, Lou, or you're finished. I've got to have it."

"I've got a story," Lou said, furious. "I've got a really juicy one."

"Good boy," O'Dwyer said, totally exhausted. "I knew I could count on you."

3

When Gibson left I knew I had to act quickly. O'Dwyer turned and smiled at me like a well-behaved mongoloid. He'd done everything the way I'd told him to and then expected a reward. But it only reaffirmed for me that he was, at this point, completely incapable of doing anything proactive on his own. This made him more than useless, it made him dangerous. There was a high-stakes card game in the back of the waterfront hotel of power. I wouldn't be there with him if I wasn't desperate. In fact the whole country was desperate in 1951, and every gambler knows that citizens of a high-class rat's nest do not like uncooperative guests.

"Jim," I said. "I feel sorry for you."

"You do?" O'Dwyer said, too confused to protect himself from me.

"It's a tough job, Jim. Being the editor of a New York City newspaper. It's more than any longshoreman or cabby or file clerk or insurance salesman like your father can ever understand. They don't know the pressure. No one knows what it's like to smile till your face hurts through the bars of your cage."

"Oh, God, Austin," he said. "I don't know if I can take it."

"Of course, you can't take it, Jimmy. Who could? It's an impossible situation. No man, no matter how strong-willed, can stand this kind of pressure day after day, year after year. You feel like a bleeding pig, don't you? And the only natural outcome is to wake up one morning underneath a pier."

"Yes," he said, too weak to refill his cup of bicarbonate. "What do you mean by that?"

"You feel almost dead, don't you, Jimmy?"

"I do," he said.

"And it's always almost until you get there, isn't it?"

"Oh, I'm so tired, Austin. I don't think I can make it through another day."

"You can't, O'Dwyer, it's obvious. You're at the end of your rope."

"I am," he said. "I've reached the end. I need a rest."

I got up and walked across the room and stood by the window.

"Beautiful view you've got there. Come, take a look."

"Yes," he mumbled obediently, standing beside me, stinking like a barnyard.

"Jimmy," I said. "Think about your son."

"My son?"

"What a hero," I said. "I'm sure you've spent many hours imagining his last moments on this earth. He, too, was exhausted. Far more tired than you feel now. But did he retreat? No. Did he go to his commanding officer and ask for R and R? No. He went into battle knowing that he had given everything he had to give to his country. He knew that death was more important than dishonor. Don't you feel that way, Jimmy? That death is more important than dishonor? It's easier. Do you really have the strength for public dishonor? You don't, Jim. You're too tired. You're just like your boy. A hero. You're ready to give up your life for your country rather than sink into the abyss of immoral power. It'll all be exposed eventually, and you won't be able to stand it. Father of war hero, a sniveling coward. You have to change the paper, I agree with you there. But what honor will there be for you personally, Jim, to be the editor of a scandal sheet? And then to be revealed as an informer? What a plummet downward. Of course, you have no choice, it must be done. But your social standing? And the legacy of your father-in-law? Your name will be cheapened, obviously. Do you have the strength to go through that hell? Aren't you tired enough already?"

"I'm too tired," he said. "I can't do it."

And he started to cry. He had his head in his hands like a blubbering baby and was sobbing openly, snot running down his face.

"You can't do it. And you can't do anything else. I agree with you, Jim. You are at the end of your abilities. Better to put an end to it now and do your wife a favor. Don't drag her through the mud. Just go."

I opened the window wide, all the way to the top. The gap in the wall was larger than my own body, it would have taken nothing for me to simply step through it.

"Come here, Jimmy," I said. I took him by the hand and pulled him into the full frame of the window. "Look. Doesn't that breeze feel good?"

"Yes," he said.

"Look at the beauty of that city, Jim. Just take one step and you will be part of it forever. No one else will ever shame you. No one will ever hurt you again. You will go down in your glory and nothing will ever take that away from you. Today you have your good name, Jim. End it now and no future calamity will ever plague you."

"You're right," he said. Empty. He had no further will. He had been destroyed.

"Do it, Jim," I said. "Do it for your son and do it for yourself." Then I backed away, slowly, leaving his profile standing stark against the backdrop of the beckoning city. The blanket of its music engulfed this lonely, stupid man. Quietly, I stepped out of the office. Quietly, I walked through the hallways, down the elevator, and through the front plate-glass door. Then I hailed a cab and went off to the Stork to see how long it would take for the news to reach me there.

CHAPTER TWENTY-NINE

Sylvia Golubowsky

1

I sat alone in my apartment. I'd been sitting there all weekend until the last mover carried out Caroline's last box. I sat there all the following week, drinking scotch and remembering, occasionally, to call in sick to work. I'd sat there as the piano hung forlornly from its ropes while the workmen slowly lowered it out the window. I sat and waited for the knock on the door that never came and then went out for another bottle of scotch. I sat on the floor and wailed and then went down for one more bottle. Even the lady at the liquor store commented on how badly I looked.

"What's wrong, honey? You're as limp as an old girdle. You've lost all your zip."

I'd bought two bottles that day to avoid having to face her again anytime soon. I resolved never to return to that store. I sat waiting for the phone to ring. I wailed. I passed out. I waited. I stared at the phone. I cried. Drank. Slept. Now it was Friday night again at six o'clock. If I didn't get myself to the office by Monday I'd be on the unemployment line. Then the phone rang.

"Yes?"

"Hello?" The fact of a man's voice revealed to me that I still harbored an expectation that Caroline would call. Would come back to me.

"Yes."

"You must be Sylvia," the man said.

"I am, but must I be?"

"Look, Sylvia. This is Charlie from the office. I want to talk to you about the Hewitt business."

Usually in my house there is music behind everything. But music was too filled with feeling for this. And yet there was something so mundane about Charlie's voice on the phone that I missed that jump of clattering bouquet. I looked around and recognized my records scattered on the floor like a posse of old, true friends.

"What about it?"

"You were a friend of Hewitt's, right?"

"I don't know." I saw my own matted hair in the mirror.

"There was a big showdown at work a couple of years ago. You remember."

"Yeah, Hewitt was a good guy. What do you want, Charlie?"

"He committed suicide."

"Suicide?"

"You didn't know?"

"No," I said. "I thought he was fine."

Where was that Bud Powell?

"I'm sorry to have to break the news to you this way. Jesus, but Hewitt hasn't been fine for months. He was blacklisted, you know, couldn't feed his family. All kinds of doors slammed in his face. Poor guy."

"Poor guy," I said slowly.

"The thing is," Charlie said. "We're afraid that some other people might be about to meet the same fate at the paper. Seems like a bunch of us signed a petition at Hewitt's instigation, and now there's a risk that our names might have ended up in the hands of the FBI."

"Why?"

"Because . . . look, Sylvia. I think your name might be on one of those lists. It doesn't mean that anything is necessarily going to happen to you, but it could."

"I don't have an important job, Charlie."

"Yeah, but there are plenty of people who would like it.

Look, Sylvia, a lot of people's jobs could be at stake. I'd like to talk it over with you in person."

"I don't know. This isn't the best time."

Freddy Green backing up Lady Day.

"It's Friday night. You're getting ready to go out on a date. But, look, I'll be at the bar at the Minetta Tavern. South of Washington Square Park. Meet me there in an hour. I'll wait for you, and we can talk it all over."

I hung up the phone and sat, silently. It was too much information for someone in such a profound state of grief. And then, for no reason, the phone rang again.

"Caroline?"

"No, it's Lou."

I hung up immediately.

The phone rang and rang. Rang and rang. It rang until I was sure my head would explode. I turned on the bath water. Full throttle, closed the bathroom door and immersed my head in the water, trying to shut out the sound. By the time I dried myself off, got dressed, and combed my hair, the phone had still not ceased to ring.

"Hello."

"Look," Lou said. "There is something you need to know."

"Is it Pop?" I asked, expecting another thing, another layer of punishment.

"No," Lou said. "Look, I know all about you. I know where you go on Friday nights, and I don't owe you anything. But I've thought it all over, and I have to do what is morally right. It wouldn't do for Ma and Pop to have your face on the front page of the *Star* being led away in handcuffs. Whatever happens, don't be near that dive at ten o'clock tonight."

"Lou," I said. "I want you to go to Pop right now and tell him that what you did to me was wrong. You were wrong to take the job. You were wrong to go running to him. Tell him that you knew I would never get a fair hearing in the family and that you used that fact. Tell him that the way he and Mama acted toward me was wrong and you knew it would be."

"It's gone too far for that."

"Lou, do it now. While Pop is still alive. Do this now and

your whole life will be better. If you don't do it, everything will go a different way."

"What are you talking about?"

"Someday Mommy and Daddy aren't going to be here anymore. And you're gonna need someone on your side. And, face it, Lou. You're not a very bright boy. I hate you."

"Well, I hate you."

"Of course you do, Lou. Because you are a conformist. You hate me because I hate you. Mama and Pop trashed me so you did too. You have no independence. You just follow everybody else's lead."

"You're a freak," he said. "You're a bitter, angry, crazy woman."

"Where would women like me be," I said, "if it weren't for men like you?"

2

Serves them right, I thought the whole way to MacDougal Street. Those scumbags, throwing me out on my ass just when I needed friends the most. Those drunks sitting at the bar wouldn't lift a finger to help another gay girl if their lives depended on it. And Jimmy and Danny, those bums, taking every last dime off of hardworking girls. They deserve whatever they get.

But the real pleasure, the thing that actually made me smile for the first time in a week, was the thought of Caroline, led off to the paddy wagon, spending the weekend at the Women's House of Detention. Cal would really love that one. Her picture in the *Star* would make a great impression. She deserved the humiliation, her and those other freaks. Being paraded through the streets in handcuffs. The strip search. Being knocked around by the cops who'd put their hands down your blouse and any other part of their bodies any place they'd like to put it. Those girls with their names in the papers. Losing their jobs. The works. I'd certainly heard the scenario enough times. I'd seen enough battle scars to know.

Charlie was sitting at the bar waiting for me in his leather flyer's jacket. It was the first time I'd seen him out of a suit and tie.

"I didn't know you were a flyer," I said, climbing onto the bar stool.

"I was a bombadeer," he answered, not wanting to dwell on that part of things. By this time war stories had become an old conversation. They only became reborn later when his kids' generation didn't want to go. "Bartender, a vermouth cassis for the lady." I started to giggle. "Or, would you rather just have a beer, Sylvia?"

"Sorry, Charlie," I smiled through my fingers.

"Jesus, Sylvia, have whatever you want."

"Thanks."

I'd never really noticed Charlie before. He was a wide-eyed one whose sadness hadn't defeated the wonderment. A stumbling one. Fervent. Honorable.

"Forgive me for being so blunt, Sylvia. But I need to know before we go forward, exactly where do you stand?"

"Where do I stand?"

"Yes."

"Regarding what?"

Charlie looked at me, a bit puzzled. Obviously he'd thought that all of this was clear.

"Well, regarding the Hewitt affair, of course."

"I've told you," I said glibly, feeling blasé about this whole conversation. "I liked Hewitt. I signed that petition of his gladly, and I'd do it again. Just because they drove him to his death doesn't change all of that. Those monsters could do it to anyone."

"Good show," Charlie said, slightly confused. Then he smiled with a sigh of deep relief.

"Hewitt was a Communist," I guessed.

"How do you know?"

"He told me," I said, effectively lying. "He'd been in the Party for many years."

"Since he was a boy."

"Of course." I reached for a cigarette.

"I'm not in the Party," he said. "Never was."

"I am not now and have never been a member of the Communist Party," I said.

He stared at me.

"Oh, would you like another drink?" Charlie asked, somewhat surprised at the speed with which my glass had been emptied.

"Why, yes. Thank you. I'll have another one of those lady drinks that you know about, Charlie. What would you recommend?"

"Champagne cocktail? With a brandy float? It's not too strong."

"You heard him, bartender," I said as Charlie put his cash on the bar.

"The thing is," Charlie went on, "in the '30s when Hewitt joined up, everyone who was really interested in a better future was interested in the Soviet Union."

"Why was that?"

"Well, you heard about so many exciting things there. Abortion was free, divorce and marriage were up to people to decide, they had no unemployment while we had tremendous unemployment."

"That's true," I said. And actually, I'd never quite realized that before.

"But the important thing was," Charlie continued, "when you looked at what the Communist movement in America was doing, these were not people with state power. These were people fighting against great odds for the most important things that a healthy society must have."

"What are the most important things that a healthy society must have, Charlie?"

"Well," he said. "It was the Communist movement in the United States that raised the slogan 'Black and White Unite to Fight.' They spoke out against world racial discrimination. It was the Communist movement that first proposed

Social Security and Welfare, which became the law of the land. They did the first organizing of the CIO and the industrial unions."

I flashed, unexpectedly, on a picture of Spin standing behind her cash register.

"But most important of all, when you read the Marxist classics, you find the noblest ideas ever written by man. The fact that they may be ill-realized doesn't take away from the beauty of the source. Where else do you find the desire to end all forms of human exploitation? Wage exploitation? Exploitation of women by men? The exploitation of blacks by whites?"

And that little butch from New Jersey.

"Don't forget," Charlie said. "When fascism happened, all of Europe dabbled in it or embraced it fully. Even England and France. I don't have to tell you as a Jewish person that only the Soviet Union opposed it. And they were the only friend that Republican Spain ever had. Look, Sylvia."

"Yes?" I mumbled, distracted.

"This fight at work, there's nothing personal to be gained out of joining it. It may be time-consuming and replace a lot of other more lucrative or pleasurable activities. But it might be a contribution toward making the world better. And that is something that most people never do. It might just be nothing more than a matter of personal integrity."

"Integrity," I snorted. "That's a strange word. It gets tossed around like a hard-boiled egg. But what does it really mean? No one seems to know."

"You're right. Sylvia," he said. "We're writers. We know that language is the irrefutable key."

That stopped me cold. No one had ever called me a writer before.

"That's right," he continued. "Look at the papers every day. Look at that rag we work for. J. Edgar Hoover, now he knows how to use language. Regular folks on your block are no longer people. They're *individuals*. Friends? Nowadays they're called *contacts*. It puts a sinister spin on everything personal. Yeah,

Hoover knows the meaning of language, Sylvia. And so do I. And so do you."

3

It was already nine o'clock when I stepped out of the bar. It was a gorgeous, clear night. Old Italian women clacked on the cobblestones of MacDougal Street as they walked past the slaughterhouse on the corner of Bleecker. In the morning they'd bring their rabbits there to be freshly killed for supper. Bohemians were drinking espresso at the Figaro. I ran past the Provincetown Playhouse through Washington Square Park. Soon it would be warm enough for little kids to dance into the fountain in their underpants. In the meantime chess players were studiously at work, even in the dark. The statue of Garibaldi presided over the park. Rumor was he turned his head when a pretty girl walked by. I went up University Place, passed the galleries on Tenth Street, glancing into the Cedar Tavern, which was already packed with artists and would-be's. I passed Klein's Department Store, hovering over Union Square like a grand maharajah. Would there be another Communist Party celebration this May Day? Last year the marchers were assaulted and pelted with eggs. There was a guy selling windup toys on the corner. A woman bought a pinwheel for her son. A double-decker bus went by. Two guys were on a hammer drill in front of the subway station.

One more year, then I'll take a real breather, I decided. That's when I'll write my first novel.

I got to Sixteenth Street at nine-thirty and swore I saw a police sedan waiting at the corner in preparation.

'Tis a far, far better thing I do now than I have ever done, I thought, and then smiled at how much I had become exactly who I was raised to be. I had become a hardworking, intelligent, ethical, self-aware girl who made a contribution to my society. I had grown up to be brave, truthful, and dignified, just as my mother would have wanted me to be. A girl whose last thoughts turn to Dickens as she faced the firing squad.

"Hey, Jimmy," I smiled, trembling, walking back into the familiar cage.

"Surprised to see you here so soon," he said. "Behave yourself."

"No sweat," I said, sweating.

Spin put my drink up on the bar, so I guess everything was copacetic. Caroline was still at the piano. She noticed me all right, but made no acknowledgment. I imagine she expected to go on like the rest of the girls in the place, moving from lover to lover and corner to corner in full view of our entire pasts.

"Think it may rain and cool off?"

It was the little squirt from New Jersey.

"Such things have been known to happen," I said, lighting a cigarette.

"Can I buy you a drink?"

"Go down to Gimbel's bargain basement," I said. "You've got the wrong department."

"Hey, let's go to Sheepshead Bay tomorrow," the girl said, still trying. "We can fish off the pier. Better yet, let's have a real adventure. Let's go see America. It'll be swell with a girl like you."

"Oh yeah, Miss Operator." I smiled. "And how are we going to get there?"

"I've got a 1940 Chevy. It'll be great. A seventy-five-cent hotel over a waterfront barbershop. A pitcher, a basin to wash up in in the morning. Pork and beans out of the tin warmed over a trash-can fire. Nothing to worry about except who won at the horses."

"You wanna leave tomorrow?" I laughed.

"Nah," said the Squirt, backing down from her boast. "I've got to finish secretarial school first."

"Yeah? What happened to the drive-in? Give me another one, Spin."

"Gee, here we are, out of conversation it's still so early."

"What time is it?"

"Ten to ten," she said. "What's the matter, don't you like to have fun? You're chewing up half your smokes."

"You have a line for every occasion," I smirked. "Don't you know that this is New York where *hello* means *good-bye.*"

"Well," the kid said. "Don't go into prayer and fasting about it. Why are you so angry all the time?"

"People got things on their minds in this town." I blew smoke rings over the bar.

"Statistics tell us everyone has problems. You want to dance?"

"I think we have to wait," I said.

"Until what, school opens?"

"No," I said. "Just two more minutes."

The girl sucked on her drink. "I'd love to ride you down to Florida beach in a nice yellow convertible."

"Okay," I said, stamping out my cigarette. "I'm ready."

"For a ride to Florida beach?"

"No, Einstein. I'm ready to dance."

It was three minutes to ten. Squirt and I stepped out into the back patch of floor space in the crowded bar, and when Caroline saw us she started tinkling on the keys. "I'm in the Mood For Love," of course, that sadist. Well, she was gonna get hers so I could even enjoy it. She didn't play it in that chintzy, bad taste, barroom kind of way. She played it like Miles Davis would have played it if he still played the piano.

"Hey," the kid said. "What kind of music is that?"

"Just hold me," I whispered, laying my face on her shoulder. "Just hold me around the waist and no matter what happens, don't ever let me go."

"All right, sweetheart," she said tenderly. Understanding something inexpressible, she took me entirely into her arms. And I was home, in that place between the shoulder and the breast that has no name. I was safe and free and complete as we slowly sang with our bodies in the shadow of the music.

At that moment, there was a crack in the world of people without power and their powerless universe. There was a commotion in the front as the doors burst open. I could feel the girl's muscles tighten as she instinctively tried to pull away. She tried to survive, as she already had a thousand times before. Like a panther escaping a flame. But, there would be no pretense of escape. I held her viciously and would not let her go. The two of us stood frozen, as all around us trapped animals panicked, cried, and burned. We stood, silently, until the flashbulbs began to blast.

AUGUST 2 1996

BILLBOARD MAGAZINE'S TOP TEN HITS

1. Because You Loved Me .... Celine Dion
2. One Sweet Day .. Mariah Carey and Boyz II Men
3. Un-break My Heart .... Toni Braxton
4. Give Me One Reason .... Tracy Chapman
5. Macarena .... Los Del Rios
6. Ironic .... Alanis Morissette
7. 1,2,3,4 (Sumpin' New) .... Coolio
8. Nobody Knows .... The Tony Rich Project
9. Sittin' Up In My Room .... Brandy
10. Not Goin' Cry .... Mary J. Blige

Austin Van Cleeve

1

Jim O'Dwyer did die, but it was not by his own hand. Instead, his demise took place later the same evening. He was in the process of receiving a blow job from Theresa Calabrase, that little petunia. And at just the right moment, her boyfriend Bruno decided to stop home on his way out to a job.

Bruno was sent upstate for life, and Theresa moved to Bensonhurst where she attempted to disappear into Guinea heaven. There, she quickly married a longshoreman named Anthony Vitti, with whom she raised six children. But this girl was not fated for anonymity. I wasn't surprised when she popped back into the news in the early '80s. One of her sons was implicated in the beating death of an innocent Black man who had dared to stop in an Italian neighborhood to buy a bagel. A lynching. According to the newspapers, she operated a part-time manicure business out of the garage of her two-family home. Two years later, at the time of her son's trial and conviction, the papers reported that she had taken on a second job as a dispatching operator for a Brooklyn-based trucking company. She died of diabetes in 1993.

Of course, Jim's death left a power gap at the *Star* for about an hour and a half. Without hesitation, Amy replaced her husband as editor in chief. With an influx of funds from her personal fortune, she transformed the paper into New York's first full-color weekly tabloid. She initiated the tradition of selling newsprint publications exclusively in food chains and quickly dominated the scandal market. Amy was subpoenaed by Congresswoman Elizabeth Holtzman, right after our divorce became final, to testify before the congressional Investigative Committee on the Watergate scandal. Of course she never actually appeared. Later, she became a major funder for Ross Perot's first presidential bid and died, at the age of ninety, the evening after attending a fund-raiser for Robert Dole.

As for me? Oh, there are petty biographical details. I was convicted of income tax fraud in 1963 and served six months in a federal penitentiary. The next year I bought a second home in Newport and learned how to position from afar, whenever necessary.

And now you find me, an old, finished man on my deathbed. I was a shit, and I loved it. The body, finally, has failed. But no regrets. It served me very well. And in some ironic way, today has been a very happy day for me. My grandson, Calvin Kinsey, sat by my bed quietly reading the paper out loud. It was a moment of tenderness. Even love. The lead story in this morning's *New York Times*. It was very sweet when his voice revealed to me the shocking, pleasurable truth that President Clinton had finally dissolved Welfare. Twelve million cockroaches off the dole. It may sound strange, but in some way I feel that with this huge event, I can die happy. It took us sixty-one years to defeat the New Deal, but finally, it is over. Me and my kind have triumphed. That spend, spend, spend way of thinking is no more, and America has returned to the values and structures that I have always fought for with great vigor and vicissitude. Now I am old, but I have won. The America you inherit is the one I wanted for you. And with that, happily, I wish you and yours Godspeed.

Sylvia Golubowsky

2

My brother left the newspaper business, of course. He moved back home with our parents for a year until he met and married Doris Solowitz, an accounting student at Brooklyn College. The two developed a cheesecake distribution company that sold to the finest restaurants in New York City, New Jersey, and upstate New York. In the 1970s, their company, Doris-Lou, attempted to branch out into low-fat cheesecake. But they were too far ahead of their time and the venture failed. In 1983 they opened a bagel shop in Woodstock, New York, and soon became the largest distributors of bagels north of Riverdale. Their son, Wellington Monroe Gibson, was an associate editor at *Spy* magazine and later wrote the bestselling book *Why Political Correctness Is Destroying America*. Their daughter, Suzette Karen became a heroin addict and later, a methadone addict. She worked as a bagel packer in the Monticello store until she died of a heroin overdose in 1992.

Many times I have considered what my brother's life would have been like if he had stood up for me. Truthfully, I believe that our dreams would have come true. I think we would have become a great writing team, like Comden and Green. Very successful. We would have had an office together and his wife and my lover and his kids and our friends would all have been one big family. Barbecues. High school graduations. Shared summer vacations. We would have borrowed each other's cars. I think we would have had very happy lives. And we would both have known something very incredible about loyalty and love. Whenever anything horrible has happened to my brother, I have been glad. When his daughter died, though, I did feel conflicted.

As for me, after my arrest, of course, I was promptly fired. After some unconveyable suffering, I started working at Orbach's as a salesgirl. I stayed there until 1955. At that time I secured a job in the Research Department of the *New York Times* through Irving, God rest his soul. I continued to be employed there until my departure in 1983, at which time Agnes and I moved to Vermont and I began teaching as an adjunct at the local university. In 1990 I was awarded $40,000 in back pay as part of a class-action sex discrimination suit settled out of court by the *Times.* Agnes used this money to retire, but I kept working, eventually securing a position in that university's Master's program in Writing. You see, all this time, since I began in housewares at Orbach's, I was writing books. Throughout the '60s I used the pseudonym Caroline Lewis to publish a long, complex series of novels for young women that followed the adventures of a gang of career girls trying to make it in New York City. Last year, my life's greatest achievement, my memoir *Freud Was My Co-Pilot,* was published by Harper's. It documents my experience of ten years in psychoanalysis. Interestingly, the gay crew was very taken with the book, and I was nominated for a Lambda Literary Award for Lesbian Writing. Agnes and I flew to Chicago for the awards dinner. We met some very nice younger women, the men had nothing to say to me. But the prize went to something called *Dykes to Watch Out For, Volume Twenty.* Whatever that is.

Today on National Public Radio they were interviewing a wide range of people about their views on the dissolution of Welfare. Everyone seems to be in a fog. They couldn't really understand how this had happened to them. Idiots. I know exactly how it happened to them. I know the mentality. I know the enemy better than I know my own self. And in that sense, I have given them myself. There is a great deal of joy to be found in personal integrity. But, in the end, the masters do win. They do take your soul. They take your brother. They take your lover. And now they take the food out of your mouth.

N . T a m m i B y f i e l d

3

Well, I am entirely Black after all. Of course, as Thomas says, if you're one drop, you're Black. My mother says I would have been just as Black, even if Caroline was my grandmother. But I'm glad I'm one hundred percent.

Last night Thomas and I went to a Columbia "dance" party. This white girl next to me goes, "I love this song." It was *Sweet Home Alabama*.

"Let's get out of here," Thomas said.

I think we might be in love. My mother likes him. His mother likes me. His yummy, delicious, irresistible body is the primary thing on my mind these days, so my schoolwork has gone to hell. All I can think of is how he takes me in his arms. But he wants me to do well and go get that Ph.D. He loves my body, he says it is a reflection of my life. Isn't that cool?

I had to go ahead in my grandfather's memoirs to find out what happened to his first wife. There was a lot of silence but he did get around to it, as I knew he would. His sense of historic imperative was stronger than shame. As soon as Caroline got out of jail she packed up her stuff and left my Aunt Ide's house for good. She did remain in New York playing at small clubs and offering music lessons for a few years, but not peacefully. After her third arrest for disorderly conduct and public drunkenness, she finally got smart and returned to North Carolina. There was no place for her here.

In my grandfather's papers there was a letter from Caroline. I can't read the exact date on the postmark but the year was 1970. It was a confession.

Dear Cal,

Many years have passed, and you may not know that I'm back home in Flat Rock. I played piano in a honky-tonk here for a number of years and finally I did manage to open my own club, Caroline's. In 1967 Jerry Lee Lewis stopped at the bar for a beer and we played a set together.

After my mother passed on, I had a vision in which Jesus came into my heart and told me to follow Christian ways. I renounced my sexual perversions and alcohol and I accepted Jesus Christ as my lord and savior. I know that Jesus has forgiven me.

I am writing to ask you, too, to take Jesus into your heart.

It was through my church, First Baptist Calvary of Flat Rock that I met Monroe Wilks, a machinist, and we married last year under the loving eye of Jesus, our Lord.

I know I caused you suffering with my sinful ways. I hope that you can forgive me in Jesus' name.

Yours In His Name,
Caroline Wilks

My grandfather saved the letter. I guess it meant something to him in some strange way. Monroe Wilks sent Aunt Ide a death notice in 1975. The Lord used lung cancer as his tool to call Caroline back to the kingdom of heaven.

Before the divorce was even final, Ide introduced Cal to Marion Woodson, my grandmother. She was a young law student at NYU. With her emotional support my grandfather completed an MBA. Then he worked his way up through the ranks to partner at one of the first Black-owned advertising agencies in the world. Now, he is often credited, within insider circles, as the conceptual father of niche marketing to Black consumers, which is the principle at the basis of my mother's import business. He championed the representation of African-Americans in mainstream advertising in both Black oriented and general-interest magazines. But there wasn't a happy ending because he finally retired as an act of protest against a campaign his agency took on for *Uptown Cigarettes,* a smoke for the Black consumer. He was very bitter about that one until the end. My grandfather.

Grandfather? I wish you could see me today. I will be everything you dreamed of for the Black race. I look at your life, how they took your dreams away, and I swear on your grave I won't let them do it to me. I won't. I see injustice very clearly, and I will learn from your suffering, Grandfather. I won't let them do that to me.

Thomas is much softer than I am. I worry about his soul. This morning at breakfast, my mother read to us from the paper about Clinton's new Welfare Bill. Steve didn't say a word, but my mother was literally crying, thinking about the unnecessary suffering of the poor. How much more of it was in store. How much of her life she'd fought to alleviate it, and how little she'd accomplished, in the end, for others.

"I don't understand," Thomas said, love and sweet empathy on his face. "What is wrong with your country? How could any-one be so cruel? Who would make this happen?"

I watched him sit, my mother quietly sobbing.

"What kind of person would do something like this?" he asked me. "Who?"